FIRST EDITION

China Grove Press / IsoLibris Publishing
ISBN 978-0-9852-6713-1

The Hard Times

a novel

Russell Scott

The Storm's Edge

The sky is dark this morning.
There is no movement in the air.
The trees and weeds stand at attention,
Immobile, stock still, and waiting.

The world is breathless,
In anticipation of the coming storm,
And the frenzied dances,
That it brings.

Scott Anderson

One

Charlie Lee wasn't dead yet. That was one of the few things that he was relatively sure of. He was hurting way too much to be dead. But, if something didn't happen pretty soon there was a good chance that he was headed in that direction. He was lying face down in the middle of his kitchen floor. He focused on the dust particles that swirled and danced in the shaft of sunlight that spilled across the tiled floor. Brownian motion, atoms at work, the particles driven in random directions by collisions they could neither anticipate nor avoid.

It felt like somebody had parked a truck on top of him. He fought to try and draw in a deep breath, trying with all his strength to let his ribs expand. But, no matter how hard he tried, he could not.

He was running out of time. Not enough oxygen was making its way to his brain. The dust motes became, briefly, flashing points of light, then darkness obscured his vision. He wasn't afraid, there was a calmness, a peacefulness to it. It wasn't the darkness of a cave, with the realization of the dark as a concrete fact, but a darkness of absence, as if he were not there, the darkness of slowly falling asleep. He was removed, and somehow, protected from it.

Charlie let the darkness spread until he heard his wife's voice coming from the depths of velvet folds. What was she saying? He could make out his name but nothing else registered. Then he was on his back. Millie was shaking him, still calling his name, louder now, strange, a new voice even to him, unsteady and shrill. Their dog, Suzy, ran in circles around him, barking. He tried to answer his wife, he tried to tell Suzy to shut up, but nothing came out.

He could only see Millie in bits and pieces, just when she was directly above him. In the glimpses he caught he could see her eyes, terrified eyes, drilling into his own, searching. It made him forget about himself. He wanted to put his arms around her and tell her not to be afraid. That everything was going to be all right. He'd be fine in a minute. He only needed to catch his breath.

Instead though, the truck became heavier and heavier with every second that passed. Crushing down, until it seemed as if the weight of the universe was centered in his chest. It was only by having to focus so intently on the sensations in his chest that he came to realize that his heart wasn't beating any more. He hadn't paid any attention to it before now. But instead of the steady, lub-dub he never really noticed, it felt as if a bag of snakes were crawling around in the center of his chest. That was a bad thing.

The pain built. He rode it like a wave. He didn't have a choice. As a doctor, he'd watched people die for thirty-five years. He knew what it looked like, but only from an observer's perspective. Now, he was seeing it from the inside.

His wife started to blow air into his mouth. The air just blew back out his nose. Then she remembered her CPR and pinched his nostrils shut so the air couldn't escape and would be forced into his lungs. Within a few breaths the pain improved. Subsiding little by little as she blew into his mouth. Millie dialed the phone between breaths, no answer. She dialed again. What was she doing? Dial 9-1-1, Charlie thought. Somebody's going to answer that. Finally, she spoke to someone and checked his pulse.

"No," she said. "He doesn't." Suzy, old and overweight like her owners, had thankfully gotten winded and sat quietly panting under a chair. Unsure of what was going on, but unwilling to go too far, lest something interesting happen while she was gone.

Millie began to pump on his chest as well, but she was doing it all wrong. The sequences were crazy. There wasn't any rhythm at all. Five pumps-one breath then eight compressions and two breaths. On she went, crying as she did, four-one, seven-two, six-one, eleven-three. It was maddening, but apparently it was working. He was still here. Dead people weren't irritated by the irregularity of their wife's chest compressions.

He needed to lose weight. The fat on his stomach shook as his wife continued pumping with her erratic rhythms. He was going to have to go on a diet.

He could feel Millie wearing out, pumping slower, needing to stop to catch her breath before she could blow into his mouth again.

"Charlie, please, I can't do this…" she whispered.

The back door opened. Suzy, startled, jumped up and resumed her barking, serious this time, protecting her masters.

"Mrs. Lee, we have it from here," someone said, and lifted Millie to her feet.

Charlie recognized the paramedic's voice. It was Bobby Pierson, from Metro. A mask was placed over his face and he could hear the hiss of the

2

oxygen from the tank as it filled the Ambu bag. New hands, professionals, began to compress his chest in a regular counted rhythm. His shirt was cut off with scissors. He knew what was coming when he heard Bobby say in a loud, firm voice, "CLEAR".

Electric shock was the only thing that could stop the chaotic impulses that were keeping his heart from beating normally. Nothing you thought you knew could prepare you for what that felt like. The horrible jerking energy of the defibrillator threw him out into space. He spun, rigid and awful, away from the world and drifted back just in time to hear Bobby call, "CLEAR" again, and it happened all over. This time it was harder and it was taking longer to get back. He never made it, because they hit him the third time before he did, 360 joules and he was gone again, somewhere else.

This time he was nowhere, a black speck looking across a blinding plain. Three men moved across the expanse. The man who was closest was alone. He felt familiar somehow, familiar, but beyond recognition, faceless in the light, blinded, unseeing. The two other men moved, traveling together, coming from far away. He wasn't sure who they were, or why they came. But the three men were connected, to each other and perhaps, somehow, to him. He was not what they were seeking nor did they recognize he was there. He was simply the convergence point for their journeys. But, he wasn't a person anymore and this was no longer a place. It was no more than a pinhole in the light around him.

Then, suddenly, it wasn't. He was back in the world. He felt the bumping as they locked him into place in the back of the ambulance, felt his wife's hand. He could hear her voice coming to him. He couldn't see her. He felt her squeeze his hand. Even though he couldn't really make out what it was that she was saying, he began to feel better as he listened to the rhythm of her voice, and he knew that whatever it was that they were doing now, it was working. He wasn't going to die after all. He felt so much better.

Ray Moffett walked across Twenty-First Avenue and headed into the ambulance entrance to the Emergency Department. He had on a fresh set of blue scrubs. His hair was still wet. The door sprang open as he stepped onto the dock and he nodded at Andy, the guard who'd triggered it for him.

"Hey Doc, seems like I just let you outta here." Andy smiled.

"Hey, Andy, what are you still doing here? You should be gone yourself. You got off at three, didn't you?" Ray countered.

Andy put a hand on Ray's back as he walked through the door. "Just working a little overtime, I'm going home at nine. Maybe get a late dinner with the wife. I guess I know why you're back."

"Part of being the boss." Ray had only been gone for six hours.

One of his partners, Grif Ryan, was supposed to be coming on now. Grif had called him that morning, right after Ray'd fallen asleep. Diarrhea and fever, he'd needed someone to cover for him. Maybe, if Ray had been more awake he'd have taken the time to call in one of the other guys to fill the shift, but he was too tired to get out of bed and start calling around. Lying in a warm bed, it seemed easier to just get a little shut-eye and do the shift himself. So he'd set the alarm clock, closed his eyes, and went immediately back to sleep.

"Sorry about it anyway." Andy offered.

It was a kind of a strange comment, but Ray let it pass. Everybody who worked in the ED on a regular basis was used to working weird hours. Andy was working overtime, Ray was coming back after only six hours off. That was just the way it was, there wasn't anything to be sorry about.

Ray walked to his office and grabbed one of the white coats that were hanging on a rack beside the door. He pushed the door shut and glanced at the mirror on the back of the door as he slipped his arms into the sleeves. His hair was sticking up already. It was drying and starting to sprout wings. He should have put some hair gel on, to hold it down better. The more he smoothed it the more it stuck up. He needed a haircut. Ray's hair was still mostly the same red it had always been. He had a little gray. You had to expect that at fifty. "Guess I'm lucky I've still got hair," he murmured. His dad had been almost totally bald by this age.

Satisfied he'd done the best he was going to, Ray turned and walked down the hall.

His eyes went immediately to the status board as he came into the nursing station. Three rooms and the big trauma bay had patients in them. He glanced around the collection of countertops, computers, and chairs that served as the nerve center of the department and tried to get a read on the mood of the staff. That would tell him as much as the board did.

The first thing that struck him was the quiet. Not a natural quiet. It was a quiet that was about him. Even through the fog of fatigue Ray knew that there was something wrong. No one met his eyes. No one spoke, no nods, no jokes about being back already, nothing. Several of the younger staff watched him intently, then averted their eyes when he returned their gaze Their faces convincing him of what he already suspected.

Bill Evans was the doctor he was scheduled to relieve. Bill sat with his back to the door writing in a chart, not yet aware of Ray's arrival.

"What's up Bill?" Ray asked.

Ray could see the tension in Bill's face as he spun in his chair to face him, a muscle twitched under his left eye as he looked up tapping the chart he'd been writing on with the tips of his fingers. Bill's lips were a tight line as he picked up the chart, and stood, holding it in front of him with both hands, but didn't speak.

Ray was too tired to stand around trying to figure out what it was that everyone else in the room obviously already knew and he didn't. He spun the index finger of his right hand to try and prompt his younger partner.

"Charlie Lee came in a little while ago, Ray." Bill said, setting the chart back down on the desk.

Ray could see the emotions moving around his younger partner's face, just under the surface, as he struggled with where to go next. Charlie Lee had put their group together. Picked every doctor on the department's staff. He was also Ray's best friend.

"Is he okay?" If Bill was this upset, something had to have gone wrong. His mind raced ahead preparing for the possibilities. Damn, he hoped they hadn't screwed up and done something to piss Charlie off.

Bill's face settled, his eyes locking onto his boss's. "He didn't make it, Ray. I'm so sorry…I thought you knew," Bill said, stepping near him, and putting his hands on Ray's shoulders.

Ray stammered, "What do you mean he didn't make it?"

"I'm sorry," Bill repeated.

"Charlie, our Charlie, the guy that built this department?" Ray stumbled.

Bill nodded silently.

"He's dead…dead? Not in the unit or something?" Ray was suddenly transformed from head of the Emergency Department into being just another guy being told about something he didn't want to accept. That was the overwhelming power of personal tragedy. Anxiety rose in his throat and choked him. "We didn't kill him did we?"

"No Ray, he was dead when he got here."

"How can that be? He doesn't have any history of heart disease…I just saw him…He just retired." None of this made sense. There had to be something he wasn't understanding yet.

The doctor in him knew there wasn't. He'd said those same words himself too many times, to too many people, not to grasp the truth in them. He needed to see the details.

"Is that his chart?" Ray asked, extending his hand.

"Yeah Ray, I'm sorry," Bill put the chart into Ray's outstretched palm and started to present the case. "He collapsed at home about four-thirty. Millie called 9-1-1 within two minutes and started CPR, but he was fixed and dilated when the paramedics got there." Pupils that were fixed in the dilated state and failed to respond to light were one of the first indicators of brain death. "We ran

5

a strip over the telemetry, as soon as they got on scene. He was in v. fib. on the first tracing. Bobby Pierson was the paramedic on the scene." For the first time, there was a crack in Bill's voice. "It was pretty hard on Bobby. Charlie trained him. Hell, Charlie trained all of us. The whole code was by the book. They shocked him three times on site and gave him three rounds of meds. We coded him all the way in, but there was nothing there Ray. He went into asystole on the way in, by the time he got here he was gone. I'm sorry."

"God damn it, why didn't you guys call me?"

"We tried..." Bill started.

Ray pulled out his cell phone and stabbed the button...nothing happened. He pushed it twice more. It was dead. He'd forgotten to plug it back in when Grif had called to tell him he wasn't coming in.

"Shit," he muttered and pressed the phone to his forehead.

"What were you going to do Ray? He was gone."

"I just wish somebody would have gotten me." Ray murmured.

"A ten-year-old girl went through the windshield of her grandmother's car. She came in at the same time. Nobody had time to look for you." Bill said, his voice gentle despite the hard words. Words that cut all the deeper, because Ray knew that they were true. Their job was about saving those that could still be saved and having the courage to understand that there were those that couldn't.

"Where's Millie now?" he asked.

"One of the kids came down and got her, I think it was Sissy, they just left." He looked at his watch. On a busy day, when a lot of things were happening at once, time was a hard thing to be sure of. "I don't know how long they've been gone. I got tied up with the kid. They've been gone a while I guess. I gave Millie a mild sedative here and gave her a script for a couple more. I figured that you'd be over there to check on things if she needed more than that." Bill answered.

"Yeah, I can take care of that...can you stay for a while? I need to try and ..." Ray started.

"Don't worry about it Ray, I called Fred, he can get here by eleven. I can stay til then. You need to go and do, whatever you need to do. Nobody expects you to be here right now."

"I should try to be there for Millie." Ray muttered, looking at his shoes. He felt Bill's hand squeeze his shoulder.

There was a sad mix of empathy, compassion, and a degree of misplaced guilt that went with the telling of terrible things. Despite the best efforts to be gentle, there was a guilt that came with being the bearer of that kind of news. Knowing that the words, once said, would shatter the listener's world. Ray knew that this was what his younger partner was feeling now.

"You did everything you could, I'm sorry you had to be the one to do it." Ray handed Bill the chart back and nodded.

As he walked away from the desk Ray could feel tears trying to well up in his eyes. He didn't let them. He'd been "Doctor Moffett" long enough to know how to hold it together until he could get out of the department. As he left, several of the staff touched his face, or shoulder, or took his hand murmuring their condolences. He didn't really hear them. He just said something, anything, in return. He wasn't sure if the things he said even made sense, it wasn't the words that mattered.

He walked past his office without stopping. He left the white coat on and kept walking, through the door to the main hospital and down the hall, past the cafeteria, and on past the receiving department. It wasn't until he turned into a low ceilinged corridor that he knew where it was he was going. He took a deep breath and pushed open the double doors.

Stillness is the single most defining characteristic of the dead, Ray flipped back the thin sheet that covered the body on the stretcher. The face was Charlie's. More relaxed, younger than Ray had seen him look in years. The lines of tension smoothed away. There was an unreal quality to it. He wanted Charlie to sit up and yell, "surprise." It would've been a good joke.

"I really fell for it this time." He felt the words form on his lips. But it wasn't a joke and Charlie didn't move.

In sleep or even in a coma there was movement that could be detected by a trained eye, the movement of the chest and the flair of the nostrils with respiration, a pulse thrumming in a carotid, or even the subtle contortions of a dreamers face. They were the things of the living. But they weren't there. Ray focused harder, as if he could change reality if he just looked hard enough. He could imagine for a moment he saw a movement here, a flicker there…but it wasn't so. It was simply his own mind, unable to come to terms with such absolute stillness.

Two

On the other side of the world, in Namibia, the second of the three men Charlie Lee had seen moving toward him as he died bounced his truck across a stretch of washboard ruts that were the remnants of the rains that had swept in across Erongo from the Atlantic a few weeks earlier.

It was better to keep up a little speed going over them. That way they were more of a buzz as the tires skimmed the tops of the bumps, than the bucking and jumping that went on if you slowed down too much. Fritz thought hitting them fast was easier on the truck, too. It cut down on the amount of jarring coming up through the suspension. It was certainly easier on his sinuses and lungs.

It was the hottest part of the summer and everything was as dry as a bone. A fine red dust rose into a wide cloud that billowed out behind his truck as it traveled the dirt trails that passed for roads out here. When it settled it would coat everything for fifty yards in every direction. That was why they were called dust roads. Keeping your speed up kept the dust behind you. It was one of the habits that came from a lifetime spent driving in this country.

He was coming down, headed back toward the city. He'd spent the last three weeks getting the hunting camps ready for this year's batch of hunters. It was part of the work that went into being a hunting guide, getting things in order before the season opened. Now that that was done, all he had to do was go and find some hunters, and he was on his way to America to do just that. He was going to a place called Las Vegas, to a big hunting convention. He'd never been to America before. He'd never been off the continent.

He was in a hurry to get home to get packed before he left. He had a duffel bag full of clothes on the seat beside him, but he was going to have to find some things a little nicer than the stuff he had with him. The bush was hard on clothes. It was hard on everything. He needed things that hadn't been sewed or patched a dozen times. Everything he used in the bush was crisscrossed with tiny stitches of khaki thread or the white hairs from a wildebeest's tail, depending on which of the girls who did the laundry had fixed the rip, fine to hunt in, but he didn't think they were going to impress rich Americans.

He needed to get his heavy coat too. January and February were still winter above the equator. He didn't know what the weather would be like in Nevada, but he wouldn't be outside much, as he understood things. He'd be sleeping in a hotel room with a heater and a bed at night, and if it was cold enough during the day that he didn't have to put up with flies and mosquitoes, so much the better for him.

He was supposed to meet his boss at the airport tomorrow morning just before lunch. They had a one-o-clock flight out, headed into Johannesburg. From there he'd just try to do what his boss told him. His boss was a good guy. He'd been in the hunting business a long time. His name was Walter Lent but everybody just called him Walt. Kind of a casual name for a guy that controlled one of the most valuable hunting concessions in the world, eighty thousand hectares of land bordering the Etosha game preserve.

Fritz felt his teeth chatter as he started into the next strip of ruts. The first few weren't too bad, but then he hit the big stuff. He'd been preoccupied with daydreaming about America, what it might be like, and hadn't noticed what was coming. The truck was going either too fast or too slowly, he wasn't sure which, but this strip he was on was worse than most. Before he could do anything about it, the truck was hopping like a scared springbuck. Everything in the truck flew into the air, only to get slammed right back down, as the nose of the truck alternated trying to go straight up or straight down. Thank God he wasn't carrying a truckload of hunting trophies, they'd be all over the road and broken to bits. Without a seat belt on, his head slammed into the roof, then against the steering wheel before he got himself braced. He gritted his teeth and hit the brakes, knowing what was coming as soon as he did it. The boiling cloud of red dust was everywhere now. The dust cloud swallowed him up at full strength. He found himself trying to breathe a mixture that was half air, and half dirt. His eyes squinted and burned as the dirt turned his tears into mud. With the truck fully stopped all he could do was to sit there with his mouth and eyes closed tight, and try to hold his breath for as long as possible. One breath, and then another, cautiously through his nose. When he could finally breathe without choking he slowly opened his eyes, one at a time.

"Well, that was nicely done," he said, looking at himself in the mirror. Red mud coated the rims of his eyes and the corners of his mouth. He felt like boulders had formed in his nostrils, he snuffeled and blew as he fished a cloth out from behind the seat and blew his nose into one corner, careful to note which one.

"Damn it," he said, spitting as he tried to shove his hand far enough under the passenger's seat to retrieve one of the bottles of water that had flown off of the seat and rolled back just beyond his reach. Finally, with one more grunt and curse, his fingertips brushed one of the plastic lids. The first thing he did was rinse out his mouth. He spit the first mouthful out the window to keep from swallowing dirt. Then he wetted the unused corner of the already dirt stained rag and began to wipe his face. "I guess that's reason enough to stop for a beer on the way home," he consoled himself as he wiped grit and dust from the corners of his eyes.

Okahandja was still thirty minutes away. That was the closest good place to get a beer. He washed as much of the grit out of his teeth as he could with what was left of the water. Then he shoved the transmission into gear and let out the clutch. Within seconds the red cloud was behind him, where it belonged, as he traveled south across the burned brown landscape.

The road widened and he began to pass more houses. Okahandja was more of a collection of low single story buildings clustered along the highway than a real town, but it had a bar of sorts. He'd heard that it belonged to an old friend of his now. A guy named Bink.

To someone who lived in a town, calling it a bar would seem an exaggeration. It was a simple cinder block rectangle with a tin roof, a dirt floor, and an empty door frame in the front of it, but it had what was important, a plank bar, a couple of handmade stools, a ceiling fan, and most importantly, cool beers resting in the bottom of a fifty-five gallon drum of water.

"Hey ya fat bastard," Fritz crowed as he walked through the door.

"If it's a bastard that you're looking for, look in the mirror you got hanging off the side of that scheisse truck you drove up in." The man behind the bar answered, smiling as he shoved out his hand.

Fritz reached for the hand but gave the man a quick punch in the center of his chest instead. "Come on now Bink, don't go calling my truck shit. It might hear you. The last thing I need is for it to get depressed and break down on the way home."

"Still as superstitious as ever?" Bink asked.

"Just don't want to take any chances." Fritz answered.

"Yeah, sure. That'll be the day won't it boy?" Bink said, flipping a cigarette butt onto the floor so that hundreds of red flecks shot out only to die in the red dirt. "What're you today, a professional hunter? Now that's as safe as mother's milk, isn't it?"

Fritz shook his head as he stepped on the glowing ember of the butt.

The big man was just a bit taller than Fritz, but probably weighed half again more. He may have had a bit more of a span around the middle than he'd had the last time Fritz had seen him, but there wasn't much of it that was fat.

He raised a hand like a ham and held up a meaty finger. "You've always been a safe sort haven't you? What were you when I met you?"

"A kid?" Fritz answered

"Not a minute of it. If you were a kid you grew out of it faster than anybody I've ever seen. You were a hard trooper boy, a steady hand, and a sharp eye, even then you were a killer." He put up a second finger. "Then you were running guns over four or five countries. No borders for you were there? Had all of us jumping and stepping trying to catch you, and we didn't ever know who the hell it was that we were chasing in the first place, a real wil-o-the wisp back then."

Fritz smiled as he walked around the bar and fished one of the beer bottles out of the bottom of the barrel, "Weren't supposed to. But you figured it out soon enough. Want one...they're on the house."

"I'd hate for you to have to drink my beer alone," the big man replied returning to the stool he'd been perched on when Fritz entered. "Hell, we were seeing the same guns over and over. It wasn't hard to figure out one of our own was reselling whatever we captured. I do appreciate you and your boys making sure you never shot any of us when you returned fire, always shot high enough to make us get down, never low enough to hit anybody."

Fritz took a swig of the beer as he came around the corner of the bar. "We both ended up making money, I always left some along the trail, so you could get a bounty out of it."

"Yeah, yeah, that's why I have all of this." Bink said sweeping his big arm in an arc to indicate the bar.

"Well, you've ended up the better off of the two of us. I've got a rifle and these boots, it's not even my scheisse truck," Fritz countered. He sat the beer in front of his former sergeant, "to fallen comrades," he said and raised his own.

"To the lost past," Bink answered clinking the necks of the beers together, the sad toast of defeated troopers.

They'd met back in Katima Mulilo in the Caprivi Strip. Fritz had just come out of school and Bink had been his nursemaid, he'd watched over them all, all those stupid kids, just boys, sent into the jungle to save the country for the white man. Most of them were dead now, served honorably, but they'd never really had a choice in the first place. They'd all had to serve back then, no exceptions. Sent off to save the country, and what good had it done them? Dead friends and a lost country...not much good at all.

Both men took a long pull of the cool liquid.

"Now back to what I was sayin'." Bink continued, holding up a third finger. "Then after we figured out it was you running the guns, you ran off across the border and tried settling down and being a gentleman farmer, right?"

"Well, the gentleman part is a bit of a stretch..." Fritz protested.

"Off the Wankie wasn't it?" Bink asked. "I'd heard you were hunting the game preserve there."

"Yeah right between the Wankie and the tribal lands," Fritz drew the outlines with the condensate off of his beer on the wood of the bar. He drew a square to represent the Wankie and a few lines as the tribal lands. Then pushed his finger down between. "This was me here, them they were all over here." He ran his finger around in the puddle that was supposed to be the tribal lands. "That's what caused it to happen so soon. That and Mugabe."

"May he rot in hell." Bink pronounced raising his bottle.

Fritz echoed the sentiment by raising his own and draining it.

"Time for another, huh?" Bink asked, pulling two new bottles out of the barrel.

"The hunting was good, just like the Caprivi is now." Fritz started in, getting pulled back into the story despite himself. "I was growing a little coffee and a little tobacco. I had good workers, too. I hated to lose that. When Mugabe told them that whites couldn't own property anymore it was first come, first served. They came pouring out of the tribal lands like a flood. They were taking the place and they didn't care who they had to kill to do it. They were ringing anybody they could get their hands on with a stack of tires, dousing them with diesel and setting them on fire while they were still alive. They killed two of my neighbors that way. The same bunch has drifted over here now. Now that it's gone to shit over there. They've started squatting wherever they can. They still have the mindset that if they've been there a couple of weeks and haven't been run off that the place is theirs. When the owners come to run them off they've torched a couple of 'em here too."

"It must have been hell, just watching them take everything you'd worked for." Bink said, truly sympathetic.

Fritz looked up at his old friend. When he saw the solemn look on Bink's face he remembered how much they'd both lost. Bink's wife and son had died at the hands of the black "freedom fighters." Shot to death on their own farm "It was hell for both sides, like it was here. It was give and take, trading shots, just like it was for us in the war. That's what brought the police. But there was no law to it over there if you were white."

"From the way we heard it here, a half-dozen of them got killed that morning they came to arrest you," Bink continued.

"They didn't come to arrest me. That was pretty clear when they killed the maid and the houseboy. I figured I was next. Just lucky they didn't know I had a rifle hidden in the barn."

That day replayed itself in Fritz's memory. He'd been out hunting alone to get some meat for the house. He was riding his old horse Buck. He'd ridden down the hill, coming to the house, when he'd seen the police cars in the yard.

"Mr. Dietrich, you are under arrest, for the murder of a tribal elder." A tall policeman had shouted as he came through the gate.

He should have known then not to get off of the horse, but he did, he still had his pistol in his belt. Since that's all they were armed with, he left his rifle in its scabbard as he got down. He'd wanted to try to keep things from getting out of hand if he could.

"I didn't shoot at anybody who didn't shoot at me first. A man has a right to defend his property," Fritz answered.

As his weight came off the stirrup, a man he hadn't seen was behind him. He knew he'd made a tactical error when he felt the barrel of the gun shoved into the back of his neck. He tried to turn his head, but the man behind him pushed forward hard with the barrel of the gun, pushing his face into the skirt of the saddle and grabbing Fritz's pistol out of his belt at the same time. From the distance between them when he did it, Fritz knew that the man was holding a rifle.

"They can do as they wish. President Mugabe has given them the rights to this land," the man growled into his ear.

"This is my land, I've bought and paid for it." Fritz argued, as the man behind him slipped a loop of rope around his hands and started to tie them behind his back.

"Whites may not own land in this area anymore," the tall policeman in front of him had explained, as if that made it all okay.

He remembered how Kalinda, his maid, had stepped through the door and opened her mouth to say something. She'd never gotten it out. The short fat policeman shot her in the chest with a pistol. Instead of words, what had come out of her mouth was a keening wail followed by a gush of blood. Her son Joseph, his houseboy, ran out of the house trying to get to her as she fell, the man behind him let loose with a burst of automatic rifle fire. Fritz hadn't waited to see what happened next, he'd ducked under the horse and run towards the barn, a mixture of rifle and pistol fire behind him.

He hadn't been sure that they were shooting at him until he'd heard the high-pitched whine of the bullets as they passed by on both sides of his head. There was nothing else that sounded like that.

Now he was back there...they were shooting high, so he went low, ducking and working his hands frantically to get them out of the rope.

He dove through the door, bullets splitting the wood just above him.

As he rolled to get out of the doorway his right hand came loose. He made a dash up the stairs to where he'd hidden his rifle, shook the rope off of his left wrist, and clicked off the safety. He moved silently across the loft, using his ears first. Getting a sense of who was where. The last thing he wanted was another surprise. There was no one downstairs yet as far as he could tell. He looked between the floorboards, to the splash of sunlight streaming through the open doorway and saw the shadows of two men as they peered through, unsure of entering.

"Come out now, you are under arrest." The taller policeman shouted through the doorway. The shorter policeman began to talk into his radio.

"I can't let them call for reinforcements," Fritz whispered to himself. Without pausing he brought up his rifle, shooting through the floor and killing each of them with a single shot to the head.

The front wall of the barn exploded almost immediately, as a burst of gunfire tore through the boards. The third guy, the one he'd never seen was still out there.

He held dead still behind a pole, not moving an inch, until the shooting stopped. As long as he stayed still, and his attacker was shooting through the front wall he was safe. The bullets were coming in at too steep an angle to hit him. The man shooting from below didn't know how to adjust for an upward angle of fire and the bullets were just tearing off the roof three feet in front of him. As long as the man didn't back up or come through the door Fritz was safe behind the pole. If he came through the door he'd be a dead man, just like the other two. But he knew that. His two pals had already taught him that lesson.

That was something Bink had beaten into them. "Your enemy will learn from everything they see you do, they'll adjust, so expect it, adjust first, look for them to come at you differently."

Fritz stood quietly, listening, trying to adjust. The man wanted the radio. That was something Fritz was sure of. The man outside needed help. He'd lost the advantage. The radio was his bait.

He heard footsteps retreating and he bent his knees, lowering himself first to a sitting and then to a prone position. Adjusting his height to keep himself safe.

He couldn't move closer to the wall without risking being hit, so he couldn't see what the man was doing. The man had moved back near the vehicles, probably taking cover himself. He thought about sneaking down the stairs and slipping out the back window, but if he moved he couldn't cover the radio. It was a waiting game. The winner would, in all likelihood, be the one who moved last.

If the man tried to leave, Fritz could make it to the hill on the horse,

14

or in the other car, and ambush him before he made the big sweep around the front fields to the road. He heard the man doing something at the cars, and then the sound that was unmistakable, the clatter and click of a new magazine being slammed home. Fritz ducked his head behind the beam, just as a new fusillade of bullets was let loose at the front of the barn. The bullets were tearing through the roof well behind him, but were moving toward him quickly. The man was running toward the front of the barn as he shot.

Fritz aimed his rifle, looking through the cracks in the floor to where the radio laid still gripped in the hand of the dead fat policeman. He strained, tension in his index finger took up the slack in the trigger. Ready to fire the rifle as soon as he saw the first glimpse of his target. He wouldn't get much time. Sweat trickled down the nape of his neck, and he couldn't swallow.

There was a crash above him, breaking glass, and then the thump-woosh of the petrol as it ignited. Flaming liquid rained through the holes in the roof all around him. He rolled, and as he did he saw a shadow grab at the radio and it was gone. The fire rain ignited the boards around him. There was no waiting anymore. With the radio lost there would be twenty more policemen here before he could get away if he didn't do something quickly.

Fritz ran headlong across the decking away from the flames, he became aware of a searing pain in his left leg and looked down to see his trouser leg on fire. He tried to beat it out with his hand as he ran. He started down the top of the stairs and bullets tore into the barn through the open door.

The smoke burned his eyes and filled his lungs, the entire loft of the barn was billowing smoke as the flames spread rapidly towards him.

"At least I won't burn to death," he thought. "I'll be dead of smoke inhalation before it gets to that."

He kicked at the back wall, but the plank held. He saw an axe, a pick, and a shovel leaning against the wall near the bottom of the stairs, and he knew that the shooter would never let him get there.

He was running out of time and air. Only one thing left to do. Two quick shots and the board broke on his next kick, he pressed his face through the opening and gulped the air. Two more shots and its neighbor did too. He sucked air into his lungs, turned and fired two shots at the police cars for good measure. Then he squeezed through the opening and dropped the twelve feet to the ground. He ran straight away from the burning building until he felt thorns tearing at his face. Then he knew he was safe. He circled high on the hill, staying in the thorn bush. As the flames grew he used them to his advantage as a visual shield. The heat waves would hide him. He continued to circle until he could see his target, a man in an Army uniform leaning against the fender of one of the police cars, his rifle resting on the hood. He was shielded quite well from the barn, but that wouldn't do him much good now.

Fritz estimated the distance to be about three hundred meters. He leaned into a tree and laid the rifle's forearm on a branch. He put the blade of his sight on the top of the man's head, took in a deep breath, let it halfway out, and squeezed. The body flew forward as the bullet hit his spine, then spun against the fender of the car and ended up in a sitting position, paralyzed from the chest down. The soldier's head jerked back and forth looking for his assailant. His hands grasped the front of his shirt trying to stop the blood. Fritz again aimed the rifle, and with detached deliberation, finished the job.

Fritz hooked his stock trailer to the old pick-up, and loaded the horse. The flames had spread to the outbuildings, and the thatch roof of the house was starting to smoke. "Let the bastards take it, now," he screamed at the flames. He drove to his neighbor's house, but it was already empty. So, he turned the truck onto the road and headed toward the tiny point where the Caprivi Strip poked a finger into Zimbabwe. Twice he encountered the police, and twice he killed them. He stopped a kilometer from the border crossing and unloaded the horse. He shoved a rope into the gas tank and then withdrew all but the last few feet. He lit a cigarette and folded the book of matches around it so that the match heads were right against the cigarette paper, about two centimeters from the glowing tip. This he lay in dry leaves right next to the gas soaked rope.

Then he got on his horse and followed a trail that would take him just into Botswana before he came back up into the Caprivi, and home. By the time the soldiers at the border crossing got to the truck to investigate the explosion, he was gone.

The sound of Bink's voice jerked Fritz back to the present. "I taught you well my boy. Always keep a hideout where you can get it if you need to."

"Well it saved my skin, that's for sure." Fritz acknowledged.

"At least they didn't send you back, to stand trial for it. Most of us thought they were going to, you know?" Bink said. "They would have too. Good thing your brother's got some pull with the government."

"I wouldn't be here if he didn't." Fritz replied.

"How is Manny?" Bink asked, a bubble of foam, still sitting on his upper lip.

"I don't know, I've gotta call him. I can't go back home to Luderitz any more. Not with a criminal record and all. Everything's tightened up all along the coast now. The whole region's being treated like it's in the Restricted Zone and Luderitz is right on the edge anyway. Hell, I couldn't even take a boat out if I wanted to, now that the diamonds are mostly marine recovery." Fritz complained.

"Mining from boats, what'll they think of next?" Bink said thoughtfully.

"Who knows? Floating shovels I guess," Fritz answered, peeling the edge of the label from the bottle.

"So you headed up or down."

"Down," Fritz answered.

"If I know you, you're sharing digs with a blonde? What's this one's name?" Bink asked with a lecherous smile.

"Reese." Fritz said, rolling the wet label into a tight little ball with his thumb and index finger.

"That her first name or her last?" Bink pushed the question.

"First, her last names Stern."

"And is she? Get a bit of the whips and chains going, huh boy?" Bink slapped him hard on the shoulder.

"I don't guess I'd care if she dressed up a bit, but I'm damned sure I'll never let myself get tied up again," he said flipping the rolled up ball of paper at his friend's head.

He was glad to get off the subject of his life, better to talk about women. He didn't really want to go through it again with Bink. Bink knew what war was like, what it was like to take and return fire, what it was like to have to kill, there was no need to say anything more to him about what had happened in Zimbabwe. Women were easier for men to talk about. There was a rhythm to it. No one even considered you were telling the exact truth, they were happy with exaggeration, or minimizing, or even a downright lie, as long as it was entertaining. Hell, with women nobody really knew what the exact truth was. Every man knew that.

Three

A hundred kilometers South, Manfred Dietrich walked through the front entrance of Windhoek Central Hospital, with his wife Gretchen locked securely onto his left arm. It was difficult to tell if she held him so tightly to provide some form of emotional support, or to keep him from trying to make a run for it.

"I don't have time for this right now, you know?" he said frowning. He wore a conservative suit with a tie to add a splash of color, but not too much.

"I don't suppose you have any choice in the matter," his wife said quietly. "Now is when the doctor sent you, so now is when you're going to make the time."

"I need to be back home, not here, messing around with a bunch of absolute nonsense," Manfred grumbled.

"A mass in your lung isn't something most people consider 'absolute nonsense'," she answered. Her voice was honey but there was iron underneath, the iron of thirty years a nurse. She was the head nurse for the Clinic in Luderitz that had diagnosed the problem with Manfred's lung in the first place. The doctor had ordered everything, but it had been Gretchen that had arranged it all, and it had been Gretchen that read through each of the reports before filing them, and it would be Gretchen that made sure that everything that needed to be done for her husband's health would be done... if he wanted it, or not.

Manfred recognized the resolve in her tone, and let up on the complaining. There wasn't any use trying to argue. What was he going to tell her anyway? The truth? That he had to get back home to try to find a way to hide a couple hundred million dollars worth of black-market diamonds from the United Nations and the World Trade Commission. That would go over well.

They stopped at a directory and Gretchen finally let go her death grip on his arm. She ran her finger down the glass until she found the word Pulmonology. His first appointment was a consultation with a lung specialist, so they could decide what it was they needed to do to try and find out what was going on. That would be the easy part. Next, they were going to run a tube

18

down his nose to have a look at his lungs from the inside. Gretchen had called it a bronchoscopy. That was tomorrow. This morning was just the consultation. Asking questions, listening to his chest, poking and prodding, that kind of thing. Then, a CT scan in the afternoon. Manfred hoped the consultation wouldn't take too long. He wanted to stop by their son's school. It would be nice if they could manage to have lunch with him before the scan. Fritzy was their only child, named for Manfred's younger brother.

As Gretchen reached to push the elevator button she took his hand. Manfred felt the hand holding his tighten for just a second. He looked at her and smiled. She was biting her lower lip. She was nervous. She'd hidden it well up to now. He hadn't seen it. He should have realized she would be. This was worse for her, than it was for him.

For him, it was nothing, just a scare to get his attention, make him quit smoking, take his health a little more seriously. It was a lot more than that for her. Her father had died of a lung cancer. A cancer that had already spread to his brain by the time they'd found it. The old man had done badly. He'd died two months after the diagnosis. Poor old bastard, Manfred thought, then looked at his wife and added, poor Gret. This had to be torture for her. She didn't have to imagine the worst. She'd already lived through it once.

The lung guy was a pretty straight shooter. After a thousand questions, most of which Gretchen answered, the doctor asked him pull off his jacket and shirt and moved a stethoscope around his chest.

"Smoked since you were a boy, have you?" the doctor asked, looking at Gretchen. She nodded, so as to avoid interrupting his listening. "Well the lungs sound like it, nothing moving at all in the upper part of your left lung here." He tapped on Manfred's chest just below his collarbone. "That's where the problem is. You can see it clearly on the x-ray, but we need to see what we have on the CT and the bronchoscopy should tell us for sure what were dealing with if we can get a piece of it. The big three, right now, are TB, a fungus of some sort, or a lung cancer."

"Couldn't it be just a case of pneumonia?" Gretchen asked.

"Or silicosis." Manfred offered hopefully. He knew a lot of guys with silicosis. It got bad in the end but that could take years. He could stand that. He could stand the being sick if it didn't come for a while.

"Not likely, too round for silicosis, and it hasn't responded to antibiotics like it should if it were a simple pneumonia, but we can always hope," the doctor replied unconvincingly. "All right, I'll see you tomorrow morning," he said over his shoulder as he walked out of the room, then turned to add, "Remember, don't eat anything after midnight." The trailing nurse closed the door behind them and they were gone.

Manfred buttoned his shirt awkwardly, trying to avoid Gretchen's eyes. It was strange. For some reason he felt embarrassed, like he'd failed her somehow. When he finally looked up, she was watching him. He gave her his most reassuring smile.

"Looks like we have plenty of time to go by and get our boy before the CT," he said, concentrating on his third button as he spoke. Manfred kissed her cheek as he tucked in his shirt and turned for the door where his jacket and tie were still hanging.

"Let's get out of here, and get some lunch," she said, her voice strangely quiet over his shoulder.

She stayed quiet as he drove their Land Rover through traffic to the school. Her hand rested on his knee but her eyes remained on the passing city.

"Would you mind running up to get Fritzy, while I keep the car running?" he asked when they stopped in front of their son's dormitory. Manfred was fairly sure he wouldn't be able to walk up the three flights of stairs to their son's room without stopping to catch his breath. He was hoping she would spare him that indignity. Boys could be cruel. He didn't want to be an embarrassment to his son.

"You wait here, I'll pop up and get him," she offered without hesitation.

He squeezed her hand before she got out.

"We'll be right back down." She winked and then turned, to walk away.

He watched as she entered the front of the dormitory and thought how much he loved her. The changes had already started. He needed her to walk up the stairs, because he couldn't. If this was a cancer, it was only going to get worse. Gradually, their roles would reverse. She'd be forced to take on more and more of the responsibilities, while he became progressively more dependent. She was a tough one. She could take it. He wasn't sure he could.

His whole life had been spent taking care of the people around him. First it had been his alcoholic mother, after his father'd died, and then she died and there was his little brother Fritz to take care of. Now he had Gretchen and their boy, little Fritz. How shitty would this be for the boy?

He remembered the anger he'd felt at his own parents for dying. Dying when he was so young, twelve years old and he'd been left to raise his little brother alone in Africa. No family had come and damned little money. He would need to make sure his own family was spared that. He hadn't spent much time up to now planning on dying. He'd planned on being there until the boy was grown, and that was still the best plan, as far as he could see. Now, if he could only convince God of that fact. He hoped God was paying attention. He laughed to himself at the thought.

"What's so funny?" Fritzy asked pulling the back door open to get in.

"Just having a little joke with God." Manfred answered, trying to hug his son around the seat back.

Gretchen made sure that lunch was filled with talk. Nothing important, what was happening at school, sports, and a little bit of what was happening at home, a mindless family rhythm, to occupy the time before his first test. Manfred sipped his tea and listened quietly.

Fritzy came to the hospital with them. Manfred knew it would make things easier, give Gretchen someone to talk to during the scan. It also gave her someone to hold on to as he followed the technician down the hall into the Radiology department.

There wasn't much to the scan itself. All he'd had to do was lay there. Except for the moment, right after they'd started the IV, when the technician shot the dye into his vein. He'd felt a heat moving through his body, and had the taste of metal in his mouth, like iron, but different. When the warmth hit his crotch, it spread like a flood.

"Oh boy, I think I've pissed myself," he warned the technician. He was ashamed to have to admit it, but he didn't want the man to step in it.

The technician patted his arm. "Not to worry, most people get that feeling about now. Just lie still. I'm going to move you into the tube."

Sliding into the scanner was a bit dim and claustrophobic at first. But when his head moved on through the ring, and he could see out the other side, it was better. A little buzzing and a few clicks, then he was back in the lobby.

His wife and son bombarded him with a barrage of questions, speaking simultaneously. But, there was almost nothing he could tell them. The technician had been a good enough fellow, but never said anything, except that the radiologist would read the films later that afternoon and that the report should be ready for his doctor sometime tomorrow. They'd all just have to wait until then.

Gretchen nodded as he explained, but he could see her mind racing, trying to examine the subtext of what she wasn't hearing.

"If everything was fine, wouldn't they have said that?" Fritzy asked.

"Probably not," Manfred said. "This is a cancer center. There'd be hell to pay if they did and then turned out to be wrong about it."

"Is that right, Mother?" Fritzy asked.

"The technician can't say anything like that," she assured them both. "Each test is just a piece of the puzzle, the doctor's the only one who has all of the pieces. So, it's up to the doctor to put them together for the patient. Nobody else can do it."

They drove back to the hotel and changed into casual clothes. Manfred was glad to get out of his suit, and walk around town for a while. Windhoek was a real city, much larger than Luderitz. He had walked the town, from one end to the other when he was younger, but today was different. He wore out quickly and had to lean against a wall to rest several times before his wife suggested that they stop at an Italian restaurant to eat. Fritzy ordered a pizza and Gretchen shared it. Manfred ordered spaghetti with a white sauce and capers, but didn't eat much. He didn't have an appetite lately. He'd attributed that to the stress of having to deal with the diamond problem. The lung doctor apparently thought otherwise. He'd really zoomed in on that one during the interview. He started asking a lot of questions about how much weight Manfred had lost and over how long a period of time. It was clearly something that had more significance than Manfred had imagined when he'd checked the box on the history sheet.

Manfred coughed, and held the napkin to his mouth. He saw the spot of blood and folded the napkin quickly before anyone else noticed it. It was worse at work, the dust, perhaps? He wasn't ever underground anymore, but the dust was everywhere. It clung to clothing and to shoes. You could see it blowing in the air on the desert wind. Sometimes he'd cough so hard at night it felt like he was going to pass out. He'd been coughing up bits of dark blood for the past six months. It was brighter now. That was probably a bad sign. They took a taxi back to the hotel.

The whole idea of the endoscopy laboratory was kind of disgusting. It was a place that would stick a tube in any orifice a person had, up this or down that, who knew. Manfred was only sure of one thing. He didn't want any scope that had been up anybody else's anything being shoved down his throat. He didn't care how many times they washed it or soaked it in cleaner. Because, how could you tell if it was completely clean or not? There was always the chance of something getting missed. He thought perhaps he should mention this to Gretchen on the ride to the clinic, but the opportunity never really came up.

The first thing they did, once they got him checked in, was to take all of his clothes. They even made him take his watch off, and put on one of those gowns with no back. While Gretchen read, the nurse started an IV line in his arm. He hadn't had a needle stabbed in him in years and now he was averaging two or three pokes a day.

The anesthetist was an older man with a big mustache. "Fancy a nightcap?" he asked, jokey and smiling.

"I guess it beats gagging and puking while they shove a tube down my throat," Manfred started.

Gretchen gave him a hard look. He knew he wasn't going to mention being sure they'd cleaned the scopes.

"Here we go then," the man said giving the syringe a little push. "Do you feel anything yet?"

"Not yet," Manfred answered, and the man gave the syringe a bit bigger push.

Manfred felt kind of like a steak getting tilted from platter to plate as they transferred him from the little bed to the stretcher. He helped as much as he could, but things were starting to get a little wobbly.

"Still with us?" A walrus with a huge mustache shouted down into his face as he lay on a beach and looked up at the sun.

"Good as new." Manfred answered automatically. Then the bottom fell out of the world and Manfred disappeared. After that, Manfred didn't remember anything about the bronchoscopy. The next thing he knew, he was back in the hotel and his wife was beside him on the bed watching television.

"Is it over?" he asked.

"Yes, Manny, it's over." Gretchen answered tersely.

"Did everything go okay?" he continued, confused by her tone.

"Yes, Manny, everything went okay, but they found something that wasn't just normal in the upper part of your left lung. They took a piece of it to look at under the microscope. The doctor will see us in his office in two days and tell us what they find when they do that." She said in a rush. She seemed agitated.

"Are you mad at me?" Manfred asked.

"No sweetheart, I'm not mad," she said, her voice softening.

"What's wrong then?" he continued.

"It's just one of the side effects of the drug they gave you to put you to sleep for the procedure. It's a medicine that causes sedation, but it also causes amnesia. So you don't remember what they did to you. If I sound a little short it's only because I've answered these same questions…probably a dozen times now."

"Sorry," he wasn't sure what to say, or if he'd said that before too.

When she saw the look on his face, Gretchen rolled over quickly and hugged him. "I don't mind if I have to answer them two dozen more times before the medicine wears off." And she meant it.

"Have I asked the same questions every time?"

"Just about. Every time you wake up you ask the same two or three questions then you go back asleep, until you wake up again. So I was trying get through those. That way you could move on to anything new you wanted to know, before you fall back asleep. That's why I was rushing, kind of. Not because I was mad."

Her voice no longer quavered, braver for the repetition. Luckily,

Manfred would never remember her breaking down the first time she told him that they'd found a mass. She hadn't said the word again, after that she just said that they'd found something. Something was much easier to bear than a mass. Something could be anything.

"Where's Fritzy?" he asked looking around the room.

"Well, here's a new question," Gretchen said, pleased. "That's a good one. You're starting to notice your surroundings. You really are waking up. I dropped him at school on our way here. He had to go back to study. He has an exam coming up next week, but we'll see him on Friday before we go home."

He nodded, and then from some fuzzy depth he remembered she and the nurse trying to get his clothes on him back at the clinic. "Did you have any trouble getting me up here? From the car I mean."

She smiled at the question. "You were too sleepy to be much help yourself. I got the bellboy to help me. They have a wheelchair downstairs. Lucky for me. I thought I was going to have to bring you up on a baggage cart."

"I'm sorry," he said, as he started to go back to sleep again. Suddenly something about the amnesia worried him and his eyes shot back open. "I wasn't talking about work any, was I?"

She touched her lips and thought for a moment. "When you were first waking up you were talking about diamond dispersion for a little while?"

A moment of panic kept him awake. "Did it make any sense?"

"Not to me. It was kind of mangled up, and by the way, who is this Kimberly woman you kept going on about?" She asked with a raised eyebrow.

"She's not a woman...she's a place...besides its no fair using the anesthetic for a truth serum."

"Don't worry, your secrets are safe with me," she rubbed his head and stood up. "Would you like some water...that reminds me of something you did say. When you were talking about the diamonds...you said the water was the answer. That the water was the only safe place."

"The water?" Manfred asked, but before he could say anything else he began to snore. He stayed groggy the rest of the evening, awakening several more times before Gretchen ordered some soup from room service for dinner and turned out the lights. Through it all, he only brought up the diamonds the one time, and forgot completely about the water.

They both slept soundly for the first time in weeks, he because of the medication, and she from the absolute emotional exhaustion of seeing her worst fears come true.

Four

Ray laid his hand on the back of the silver hearse as it pulled away from the hospital's loading dock. The paint was smooth and cold as it slid away under the tips of his fingers.

"How in the hell is this fair?" Ray asked, looking up at the sky, like a child talking to God. Six weeks ago Charles Lee MD had laid down his stethoscope, and retired. He had been sixty-five years old and sixty-five was all he'd ever be, now. Sixty-five wasn't very old and six weeks wasn't much of a retirement, period. What had Charlie gotten to do in six weeks? He hadn't had enough time to do anything. He and Millie had been planning a trip to Europe over the summer, but he hadn't gotten to do it. He'd managed to play a few rounds of golf, go fishing a couple of times, and work around the house some. Not much of a reward for a life's work.

Ray wasn't sure why he'd stayed there in the morgue until the guys from the funeral home showed up. He hadn't been able to pull the sheet back up to cover Charlie's face. Whenever he let the thought appear, all he could see was his own face and imagine the sheet sliding up and over his eyes, so he'd just sat there talking. Talking like Charlie was still alive. Asking him what he was supposed to do to straighten out the mess his own life had turned into. Charlie had been a great listener, but unfortunately, hadn't had a lot of answers.

Twilight's golden edge spread through the sky in front of him. The first stars of evening were just starting to appear faintly in the east. He needed to run by and check on Millie. The sedatives Bill had given her in the E. R. would be wearing off soon.

Ray walked up the hill from the back of the hospital and unlocked the door of his old Porsche. It was a sixteen-year-old Carrera, built before car's had things like remote control keys, or cup holders for that matter. He'd bought it to give to his son once he got it fixed up. That had taken a lot longer than he'd expected, so Ray had ended up giving his son his Buick instead. The Porsche had become the project of his solitude, the thing he did when he was not at work, an alter to worship at with greasy hands and bruised knuckles.

Ray unlocked the door with his right hand, opened the door and got in. To start the car Ray had to close the door with his left hand, and then transfer the key from his right hand to his left to put it in the ignition. Somewhere in the process he dropped the key on the floor. When he tried to reach for it, he hit his head on the steering wheel. "Damn it," he pounded the steering wheel with his fist. "You fucking piece of shit car, I don't know why I didn't get another Buick?"

As he was punching the steering wheel his eyes fell on the charger plug for his cell phone dangling from the car's cigarette lighter. Ray snatched up the cord and shoved it into the bottom of his phone and pressed the power button. An empty battery with a red X across it flashed on the screen until the charge indicator lit. He pressed the phone icon.

He'd missed six calls. He scrolled down from the most recent back. His wife, well his soon to be ex-wife, Lisa had called him twice from her cell phone at six. Before that, a call from the ED, then Millie's cell phone, and two calls from Charlie and Millie's house. The first one was at four twenty-two, the second at four forty-eight. According to the medical record Millie'd called 9-1-1 at four twenty-five.

Ray cranked the car's engine to life, but kept the phone cradeled in his his right hand, he made no move to put it down so he could shift the car into gear. He just sat, alternating staring at the phone's screen and staring through the windshield, trying to decide what he needed to do next. There were voice mails that went with the phone calls. He felt like he should listen to them, but he wasn't sure he was ready to do that yet. The idle slowed and revved as the air conditioner cycled, still, he didn't move. He thought of Millie panicked, calling him first, when she couldn't get him dialing 9-1-1, and then trying his number one more time. He didn't need to hear that now.

He laid the phone ofn the seat next to him and punched the steering wheel again, more softly this time, then he slid the gear shift into first gear and pressed the accelerator, speeding out of the parking lot. Once he had the car in second gear he pushed Lisa's number and the phone dialed it as he drove. She didn't answer.

When he pulled onto the Lee's street he could see that Lisa's car, already in the driveway. She must have been on the road when she'd called. It was a three-hour drive from Oxford, at best, and it was only a little after eight now.

He saw Lisa and Sissy through the window of the back door. They were working in the kitchen, going through the cabinets. He opened the door without knocking.

"How's your mama?" Ray asked quietly, closing the door behind him.

"She's still asleep," Sissy said.

"We were going to fix a little something to eat before we disturbed her." Lisa added.

"Has she been asleep for a while?" Ray asked.

"Yes she went to bed right after we got home. They gave her something before we left the hospital," Sissy answered.

Ray nodded and hugged her first. He turned and faced the woman he'd been married to for twenty-two years. They both reached out but an awkwardness kept them from really embracing. He kissed the air in the vicinity of her cheek and retreated.

"There's no sense in cooking. Why don't I just go pick something up before Millie wakes up," he offered trying to cover his discomfort.

"We've got plenty to eat, but I don't think momma's going to be up for anything much. I know I'm not. We just need to fix a little something to tide us over."

Lisa gestured towards a collection of cake boxes and Pyrex dishes on the counter. "Sissy's right, people have already started dropping off food, but I don't think Millie's going to want anything too heavy when she first wakes up. I know what'll be good in the meantime."

Ray drifted into the living room, and turned to watch them through the doorway. He guessed that there was only five years difference in their ages. Lisa was older chronologically, but her trim figure and short blond hair made her look like the younger of the two. She moved as gracefully as a cat and looked wonderful when she stretched up onto the toes of one foot to reach for the bowl she wanted in a high cabinet. She'd lost weight since she'd moved to Oxford. She looked good. He missed her.

Ray was sitting in Charlie's recliner reading one of Charlie's golf magazines when Millie came out of her bedroom. She followed the sounds of Lisa and Sissy's preparations. When she glanced into the den her mouth fell open in surprise. Her hands flew up to cover her mouth. Her shoulders began to heave silently and Ray jumped out of the chair, to wrap his arms around her.

"I'm so sorry," he said meaning several things. I'm sorry I startled you. I'm sorry Charlie's dead. I'm sorry I wasn't there when you needed me. All that came out was "I'm so sorry," because he didn't know how to say any of those other things.

"Oh Ray, when I saw you sitting there…just like Charlie, I thought you were him. It was like I'd woken up and it was all a bad dream." Millie said, sighing deeply. She laid her head on Ray's shoulder and began to cry.

Lisa and Sissy came to the kitchen door when they heard Millie's voice.

Neither of them spoke as Millie let her sadness flow out into the world. When Sissy tried to move to her mother's side, Lisa put her arms around her and held her, for just a moment. Sissy stayed where she was.

Ray looked at Lisa. She was the professional. She was the clinical psychologist. His eyes begged her to tell him what to say, to tell him what to do now. But she didn't, she just smiled and turned around and went back into the kitchen to finish making supper. Not knowing what else to do Ray simply kept holding Millie, his arms wrapped around her shoulders and gave her time.

They ate quietly. It was surprising how therapeutic tuna salad and tomato soup could be, something familiar and comfortable, just enough to be there without being overtly noticeable as food.

As Lisa and Ray cleared the table Millie started to talk, quietly, not really addressing her comments to anyone in particular, as if she were talking to herself. "The first weird thing was when William came out to tell me he was dead. He was really, very nice, but then he got up and went back through the doors. I started thinking, what do I do now? I asked Sissy, "What should we do? She said that we needed to tell them what funeral home to use, but that wasn't what I meant at all. I just couldn't imagine how we could walk out of there and go home. Where can you go when your husband's dead?"

Ray didn't know how to respond so he took his cue from Lisa and just kept clearing.

"On the way home the radio was playing. It was some happy little song. I know Sissy didn't notice it. It was playing so softly. But I thought, don't play that music. MY HUSBAND JUST DIED. People were walking along, taking their dogs for a walk. Children were riding bicycles and I just wanted to scream, 'STOP IT, STOP IT, DON'T YOU UNDERSTAND ANYTHING, HE'S DEAD, my husband's dead.'"

"How could they know?" Sissy asked.

"It's not reasonable." Millie answered. "I know that they aren't reasonable thoughts. But, that doesn't change how I feel."

"How you feel is all you can deal with right now." Lisa offered.

"Another thing that isn't reasonable is the way you feel about what people say to you, people that do know what happened. I don't want someone to tell me he's in a better place. I know it sounds selfish, but all I can think of is; he might be, but I'm not. I'm stuck in a whole new hell."

"I'm not saying it will pass," Lisa offered. "But…"

"Please don't," Millie interrupted. "I don't want to talk about how I feel anymore."

"What do you want to talk about?" Ray asked.

"What happened," she replied.

"Mother, please, don't rehash it…" Sissy started.

"I need to rehash it. Hell, I need to hash it for the first time. If you don't want to, hear it, then go and watch TV in the den."

"I didn't mean…I just don't want you to get upset again." Sissy offered.

"I'm going to be upset again, and again, and again, then I'm going to get upset again, and again, and again. I can't just stop talking because I'm afraid I'll get upset."

"So, what happened?" Ray asked sitting down to face her.

"He'd been walking on the treadmill. He got a little winded and was sweating a lot more than usual, so he got a glass of water, and sat down right here, in that chair you're in Ray. His face got a funny look on it and I asked him if he was okay. He started to say something, and then…he didn't. He fell right out of the chair onto his face. His lip was bleeding. I tried to call you first," she said looking at Ray. "When you didn't answer I called 9-1-1."

"My phone died…" Ray started. Everyone looked at him. "It ran out of power."

Millie continued with her story. "So I checked to see if he was breathing. He wasn't, so I started the CPR, but I couldn't remember how many of what to do if you were the only person, so I would just hold my breath and press on his chest until I needed to breathe, and then I would give him a couple of breaths."

"That was exactly the right thing to do," Ray reassured her.

"It seemed like it took the ambulance a week to get here."

"It took about fourteen minutes. I read the log before I left."

"It seemed like it took forever."

"I'm sure it did. I can only imagine." Lisa said.

"When they tried to load him in the ambulance, they wouldn't let me ride. So I called you again. Then I pretended you answered, and told them that you said it would be okay. I felt bad about lying, but I had to. I hope you don't mind."

Ray shook his head no.

"I didn't know if he was dead yet. I didn't want him to think I'd abandoned him. I just wanted him to know I was there. Do you think he knew?"

"I'm sure he did," Ray answered. "I'm sure he did."

"I'm glad I lied then." Millie said. "It was hard to watch, but I'm glad I lied."

Ray and Lisa stayed a while longer, and after a while hugged Millie and Sissy, and made their way out the back door. He reached out and took her hand as she came through the door and walked her to her car.

"You did good in there." Lisa said, giving him a peck on the lips before getting in. He closed the door for her, and she rolled down the window. "I just drove down when Millie called, I can get a room…"

He leaned in and put his hand on hers. He didn't speak. He just squeezed her hand. That night as they lay in their bed nestled like spoons Lisa behind, her arms wrapped around Ray, they talked gently about the only subject that seemed important, everything else dwarfed by its magnitude. How could this have happened? What would Millie do? Would she keep the house? They lay together each drifting into their own private thoughts, each unaware that neither of them were speaking aloud any more.

Finally, he rolled over and kissed her. They made love tenderly, softly, grateful for the years they'd been given together, but tinged with the bittersweet realization that all love, and all marriages, in some manner or another, eventually come to an end.

Five

Manfred woke up revived. He felt as if he'd been asleep for a week. Gretchen's dark hair was splayed on the white pillowcase beside him, his arm around her waist. He rolled over quietly and slipped out from under the covers. Today was a free day, no tests and no consultations. Perhaps they could pick up their son for a nice brunch, he thought, then remembered the boy was studying for an exam. So that was out. The mining consortium, the people he worked for, had a building here in the city. He could run by the security offices there and try to find out what had happened in the world during the past two days. That might be a bit suspicions, though. It was probably best not to. He needed to avoid anything that might appear out of the ordinary.

So, he had a day in the city alone with his wife and no agenda. What could be better? He ordered breakfast from room service, and kissed Gretchen's cheek to wake her. They ate sitting on the bed together. It was something they hadn't done since their honeymoon.

"Would you like to do a little shopping?" Manfred asked biting a piece of toast.

"That's a silly question." Gretchen said dipping her finger in the butter and smearing it on the tip of his nose.

Manfred wiped his nose with his napkin. "We could even look for a few things for you as well."

"You're right. You do need new clothes. You've lost a lot of weight," she answered thoughtfully.

Nothing he had fit him anymore. He'd had his pants taken in about as much as he could, but they still hung on him as if he were not inside them. He needed shirts too, and a new belt. The weight he'd lost had been mostly around his middle, so his belt had about a foot too much leather on it. Manfred didn't care much about shopping. He could pick out what he needed it thirty minutes or so, if left to his own devices. So, he was happy to spend the time they had alone together shopping for Gretchen.

Gretchen Dietrich was a woman that without trying, always attracted attention, whereever she went and whatever she did, people looked at her and smiled. Manfred was used to it. The cascade of dark curly hair, combined with her fair complexion, and eyes that looked to be truly violet still turned heads wherever she went. At forty-five she was largely unchanged by age. No one would have ever known by looking at her how the world had taken its toll.

Manfred had always loved to watch her face light up as she tried on new clothes. Most of the things she put on she had no intention of buying. She just tried them on to see how they made her look, she transformed them and they in turn transformed her as well, and he was happy just to sit on a chair outside the dressing room, and watch. Offering an opinion from time to time, which she would listen to carefully and nod seriously before going on to the next outfit.

He sat on a bent-back armchair in a little dress shop called Rhonda's. Around him were strewn the bags of new clothes they'd spent the morning selecting to fit his shrunken frame. In front of him his wife turned and twisted centered in the three-way mirrors. This dress didn't do much for her.

"I don't really like it as well as the last one," he said honestly.

She accepted his judgment with her charecteristic solemn nod. "I'll try something that gathers at the waist. I need to find something that at least gives me the illusion I have a shape," she said.

"You have a wonderful shape," he offered.

"Wonderful for running a train on, straight as two tracks, no waist at all any more," she said as she disappeared through the door.

"You just leave off, now. I am personally quite fond of your shape," Manfred raised his voice a bit so she could hear him, then noticed the sales girl's smile and looked at the floor.

A bittersweet tinge of regret swept through him. Why hadn't they done this more? Why was it always work now? He wondered how many more days like this he'd get and how many he'd wasted?

He let that thought float free in his mind for a few moments. But he realized, sentimentality aside, work was going to have to come back to the front for a while longer. There were things he needed to take care of, business that needed attending to. Just in case there weren't as many days left as he hoped for. Even if this thing in his lung was nothing, there was a good chance someone was going to prison if he didn't come up with a solution for the illegal diamonds, and since it wasn't going to be anybody above him, he was the most likely candidate, tumor or not.

The first thing he needed to deal with was the house. Legally it was only half his. The other half still belonged to his brother. They'd inherited it jointly when their mother died. Gret was going to need a clear title. They didn't have enough money put back for a new one. He was going to have to talk to Fritz about that as soon as possible, once they knew what was what.

"How do I look?" Gretchen asked, breaking his train of thought. She came out of the dressing room in a cream colored blouse, with a print skirt.

"Like my daughter." Manfred answered smiling.

"Do you think it looks too young for me?" Gretchen asked with mild concern.

"No, the clothes look perfect. It's the old man you're with that's the problem," he laughed.

"You're not too bald yet, and you still have a few teeth…" she smiled, and bent at the waist to kiss him on the top of his head.

"I'll be bald once the chemotherapy starts," he said before he realized it had slipped out.

"Let's not put the cart before the horse," she said emphatically. "You don't know any more than I do how things will…"

Manfred changed the subject. "You know, you're a beautiful woman. Did I ever tell you that I love you?"

"Once or twice, but pretend you haven't."

"Turn around," he instructed, twirling his finger.

She turned away and looked back at him over her shoulder. "Does it make my rear end look too flat?"

"Did you say flat or fat?" he asked smiling.

"It makes me look fat?" Gretchen exclaimed in horror and whipped around to look in the mirror.

"No, it makes you look wonderful." Manfred replied.

"I want you to know, I'm not letting you go anywhere any time soon," she leaned over and kissed him deeply on the mouth. Then, she slowly broke the contact of their lips and turned walking slowly back to the little changing room. She pulled the curtain, but not all the way. She peeked out through the small crack between the two sheets of fabric and winked.

Manfred had a sudden impulse to get out of his chair and slip through the curtain. He glanced around the shop to see if anyone would notice. The young lady had returned to the register but was still wearing an amused expression. She looked up and met his eyes. He smiled back and shrugged his shoulders. She couldn't read his mind and there was nothing to be embarrassed about, but he felt a flush in his cheeks and knew that he was blushing anyway.

In the end Gretchen bought the first dress she'd tried on, a simple thing for church on Sunday. The shops were closing as they made their way back to the hotel. It was strange to watch the shopkeepers turning over their signs and

33

pulling the security shutters down for the night. The metallic clatter as they unrolled to barricade the windows and doors sounded so alien to someone from a town as small as Luderitz. Gretchen couldn't imagine living in such a place.

It was still too early to eat when they got to the hotel. She wasn't ready for the day to end. If Manny got back to the room he'd turn on the television, and then start looking through the e-mails he gotten today from work…

"Manny are you too tired for a drink?" she asked as they passed the lounge.

"I suppose not," he smiled. "I guess I can sit in a chair and watch my wife change clothes with the best of them."

"Why don't you order us a drink and I'll carry these upstairs," she said reaching for the packages in his hand.

"I can do that."

"That's not the point, order me a vodka martini," she said taking the packages before he had time to protest.

Upstairs, she changed into a little dress he'd never seen before and pulled her hair back and tied it close to her head.

"That's not right," she said turning her head from side to side. She brushed it out and tried another tact, then another. Finally she just shook it free and headed downstairs.

Manny sipped his gin and tonic and left half of it behind when they walked across the lobby to the restaurant for dinner. She ordered a bottle of a nice South African white with her dinner and ended up finishing most of it by herself.

"I'm trying to distract you. Is it working?" She asked with only a bit of a slur over desert.

"Yes, I find you very distracting."

"Well, I'm going to distract you silly, in a minute," she announced seriously.

Gretchen stumbled slightly as they crossed the lobby to the elevator. When the doors opened, she leaned against the back wall as Manfred pushed the button for their floor. As soon as the doors closed she grabbed her husband's shoulders and turned him to face her. She rose on her tiptoes to kiss him. As she did, she slid her hand up his thigh to his crotch.

Then she let go of him and leaned against the back of the elevator again. She locked her eyes on his and slowly unbuttoned the front of her dress to reveal that she wasn't wearing anything underneath.

By the time they got to their floor, one of Gretchen's breasts were out, its areola engorged, and nipple hard, awaiting the return of Manfred's mouth, his zipper was open and her hand was lost inside. They were more engaged with each other than they were with their surroundings, and missed the opening of the elevator door.

An indignant snort broke the spell. Manfred looked up to see a white haired matron, her face fixed in profound disapproval. "Can't you wait until you're in your room?" The old woman huffed.

"This isn't our room?" Gretchen asked innocently.

"I thought it was a bit small." Manfred said straightening himself as he walked past the old woman and down the hall.

Gretchen held herself together until they got the door open. Then she dissolved into laughter. She fell backwards onto the bed, pulling Manfred along with her, on top of her, and then into her. The building tension of the afternoon and evening had reached a peak. She clung to him thrusting hard against him, but something was wrong. The rhythm of his breathing was too fast, even for what they were doing. He was gasping for air, the wheezing getting louder and louder in her ear. She pushed him away to make him stop.

"Manny, are you alright?"

"Oh my God, I'll be fine, don't stop now." He implored her. "Just let me lay back a second…let me just…catch my breath."

She wrapped her arms around him and rolled them over, so she was on top. "You stay there and enjoy." She said as she lowered herself onto him. When his eyes closed, she watched his face intently as she rocked herself over him. As his breathing eased into the rhythm she recognized from the years together, she closed her eyes and rocked faster and faster, until he climaxed. Finally, she collapsed onto his chest, and allowed the orgasm that she had been holding back, to flood over her. She squeezed him inside her as hard as she could and shook in small spasms.

They lay together, clothes on, but covering nothing that modesty would demand. Manfred was asleep. His breathing had returned to normal and he snored softly. Her fingers moved through his hair. She couldn't fathom how something so wonderful could just end, that Manfred could be gone. How could the simple pleasure of their love be taken away? How could the warmth she felt in her heart when she looked at his face at times like these, the little sounds he made, how could they be gone? It was impossible. It shouldn't happen. But, in her heart she knew it could. The wheezing had been too bad.

The fact that she knew what was coming did nothing to ease the next morning's blow. She sat, tears streaming down her cheeks, as the pulmonologist delivered a death sentence in terse details. Manfred had small cell lung cancer, a very aggressive type that spread quickly through the bloodstream. The same killer that had taken her father had returned for her husband.

35

Six

The visitation for Charles Mason Lee M. D. was held at the new funeral home on Highway 39, north of town. It was a good thing, the old one was down by City Hall, and with the renovation that was going on downtown they'd never have fit all of the cars down there. The parking lot filled almost immediately and now there were cars lined up and down the four-lane in both directions.

Ray'd expected a crowd, Charlie knew just about everybody in town, but there were more folks out there than he could have ever imagined. The line of visitors spilled out of the building and stretched halfway across the parking lot. It didn't seem to ever get any shorter as people moved through the doors into the building. As soon as some folks went in more showed up. He didn't know how they were going to get them all through in the two hours they had scheduled for the visitation.

Ray looked around him at the knots of friends and family patting backs, rubbing arms, and murmuring condolences. These same people; doctors, lawyers, he'd even seen a state senator, would never have waited in line that long for anything else he could think of.

Ray and Lisa had gone to the funeral home early, with the family, to help with transportation. They'd come in Lisa's car. The Porsche didn't have a back seat anyone with legs could sit in. Staying at the funeral home with the family hadn't seemed like a bad idea when Lisa suggested it, but it had only been an hour so far and Ray already regretted not bringing a car of his own.

At first everyone spoke with a quiet reverence, almost as if they were afraid that they were going to disturb Charlie's sleep but as time went by, the presence of a dead body became less and less of a constraint. Voices got louder, people joked, or traded stories, and Charlie became less and less the center of attention and more and more furnishing, like an end table, unnoticed in the middle of a sea of flowers.

When Ray slipped out the back door, he'd had enough in the first ten minutes. He stood on the asphalt slab looking out at scrub pine, crows cawing away in the distance. He wondered if they were coming for the visitation? He turned toward the front of the building, the line of people still stretched out as far as ever. Most dressed in black. Some of the crows had already found their way.

"How're you doing?" Lisa asked from over his shoulder.

"I'm okay," he answered.

"The way you went out the door, I was worried that maybe something was wrong."

"I just needed to get out of there for a little while."

"There's a picnic table in a little alcove around here," she pointed away from the line of waiting visitors. "Do you want to go sit?" She offered him her arm. He took it, and allowed himself to be led in that direction.

"I took Sally's little ones out there for a break earlier."

"That was nice of you," he said, as they turned to walk around the corner.

"She needed a break. An eighteen-month-old and a three-year-old at something like this is just a mother's worst nightmare."

"Which part, the funeral or their kid's grandfather dying unexpectedly?" he asked glumly.

Lisa continued, as if he hadn't spoken. "The kids are doing great, but they're little. You can't expect them to go too long without a break."

He sat on the table. She stood for a minute and then sat on the bench beside him. After a few moments he said, "That was nice, too, but it wasn't what I meant. I meant it was nice for you to come out and check on me."

"Oh…" she said.

"Not that many wives in the middle of getting divorced would be so nice to the guy they were divorcing."

"We're not sure where we are. We're separated, and after last night I'm not even sure where we are with that." She put her hand on his arm.

"You live in Oxford. I live in Meridian. That's pretty separated."

"It's what you asked for. Did you forget?"

"It was a mistake, I was wrong. Come home," Ray blurted. He was picturing his own funeral. It would be just him and the folks from the funeral home.

"Let's not do this now." Lisa said.

"Which means no!" Ray snapped. He didn't know why he was so mad. All he knew was that he was. He didn't talk much for the rest of the visitation. He sat on the couch and watched as picture after picture of Charlie's life flashed across the flat screen TV that hung on the wall over a fake fireplace. That seemed to be the saddest thing of all.

He watched Charlie grow and change from a young boy in a black and white school picture into a high school football player, then a college kid, a medical student, a young parent, and by turning his head and looking through the doorway, into a corpse laying in a casket in the middle of a sea of faces.

Then it was time to leave. Finally people remembered why they were there in the first place, and everything became very solemn again. Ray made his way outside with the last of the crowd, to let the family have a few minutes to themselves.

Lisa appeared at his shoulder and slipped her arm around him before he noticed her.

"I think it went well," she offered.

"Compared to what?" Ray whispered.

"Why do you say that?" she asked sotto voce.

"I don't know. I don't know why…" he answered through clenched teeth.

"Ray, being angry, it's natural. You're best friend just died. That's not fair. He only got to be retired for six weeks. That's not fair either. It's okay to be mad. Funerals are a time for us to reassess our lives."

"…and I don't need counseling. I need a wife."

"Then you shouldn't have been screwing your nurse for a year and a half before you asked me for a separation."

She couldn't have had a greater effect if she'd physically punched him. There wasn't really an answer for that. He hadn't been sure she even knew about his affair before those words, so calmly delivered, knocked the wind right out of him.

"Because she decided not to leave her husband, doesn't mean that everything goes back to normal between us." She continued in the same tone. "We can start working on things, but we're not there. I still love you, but we have some issues that we're going to have to confront if we're going to move on."

"What…How?" he stammered.

"That's one of the things I'm talking about."

Before either of them could say anything else, the door opened and Millie emerged supported by her son and son-in-law, tears flowing down her cheeks. Any further discussion of the subject was impossible under the circumstances.

The rest of the evening was spent surrounded by Charlie's family, for the moment brought closer than they'd been in years by the immediacy of death. For just this moment, this instant, brought back into a familial bond, by a realization that only comes about by the common task of facing the death of a loved one. They were linked by shared experiences and a major link to those experiences was gone now. The only way they could keep Charlie alive was in their hearts, in their joined recollections, and so they shared. Healing themselves and one another in the sharing and the time flew. They talked until one-by-one exhaustion and sleep claimed them. Just as in time would death.

Ray was grateful for the exhaustion. Somehow, it let the anger die and made him grateful to have been a part of a good man's life.

Ray sat alone on his back porch and sipped beer from a long neck glass bottle. He couldn't sleep. A million questions swirled around in his head in the darkness. How long had she known? How had she found out? Had she known before she left. One question led to another, then another, then another, and he didn't have answers to any of them.

Seven

The first thing Fritz noticed about Las Vegas were the colors. They were everywhere. They lit up the sky from the fronts of the casinos. They filled the lobby of the hotel and covered the bodies of the people that inhabited this place. The second thing that struck him was just how much of everything there was. The room that the Safari Club had their annual meeting in was bigger than any hall he'd ever been in, and the kind of money that was being spent in that room was unbelievable. Hunting trips that cost more than he made in two years. There were shirts that cost more than he'd spent on his entire wardrobe and guns that cost more than most houses he'd ever heard of, hell, he bought his farm for less than what a matched pair of English shotguns cost here. Everyone appeared to be rich and, as far as he could tell, the only rule was that too much of everything was just about enough for Las Vegas.

It took them an hour to find out where that they were supposed to set up. When they finally did, Fritz had to go back to the hotel to fetch the table and the two Pelican cases that Walt had shipped over to get through customs. Walt unloaded each item and instructed him in where to put it. They hung up the Red Sands Safari banner against the wall behind them and covered their little table with zebra and kudu skins. Then they laid out pairs of horns and put up the pictures they'd taken last season of the smiling clients with the biggest trophies. When Walt had the table and the backdrop just the way he wanted it, they laid their brochures in piles around the table and set up their chairs in a cozy circle, like a campfire. All that was left was to wait for clients to walk by. Walt called it setting the trap.

Fritz gathered the containers and stowed them under the table. Then adjusted everything so you couldn't see them. Walt dropped into one of the canvas chairs with a sigh. "Tell you what sport. I'll take the first shift."

"I don't mind. I came to work."

"I'm going to sit here and rest my feet. You're going to work while you walk." Walt instructed, sweeping his hand in a big arc. "Go around and see what some of the other guys have set up, so we can get a feel for the competition. Look around in here a while. Then go out on the strip for a bit. There'll be plenty of work for both of us. We've got to be here for the next five days. Believe me, that's more than enough time to sit in one spot. Boring as hell actually. So, I'll man the trap. You go and beat the bushes. Take a walk around and have a look at the place. You're a likeable guy. You've got the look of a hunting guide, so just smile and shake hands with anyone you make eye contact with, if they talk back, tell 'em who you are and try to sell 'em a hunt."

"Okay, so that's it then?"

"That, and you better keep an eye on the money in your own pockets. Everybody here is out to get it, one way or another. The casinos here are probably less crooked than the ones at home, and the whores are better looking, but they're no different otherwise, so watch yourself. Be back around two, it's ten now."

He nodded at Walt and reset his watch. He walked steadily at first, just to get a feel for the layout of the place. It wasn't exactly what he'd expected but he didn't have any realistic basis for expectations anyway. All he'd ever seen about Las Vegas was from the old movies that he and Manny had snuck into when they were kids. Las Vegas was magic then, better than Disneyland because nobody was going to get any money out of Mickey Mouse. So, Vegas was what they'd dreamed of. As a kid he'd imagined himself walking into the Sands, him and Manny shaking hands with Frank Sinatra or Dean Martin. Maybe they'd go to dinner with Meyer Lansky or Bugsy Siegel, then spent the rest of the night at the roulette wheel or the craps table. Even then, he knew that it was just a stupid kids dream, the dream of a kid that wanted to be anywhere but where he was, marooned at the end of the world without a chance of ever going anywhere outside of his own little town. Stuck between the Atlantic Ocean and the great red desert. With a dead father and a mother, who when she wasn't drunk wasn't around much. Then she was gone too, and now he was here. It had been a long time since he had thought about his parents. Well, his mother really, he'd never met his father.

"Poor old Lilly." Fritz said sadly, thinking of his mother. His childhood had been tied to the fantasies and failures of that sad and unstable woman. She never recovered from becoming poor.

In her mind she wasn't. She'd always be rich. She couldn't conceive of being anything else. In her later years she completely lost the ability to tell the difference between her real life and the one she imagined.

When he and Manny were young they didn't know any better than to believe her. They grew up telling everybody that their father had been a rich banker. It was what their mother had always told them, and it wasn't completely a lie, but it wasn't completely the truth either. They didn't find out the truth until they were older that their father, Klaus Dietrich, had only come to banking in a roundabout way. So roundabout, in fact, you could call it crooked if you wanted to.

Their grandfather had been a Scottish banker named Russell. Lilly was his youngest. At seventeen, Lilly spent a summer abroad with a cousin and the two of them spent a great deal of that time in Dresden. While she was there, it was discovered that she was in need of a husband. So her father paid a visit to sort things out.

Young Klaus admitted to being one of the interested parties who had spent time with Lilly during her visit, but as he explained to her father, he was only one of several. Klaus, being a practical man, quickly eloped with Lilly in a fit of romantic frenzy. Upon their return from a prolonged honeymoon, paid for by Mr. Russell, the newlyweds settled in Glasgow where Klaus took up an executive position at the bank. Manfred was born quite prematurely, after only six months gestation, and there was great fear for his welfare. Luckily, Manfred had grown quickly, making the most of his time in his mother's womb. He arrived weighing over three kilograms, almost a normal full term birth weight, and was one of the healthiest premature births born at the Glasgow Hospital that year.

The young family had a very prosperous start, but it didn't take long for Mr. Russell to discover that his new son-in-law was an embezzler, and not a terribly creative one at that. The old man replaced the money and covered the tracks of any impropriety. He bought a partial ownership of a new shipping interest, in Luderitz, on the coast of South West Africa, and he sent his errant son-in-law there, thinking that that should straighten him out.

But costal Africa was a rough place and Klaus was a slow learner. It took him less than two years to get himself on the wrong side of a business disagreement with a Boer from Swakopmund. The old man felt he'd been cheated, and solved it the way his family had dealt with such things for generations, with grit, determination, and a loaded gun.

Lilly had always been a happy-go-lucky spendthrift and widowhood didn't change her. The problem was, her husband's untimely demise had left her with no money and seven months pregnant with Fritz.

Her only recourse was to turn back to her father, who bought her a house, hired some servants, and provided her with living expenses, but wouldn't bring her back to Scotland. During her postpartum depression Lilly developed a taste for gin and tonic, just to prevent malaria, of course. Malaria would certainly be a danger for a nursing infant, so she got her father to arranged to hire a wet nurse for his new grandson. Lilly was so worried about malaria, that many days she consumed enough gin and tonic to protect a small village. The natural side effect of her medication was that, even by her own admission, she may have been, at times, less than an exemplary mother.

The truth was, she wasn't a mother at all. From the time he came into the world Fritz had had only one family member to take care of him, and that was Manfred. It was a wonder that they'd gotten by at all. Fritz guessed sneaking into the movies, smoking, and a little beer once in a while weren't too bad when you took everything into consideration.

By the time Lilly died, their grandfather had suffered a stroke, and their uncle had taken over management of the Russell holdings, he ravaged everything that was not his, leaving them with nothing but the house. Luckily, as orphans, they were exempt from paying taxes on it, so at least they'd had a stable place to live.

Remembering the old days, he missed his brother. He should have made a point to see him before he left to come over. He'd tried to call the house but there wasn't any answer when he'd called. Manfred was probably working, but he wondered where Gretchen was? He should have taken the time to go by the school and check on Fritzy, then he'd have an answer and not be wondering about it now.

Should have, but Reese Stern was something of a magician and he didn't know if he loved her, but he loved being with her. She could make things disappear and make you feel wonderful about it; money, beer, time, even a certain part of his anatomy were subject to her magical talents. He'd have to make time to stop by and see the boy when he got home. Before he went to see Reese this time.

But right now he wanted to do something fun, since he was here and all. He'd seen the Bellagio in that "Oceans" movie, the one with all the stars in it. He headed that way to have a drink and maybe play a hand of blackjack.

Eight

Ray stopped the Porsche in front of a large colonial with six white columns and a pair of huge magnolia trees that defined the face it presented to the street. There were cars lining the driveway. Ray parked on the street, so that people could still get out. The house belonged to a guy named Pete Early who was having a get-together for a professional hunter from somewhere in Africa. Pete was a land and timber buyer that had been a friend of Charlie's. They'd been in a hunting club together. Charlie had always been sharp like that. Who'd have better hunting land than a guy who bought land for a living?

Ray didn't hunt, well he never had. He only knew Pete through Charlie. Charlie used to bring him to the club as a guest if they needed to fill out a foursome. They'd seen each other briefly at the funeral and the next day Pete had called and asked him to come for this get together tonight. Ray didn't have anything else to do, and he was tired of his own company, so here he was?

A teen-age boy wearing a Red Sands Safaris t-shirt answered the door.

"Hey, I'm Billy, come on in," the boy said, extending his hand.

"Hi Billy, I'm Ray."

"You from around here? I've never seen you at any of the banquets or anything." the boy asked as they walked down a hallway.

"I've lived here for a while, I've just never hunted," Ray admitted.

"Well, this would be a heck of a start. I went over there with my dad twice. I only hunted antelope, but it was a blast. This guy tonight's a new guy. I never hunted with him, but he's the real thing…here's dad."

Pete turned to face them as they approached. He was standing beside a table covered with brochures and a spiral notebook with a pen tucked in the spiral on one edge.

"This is Ray, he's never hunted before," Billy announced a little too loudly.

Pete was a large man, who'd clearly been muscular once, but had gone to fat in recent years.

"Hey Ray, glad you could come out. How's Millie?" he asked, handing him one of the brochures. He gestured at the notebook. "Let me get you to sign in and give us an e-mail address"

"She's holding up I guess."

"Sorry about Charlie, he was a good guy. I always liked him."

"He sure was," Ray said earnestly, having no idea what else to say.

"Well, let's find you a drink." Pete offered and turned, finished with the conversation. Ray followed him into a room with a twenty-five foot ceiling filled floor to beams with the heads, hides, and horns of animals from every corner of the earth. Several animals, mostly carnivores, and bears stood intact, prowling the corners of the room, others crouched, lounged, or sat placidly looking down from the thick heart pine beams that crossed overhead.

"This is incredible!" Ray said without thinking.

"Well it's a start." Pete replied with obvious pride, and led Ray to a bar that had been set up with a bartender in a black and white uniform with a bow tie.

"What can I get you sir?" the bartender asked with a smile.

"I've always wondered what a sundowner tastes like." Ray said unsurely to Pete.

"A sundowner is really more of a when, than a what." Pete replied cryptically.

"You read about them in Hemmingway." Ray tried to explain.

Pete nodded. "See, in camp there isn't any TV or anything. So, after dinner, what you do is sit around the fire and watch the sun set. You have a drink, tell some stories, tell some lies. Mostly about what happened that day while you were out hunting. I usually drink Vodka and Seven-Up, but you can drink whatever you like. I always picture old Hemmingway with Scotch whiskey neat, but really he probably drank mostly beer and martinis. Then there were the old Brits. They had their gin and tonics, to keep the malaria at bay."

"It was the quinine in the tonic water," Ray remembered aloud. "It prevents muscle cramping, too."

"So what can I fix you, sir?" The bartender asked again.

"A gin and tonic seems right." Ray answered.

"That's what my brother drinks." A voice with a mixed accent said over Ray's shoulder. Ray turned to see a man about his own height and build, but much fitter, and…he didn't know what to call it, dryer, maybe. Like he had no excess fluid left in him. A man, who'd, clearly spent most of his life outside in the weather. His sandy hair was bleached by the sun and his skin had the dark even tan women spent hours in a tanning bed trying to achieve.

"You must be the professional hunter." Ray guessed.

"Ray Moffett, this is Fritz Dietrich." Pete said, making the formal introduction. "Fritz is here from Namibia, near Etosha. He's going to tell us a little about what Red Sands Safari's has to offer."

"Mostly red sands, that and a lot of thorn bushes." Fritz whispered to Ray behind his hand. Ray wasn't sure if he was kidding or not. "More water, more animals." Fritz explained succinctly. "In the desert regions, we have good trophies, but you have to work hard to get them. This is real hunting, in hard country, where everything has thorns, teeth, or stingers. This isn't the boutique hunts the game farms pass off, where some old hand-fed bull is called up by rattling a feed pail." Fritz was setting the hook. No man wants to do something that's too easy. Men who came to Africa came looking for a challenge.

"What are your best trophies?" Ray asked Fritz.

Pete pointed to several of the heads suspended from the wall of his trophy room. "I took all of these with Red Sands." Pete offered, before drifting away to greet a newly arrived guest.

Ray let his eyes drift, from one trophy to the next, reading the small brass plaques affixed to the wall below each identifying each specimen by species, country, and year taken. The most beautiful was clearly the Kudu with its gracefully arcing, spiral horns. Horns so massive any practical use was unimaginable. The oddest species was the red hartebeest. So strange it looked as if it belonged in a Star Wars movie.

"There's the real trophy." Fritz said, pointing to a large antelope with three-foot spikes protruding from its head. "That's a gemsbok, the bible calls them an oryx, and there a few different oryx, but this one is the boy. They live all over Namibia, but to take one in the desert is the best. That's a man's hunt, that. I've seen a gemsbok bull toss a wild dog in the air with one horn, and eviscerate him with the other, in mid-air. A lone lion won't even take on one of these. They're just damned tough. Hard to anchor, too, it takes a good shot with a real bullet to put one down, without a day's tracking."

"What caliber are you talking about, a .270, or something bigger?" Ray asked. A .270 or a 30-06 were what most people around here hunted deer with. They were about the only calibers Ray had even heard of.

"A .270 would do the job, but like I said it would take a good tracker and the rest of the day to get it in the truck, without a perfect shot. Have to take it in the morning to be sure to find it." Fritz continued.

"Not in the evening?" Ray asked, "Couldn't you come back in the morning, and find it?"

"You could, but it will be pretty well eaten on by jackals and warthogs by then, you could do a skull mount, but not much else." Fritz answered.

Ray felt the disappointment of such a thing, to kill such a magnificent animal, only to leave it for carrion. "What a waste." He said aloud, without realizing he'd spoken.

"That's the way to see it." Fritz said with obvious approval. "Too many hunters' next question is, 'If that happens would I have to pay?' or 'Could I shoot another?' I don't even want to answer those bastards, but you said it just right. It's a waste that can't be undone. Oh, the scavengers need to eat too, but its best that they take the old and weak, the ones out of the mating group. A big bull lost, that's not just the loss of the animal, but the loss of the strong offspring that he would have produced as well."

Silently the two men stood side-by-side looking at the antelope considering its loss.

"The offspring are lost, whether he was found or not. He's just as dead." Ray said finally.

"That's true, as far as it goes." Fritz responded, "But if they lose one, most hunters then feel like they need to kill another bull, just as good, or better, than the one they lost, so two get taken, instead of one."

"I hadn't thought of that." Ray admitted.

"You have the right sense of things. You should come. I'll guide you. You can bring your wife." Fritz suggested, almost spontaneously. That was one of the things Walt kept on about until you wanted to strangle him. "Wife and kids, wife and kids, if they come once as baggage, they come back as clients, hell, half of them switch when they're there."

"Ahh, that's complicated. We're not living together." Ray said.

"Bring your kids then. We'll get them a trophy of their own."

"They're grown. If I came, I'd come alone."

"A free man then, come and stay as long as you like. Put the pets at the boarders and hop on a jet."

"No pets either…"

The conversation was stalling. Fritz was looking around the room, looking for the next booking.

"Fritz, I'd like you to meet Richard Grieg." Pete Early said, returning with another potential client. "Richard, this is Ray. Ray's never been to Africa either. In fact, you've never hunted at all, have you, Ray?"

Fritz returned his gaze to Ray, and arched his eyebrow quizzically. Ray felt his face flush with embarrassment. He didn't answer. Pete and Richard moved on toward the bar, continuing the conversation they had been engaged in, before Pete stuck a knife in Ray's self esteem.

"Everyone starts somewhere." Fritz said quietly, and then added conspiratorially. "I guided Pete his last trip, don't let it get to you, a lot of bravado in the camp, and here in the living room, but he very rarely makes a clean shot. Gets the shakes. He'd do better with a machine gun really."

Ray smiled, relieved. He liked Fritz. If he were to spend time in the bush with someone, Fritz would be an enjoyable companion. A man he would feel comfortable learning from. A man who obviously respected and cared about the animals he hunted.

"So what would you suggest, in the way of a gun, for someone who was just starting out?" Ray asked.

"A twenty-two bolt action, not one of the kid's guns, but, one of the nice ones, like a full size Winchester, or a Remington." Fritz answered.

"Can you hunt big-game with a twenty-two?" Ray asked doubtfully.

"You could, I've heard of a polar bear killed by one, and my brother Manny and I killed a leopard with one when we were just starting out, but I don't recommend it. Especially if you want to live a long life, with all the parts you started out with." Fritz answered with a laugh remembering the near hysteria of having an adult leopard with a chain looped around its back leg and wrapped around a tree trunk. Manny had been holding onto the chain for dear life and running around the tree, while the leopard tried it's best to get either a hold on him or get away. He'd, been afraid to shoot. Scared of hitting his brother or their dog. God, what idiots they'd been, but they'd needed the money the leopard skin brought for food.

"I can't believe you killed something like a leopard with a twenty-two." Ray exclaimed.

"I can't either, but that's a story for a campfire, after a hard day and a few drinks." Fritz replied. "You need to learn to shoot. You have to be a rifleman before you're a hunter. A good shot isn't necessarily a good hunter, but a good hunter is usually a good shot. Get a bolt action so you can learn to work the action without losing your sight picture. You need to be able to do that in case you need a second shot. It's always better to shoot twice and not need to, than to be too confident and lose a wounded animal. The beauty of a twenty-two is that you can shoot a lot, for not much money, and you can learn to shoot without putting up with a lot of kick."

"What do you mean, kick?"

"Recoil, a gun kicks too much you start to anticipate it belting you one in the chops, so you flinch. If you start off trying to shoot a big gun you start to flinch every time you pull the trigger." Fritz explained.

Ray nodded.

"I'd start with just some iron sights, but if your eyes are a little older and can't see the iron sights well, there's no harm in a good low power piece of glass." Fritz offered.

"That all makes a lot of sense. I wish you were going to be around, to kind of get me started." Ray said, with the anxiety that grips the uninitiated, when they face a task with potentially lethal consequences. He wanted to embrace life, not shorten it by accidentally shooting himself.

Fritz could see the doubt etched in his new acquaintance's expression. "Look, I'm scheduled to fly home at the end of next week. Tomorrow, I'm driving to Mobile, but I have to fly back out of the airport in Jackson on the way home. If you can get a rifle and a four-power fixed scope, we can ask Pete what range he shoots at, and I can run back up here, to get you started before I leave."

"That's really a lot to ask." Ray said, hoping it wasn't. "That's about three and a half hours each way."

"Nonsense, its all business. How can you come and give me bunches of money if you can't shoot?" Fritz said smiling. "I have to drive through here anyway to get to the airport."

"You can stay at my place if you need." Ray offered. "I live alone, and I'm not much of a cook, but we can sure get a steak and a few beers."

"Done then." Fritz said and offered his hand.

As the two men shook hands Pete Early called from across the room, "Fritz, Fritz…I've got the video ready, if you are."

Nine

Ray's brain was working overtime as he drove home. He wasn't sure how he felt about the things he'd just seen in the hunting videos. He vacillated back and forth between trying to choose which animals he wanted to hunt and being appalled by the images of idiots slapping hands and whooping like a bunch of kids over killing something magnificent. He was still trying to work out the dichotomy of emotions as he pushed the remote for the garage door and downshifted to make the turn into the driveway. He whipped the wheel to clear the garden wall, and directly in his path was the back end of Lisa's parked car. He jammed both feet down hard and the tires squealed. Her car was parked where she'd always parked. It was her usual spot. He just hadn't expected her to be there. He stopped inches from her car's back bumper.

Ray let his pulse quieten back down for a second, then shifted the Porsche into reverse and maneuvered it into the outside parking spot instead. His mind was a little sluggish from the gin, so he took a quick mental inventory to try and be sure there wasn't something he'd forgotten.

It was Thursday. He was sure of that. He'd worked today. What was Lisa doing down here on Thursday? He was pretty sure she taught a couple of classes on Fridays. Maybe tomorrow was some kind of holiday he'd forgotten about?

When he turned the knob on the kitchen door, it was locked. He almost never locked it anymore. It was a habit he'd developed living alone. He figure anyone who was going to take the time to break in through a garage door was determined enough to break a window to get in anyway. He hit the button for the garage door and looked through the curtains. He could see a light coming from the back of the house as he let himself in with the key.

"Hello. Anybody home?" he called out as he crossed the kitchen.

"I'm in here," he heard her say, and followed her voice back to the bedroom. As he came through the doorway she turned her head and gave him one of her sweet half-smiles. They came, whenever she wanted to smile, but was preoccupied with something else. He called it her Mona Lisa smile. He hadn't seen it in a long time.

"Hey, I didn't know you were coming down," he wanted to hug her, but her hands were full so he leaned against the doorframe instead.

" I got Sherry to teach my class tomorrow morning." Sherry was a graduate student that was working as Lisa's assistant this semester. "You don't mind do you?"

"That's a silly question," he smiled and let his eyes drift over the collection of shopping bags. One was from Village Tailor another from Cicada, then he saw one that gave him hope for the evening ahead.

"For me?" he asked, hopefully, pointing to the bag from Victoria's Secret.

"They can be." She answered, her smile broadening to its full intensity. "But I'm not sure they'll fit you. If you wanted some you should have let me know. I'm sure I could have found something in your size."

He walked to her and wrapped his arms around her waist, from behind. "I've missed you."

"I've missed you, too," she said and turned in his arms to face him, her intention to kiss him unmistakable, but just before she let her lips make contact with his she stopped, wrinkled her nose, and pushed him away. "Yuck, where have you been? You smell like cigars…and whiskey."

"Gin actually."

"Great, I'm only back in Oxford for a week and you're out carousing on a Thursday night. Not even the weekend," her smile never dimmed.

"At least it wasn't perfume," he offered.

"If it was, you could forget about seeing this," she said, holding up a silk camisole. "Really though, what have you been up to?"

"Well, I was thinking about going hunting. There was an outfitter that was giving a presentation tonight, so I decided to go and see what it was all about."

"Annnndd…" she drew the word out making it three syllables long.

"And, it looked like it might be fun," he replied trying to end the conversation there. He didn't really want to get into a prolonged discussion when he wasn't sure how he felt about the whole thing in the first place, yet. He was still trying to get through his ambivalence about it all. He didn't want her to try and resolve it for him before he'd had a chance to work things out for himself. He wanted to be the one to decide whether or not he was going to do this.

"I didn't know that you'd ever fired a gun," she said surprised.

"I haven't," he admitted.

"Won't that make it a little bit harder?" she joined her hands beneath her chin. "The animals can be kind of uncooperative when you try to drag them back to camp, without shooting them first."

"I'm taking some courses in hypnosis at the community college," he answered, nodding seriously.

"Who are you planning to hypnotize, the animals, so you don't need to shoot them, or me so I don't try to talk you out of this?"

Ray tried to keep the mood light. The last thing he wanted was an argument. "You're here aren't you, and it's only Thursday, so apparently I'm getting the hang of it."

"I hadn't thought of that. I wondered why I was driving down here."

"Why did you think you were?" he asked, truly wondering.

"I felt bad. It was kind of mean to drop that bomb on you before I left and not make an effort to start to work through it. I thought your feelings might have been hurt by the way I did it."

"Maybe a little," he admitted, "there is something else I wanted to talk to you about though...just watch the coin in my fingers," he said producing a quarter.

"Just read my lips," she mouthed the words "No Way". "Seriously, though, why don't you think of maybe using a camera at first?"

"You want to make dirty movies?"

"No you idiot, I was talking about going hunting," she shook her head.

"Who cares about hunting? I was going to hypnotize you for something a lot more fun than hunting." He raised his eyebrows.

She ignored him. "You could, you know, do wildlife photography?"

Ray was hoping to get away from that subject altogether. "I haven't eaten. Do you want to go out?" he suggested.

"I'm serious, I think you should try something like that first."

"Look, I don't know what I'm going to do about that. I was just trying to think of something interesting to do," he explained. "I'm just taking this one step at a time. First, I think I'm going to try to learn to shoot. If I can't do that, then I'll give up on the whole thing."

"My Dad would have found this really amusing, you know." Lisa said.

"I'm sure he would," Ray laughed at himself, remembering the early days of their marriage. He turned his eyes to the sky, "OK Bill, wherever you are, you were right, forgive me."

"I don't think he needs to, he really liked you, even if you were a know-it-all tree-hugger," she said.

"He called me that?" Ray asked.

"Not just him," Lisa replied smiling. "We all called you that."

"Just because I wouldn't go hunting?"

"No because you gave endless lectures about why it was morally wrong to cut down trees and go hunting and eat meat. But he did love you," she offered.

"Well, not until I cut the pony-tail off." He smiled at her.

"My God, I'd forgotten all about that. No, he never liked the pony tail."

"Your Dad was a good man. I wish he was still here, I'd like him to be able to teach me how to shoot." Ray said looking into her eyes softly, knowing how much she'd loved her father.

"He taught me. I can try to help you, if you'll let me. You can use my guns." Lisa offered.

Lisa had grown up on a farm, with her dad and two older brothers, her poor mother had wanted her to stay around the house, but Lisa wouldn't have any of it. All she cared about was tagging along with "the boys." Hunting and fishing were the things they loved, so they were the things she loved too. She'd hunted whatever they hunted. Deer, hogs, wild turkey, ducks, or quail it had been all the same to her. And after they'd married she never hunted again. Her guns sat unused in her father's study until he died.

"I thought your brother took your guns when your dad died," Ray said.

"No, I brought them here," she admitted.

"Where? I never saw them."

"That's because I never told you. I hid them in a closet."

"Why would you do that?" Ray asked, surprised. Apparently there were a lot of things about her he didn't know.

"I don't know, I didn't want to argue with you about it, and I didn't want to give them up."

Ray frowned.

"You hated guns," she explained. "I didn't want you to freak out, with the 'guns and kids in the same house' thing."

"Do they still work? I mean, could you still shoot them?" The last thing he wanted was to blow his face off trying to shoot some old worn out gun.

Lisa laughed, "Sure. Guns aren't something that have a use-by date. At least not if you take care of them."

He wasn't really sure how to express his reservations. He didn't want to insult his wife or his father-in-law, but he didn't want to go to Africa with some hand-me-down girl's gun either.

"They should be fine for anything you could possibly want to hunt around here," she kissed his cheek. "It would be fun really, getting back to shooting again. What are you planning to hunt?"

"I'm not sure yet." He stalled.

"That's kind of important…" She let her voice trail off.

"I was thinking I'd go to Namibia." He said watching her face closely, trying to judge her reaction.

"Namibia, as in southern Africa?" Lisa asked incredulously. "Don't you think you should start off here and see if you like it or not first. Maybe get a little experience under your belt? You could go hunting this fall with my brothers. They still hunt on the farm at Garlandsville every year. They'll be happy to have you come. They may be a little bit surprised, but I'm sure they'd love to do it."

"I want Africa to be the first place I hunt." Ray said emphatically.

"I'm not arguing," Lisa explained, "but, can we at least discuss this before you make up your mind? It's not my place to tell you what you can or can't do."

"I'm just daydreaming." Ray explained.

"I remember when the Porsche started out as one of your daydreams." She pointed out.

"That was a pretty good decision," he reminded her.

"That was the start of a midlife crisis that you're still in the middle of. It was the start, then the affair, and now this…"

"Please let's not do this tonight," he pleaded. "You just got here, let's just go get something to eat, please."

"I just want you to see the pattern. It's worse now because of…look, I just don't want you to get hurt trying to chase some illusion to try and make yourself feel better about Charlie's death."

"This doesn't have anything to do with Charlie's death." Ray said sharply, knowing that neither one of them believed it.

"Okay, we can just let this go for now." Lisa said gently, "I came down to make up, and no I haven't eaten yet. If you take me somewhere nice, I'll put on my new leopard print panties, and we can play 'Big-game hunter and the Leopard Princess' when we get back."

Ray smiled at first, then he put his hand to his chin to simulate thought and forced a frown, "You didn't say anything about a leopard print bra, you can't be the 'Leopard Princess' without the whole outfit."

"The panties are the whole outfit, the leopard princess doesn't wear a bra. She's a free spirit. You may even have to chase her around the back yard and into the spa if you want her." She arched her right eyebrow.

"That's the best offer I've had in years. I'll turn the heater on before we go. Is there anywhere special leopard princesses like to eat?"

Friday morning Lisa lay awake watching Ray sleep. After a while she got up and made a pot of coffee. She poured a cup and looked for some creamer with no luck. She went to the laundry room and got a rag torn from an old T-shirt and looked under the sink to find the small can of 3-in-One oil that had been there for years. In bare feet she padded to the closet in the back hallway. As she reached into the back of the closet, she ran her hands over the cases of the three guns she'd hidden there. The first had the unmistakable large tube of a shotgun. She removed it and leaned it in the corner without removing its protective stocking. The second gun was the one she wanted to see, its barrel led to a very short action, it was the first gun her father had ever given her.

She ran her finger over the piece of masking tape on the side of the gun's case. On it was a single word, "Lisa" written with a purple magic marker, in her father's precise printed hand. She slipped it out of the case and began to run the rag over its metallic surfaces. Removing the protective coating of grease he had put on the rifle, to preserve it. The job he had done was so thorough, that there was no rust at all in the grease or oil she wiped away.

She'd have to go to the sporting goods store later, to get a cleaning rod. That was the only way to be sure the bore was cleared of grease before they could fire it. She leaned the beautiful little rifle next to the shotgun, and retrieved the last gun resting in the back of the closet. It was the gun she'd used on deer and hogs. She put the rifle to her shoulder and aimed down the barrel. She didn't know if it would fit Ray. Her father had taken off the recoil pad, and sawed three-quarters of an inch off of the butt to get it to fit her. He'd done such a precise job that it was impossible to tell that anything had ever been done.

Immersed in her memories, Lisa didn't notice Ray as he came into the study behind her. He watched as she aimed the rifle at a picture of a sunset. With a practiced respect she lowered the barrel, and removed the bolt. Then she raised the action to her eye and looked through the barrel out the window. As her head came up she caught a glimpse of Ray in her peripheral vision, and jumped.

"Holy crap, Ray, you scared me to death."

"You know a lot more than I do about guns."

"I grew up with them."

"How did you know how to take it apart?"

"You mean, remove the bolt? That's not really, taking the gun apart, its just part of how you clean it. Here, look." She began to show Ray how to replace and remove the bolt, then how to open the floor plate to remove any unfired rounds.

"I need to know all this to shoot?" he asked.

"No, you need to know all this to avoid killing yourself."

Ray nodded solemnly.

Then she showed him how to place the ball of the front sight in the bowl of the rear sight to aim. When she finished showing him with the larger rifle, she picked up the little rimfire and repeated the same thing with it. Then handed the rifle to Ray.

The first thing he did was to point it at her.

"Whoa Ray! Never point a gun at anybody!"

"Its empty, we just took the clip out," he stammered defending himself.

"You don't know that, you haven't looked down the barrel. There can be a round in the chamber. Sometimes the extractor can jump the rim. That doesn't even matter. You have to treat every gun like it's loaded, all of the time. Every time you pick it up you have to pretend that somebody might have loaded it when you weren't looking."

"That's ridiculous."

"Not if you want to stay alive. That is the one lesson my dad beat that into our heads every time we went out. His favorite saying was, 'It's the gun you're sure is empty, that shoots you.' Even if you know a gun's empty treat it just like you would if you knew it was loaded."

"Sorry." Ray said, sheepishly. "Probably a good thing you're teaching me now."

"Did you know that the only advice that my dad ever gave me about marriage was about guns?"

"He told you to shoot me?"

"No, but, it was one of the times I felt like it. It was after our first big fight. I was pregnant with Mark. Do you remember? I went home that night."

"I remember you stomped out slammed the door and took off in the only car we owned," he laughed. "I just sat there and worried. After a while, your dad called me. He said you were okay, and that you'd be home in the morning."

"You never told me he called you," she said, surprised.

"He asked me not to, I guess it doesn't matter now." Ray replied with a tinge of sadness. Her father had been a good man. A simple Mississippi farmer who'd worked hard his whole life and left this earth with not much more than he came into it with.

"Anyway, when I got home, I told him that I'd made a terrible mistake marrying you, that you weren't the man I thought you were. He just sat there a few minutes packing his pipe. Then he looked up and asked, "Do you remember the line: What God has joined, let no man put asunder? That means no woman either. You and Ray don't know the first thing about each other yet. It's like trying to shoot a gun without knowing what the trigger is. You start to run your hands around and BOOM! the gun goes off, and you don't know what you did to cause it.' He said marriage was the same way. You needed to find each other's triggers. That everyone has things that fire them up, and make them lose their temper. That it was our job, to find out what those things were, it wasn't that you couldn't go there, but at least you knew what to expect if you did. I think that was about the best advice on being married I ever got."

"I still love you." Ray said earnestly.

"I love you too, but we're going to have to work to fix what's happened to our marriage. We'll need time to do that. I don't want to lose that time because you go off and get yourself killed. Promise me you won't go to Africa until you can really shoot. When something's after you, isn't the time to realize that you need some more practice."

"I'll tell you one thing I'm sure I don't need any more practice at... cooking," Ray announced. "If you'll cook up a few eggs, I'll mix us a pitcher of mimosas."

"I think I can manage that." Lisa replied, slipping the little rifle back into its case.

Breakfast ended with them sipping mimosas side by side in the hammock. Lulled by the gentle swaying, the cheese omelets and Champagne were like a sedative. Ray stirred. Inside the house, the telephone was ringing.

"Just let it ring," Lisa said, putting her hand on Ray's shoulder, when he tried to get up. "I don't care who it is, they can leave a message. What could be more important for us right now, than this?"

"Nothing," he agreed, slowing perceptibly, and lying back, the phone in the house rang twice more before the answering machine in the study picked up. "What if its one of the kids?"

"Then we'll call them back in a little while, besides if it's either one of them, they'll call your cell in the next two minutes."

Ray slipped his hand in his pocket and pulled out his phone. He tried balancing it on his stomach, but the motion of the hammock made it slip, and it fell between her hip and his. He retrieved it and rested it and his hand gently on her lower abdomen. She reached down and moved it upward several inches. He looked at her quizzically.

"My bladder's full, I drank three cups of coffee before we laid down."

"Then why don't you get up and pee?"

"For the same reason I didn't want you to answer the phone, I miss this and I'm not ready for it to end," she replied.

"You can come right back."

"But we won't, the spell will be broken, we'll start cleaning up breakfast dishes, or moving magazines, something," she said.

The back of his hand stroked her ribs softly. "Well there's only grass under us, we can lay here till you pop, or you can just pee on the grass."

"Gross!" she said nudging him with her elbow.

"Just trying to be helpful," he smiled. They lay together silently, not needing to speak. Ray had just started to snore quietly, when Lisa heard the sprinkler heads pop up.

"Oh crap," she thought and rolled backward, landing on her rear end in the grass just as the water from the nearest sprinkler head began to pelt her in the face.

Ray managed a "What the…" before the hammock that had once been under him and was now above him, released him to the unrestrained pull of gravity. He flailed his arms frantically in what Lisa could only surmise was a desperate attempt to fly. He switched tactics mid-air and tried to get his arms under him, to break his fall, but the attempt at flight had taken too long, and he crashed, face first, splashing down in the wet grass.

"Are you alright?" Lisa asked.

"Oh it's you," he answered without moving, his words muffled by the grass. "For a moment there I thought you'd exploded." She convulsed in laughter, leaning her back against him. They lay in the artificial downpour until the control box on the sprinkler system moved on to the next zone.

"I guess you may as well pee now." Ray advised.

"Too late," she answered as another fit of laughter overcame her, "…in fact…you're laying in it now." She laughed kicking her feet, splashing the water under her.

"I thought it was nice and warm here." He answered still not moving. She laughed even harder, sliding down to lay alongside him.

"If you can control yourself…and your bladder, I guess we may as well go inside and see if I have any teeth left." Ray intoned in a flat deadpan, to the grass just beneath his face. Lisa, now helpless from laughter, could only roll from side to side.

Lisa stood examining Ray's nose, they'd showered together and stood face to face, she in a terrycloth robe, and he with a towel wrapped around his waist. "I don't think it's broken. I think what got bruised was mostly your pride."

"It hurts right here…" He answered, running the tip of his finger along the bridge of his nose.

"You should have flapped harder," she answered him chuckling. "You didn't hit until you stopped flapping."

"Alright for you, you little brat." He said, swatting her on the bottom. "Anyway, I wasn't flapping, I was trying to regain my balance."

"It didn't look like it. It looked like you were trying to fly," she teased, still laughing.

"You always said, I was your Superman. Maybe I did think I could fly for a minute." Ray conceded.

"Nice try, but Superman doesn't flap his arms." She snatched the towel from around his waist, and wrapped it around his neck and kissed him quickly. "All I have to say about that is, Thank God you're not faster than a speeding bullet."

She walked into their closet. Her head reappeared as she pulled a blouse over it, "I'm having lunch with Millie. You don't mind, do you?"

"Not if I can come too." He said only half jokingly.

"No way. You won't be able to keep quiet about this morning's water sports."

"My wife's urinary incontinence isn't an appropriate topic of luncheon conversation?"

"Only if you want a lump on your head, to go with the lump on your nose," she answered, shaking her fist.

Ten

Lisa felt a tiny flicker of guilt about ditching Ray as she drove to the restaurant. It wasn't that she didn't understand his wanting to come. It was a reasonable thing to want to do. He hadn't seen Millie since the funeral. He wanted to support her...and, there was still a lot of guilt there on Ray's part. But the truth was; today needed to be about Millie and Lisa, not Ray.

They both had things that they needed to say. They hadn't spoken much since Lisa had moved to Oxford. With the relationship between their husbands things had been awkward. Lisa had been somewhat surprised when Millie'd called saying they needed to talk. There had to be something relatively important, something more than the small talk that they'd been confined to after the funeral and around the family and children that she needed to say.

Ray being there would've prevented that. There were too many things that neither one of them would be able to talk about in front of him. He had a tendency to be so...so...judgmental wasn't really the right word; it was more that he, like most men, had a limited emotional scope. Subtleties, conflicted emotions, emotional currents weren't things he noticed, or wanted to let unfurl and drift unresolved. He wanted to identify the problem and find a way to fix things. Some things, like death and infidelity, weren't fixable...they just were... and that was that.

These were the kind of things that needed time. They were things that needed to be talked about, not fixed, discussed in person, not on the phone. They were things that needed to be talked about in a setting where you could judge the non-verbal clues, the looks, the eye movements, the facial expressions of the person you were talking to, so you could be sure what it was they were trying to communicate to you in it's full complexity.

Lisa saw Millie seated at a table by the window when she came into The Landing and waved at her from across the room, then walked past the hostess with a nod. Millie stood up as Lisa reached the table and hugged her tightly.

"You look so good. I meant to tell you that after the funeral, but you remember how that was..." Millie started.

"You had your hands full, as it was." Lisa murmured as she kissed Millie's cheek.

Their conversation started, as it had to, with talk about the kids and the funeral, but Lisa knew that there was too much under the surface of what Millie was saying not to let the conversation stay there until Millie felt comfortable with where it was she wanted to go.

"The children are fine. Everyone is back home," Millie started.

"Has Sissy gone back to work?" Lisa asked.

"She started back that Monday. She still comes over every afternoon." Millie answered looking down at her salad.

"That's very sweet of her. She's worried about you." Lisa answered noncommittally.

"It is..." Millie drifted off.

"But?" Lisa prompted.

"I don't know. It's very sweet of her." Millie repeated herself.

"Very sweet." Lisa echoed.

"It's just that I'm not used to it. I'm not used to spending that much time with her. I run out of things to talk about. So, we get stuck going over and over the same things." Millie started.

"What things?" Lisa asked.

"Charlie, then, 'Am I okay?'...then 'What am I doing with myself all day?'" Millie answered, her emotions beginning to come to the surface.

"She's just concerned."

"I know she's just concerned, but I don't want to think about all this every single night. Sometimes I just want to watch TV or read a book or a magazine, anything but talk about how my life is in suspended animation. Sometimes I just need to turn that all off and ..."

"Recover," Lisa finished the sentence for her.

"It's recover, but it's not recover." Millie looked intently at Lisa's eyes trying to judge where to go next.

Lisa nodded without speaking. Anything she said would take the conversation away from where Millie was trying to go.

"It's like I can't seem to get my life back. Can't find the balance with her there every night." Millie was struggling to express how she felt.

"Have you talked to her about it?" Lisa asked.

"I don't know what I'd say. Anything I could say would sound ungrateful, and it's not that..."

"You just have to find your own way to cope with Charlie being gone?" Lisa suggested.

"No, it started before that. It doesn't have anything to do with Charlie. It does…but, it doesn't. I lost Charlie when he died, but I lost myself when Charlie retired. My whole life, I'd had a life of my own. There was time with Charlie, but he was gone so much of the time. He wasn't just hanging out around the house. He was at work or at the office writing or fishing or playing golf. He did what he wanted to do…you know? I had my own life. But when he retired it changed everything. I had to be home to fix him lunch, or his feelings were hurt. He started to go and watch me play tennis. He wanted me to start playing golf." Millie answered, tears starting to flow down her cheeks. "…and I'm such a spoiled bitch, that I resented all of it."

"You have to give yourself a break. All those things are normal. It was a big change for you." Lisa reassured her.

"A break is what I wanted. I kept thinking, 'I can't stand this. He has to get a part time job or something.'"

"…and then he died." Lisa said.

"And then he died." Millie repeated.

"And you felt just a little bit relieved." Lisa said, being careful not to sound disapproving or judgmental.

"How horrible is that?" Millie asked, picking up her wine glass and taking a drink to mask her emotions.

"It's not horrible at all. It's natural. Most things that happen to us are like a big ball of mixed up emotions. A lot of times it's impossible to sort out what we feel. A lot of times what we feel isn't what we want to feel. So we feel guilty about it." Lisa explained.

"Well I do. I feel like I somehow willed Charlie dead, and it happened."

"You know that's not true." Lisa answered, firmly.

"No I don't. Who just falls over dead in the kitchen, six weeks after they retire? I feel like I must have killed him somehow." Millie said, her voice flat, not crying, beyond crying, needing to understand for herself.

"People don't just die because we have an errant thought about them once in a while," Lisa reassured.

"That's part of the problem, it wasn't just the occasional errant thought. I spent half of the time I had left with him after he retired furious with him for …I don't know what…for suddenly showing back up. Our whole marriage I knew that medicine came first, that everything else had to come behind that, but then it was fishing, and then it was golf. He was always obsessed with one thing or another, and every one of them came before me, or the kids even. Then he retired, and he was suddenly supposed to be the center of my life again, well for the first time really, and I resented it. "

Lisa reached over and placed her hand on top of Millie's.

"It wasn't like I knew it was only going to be for six weeks. I feel guilty about thinking any of it. All I could see was spending every waking minute of the rest of my life with him following me from room to room. Now I feel horrible. I know you don't want to hear any of this. You're the only person I can talk to. I can't tell the kids any of this, I can't tell anyone." Millie seemed to deflate as she spoke; she finished with a deep exhalation that cemented that image.

"That's what real friends are for, the hard stuff, the stuff that you can't really say, even to yourself. You get so that you ball yourself up trying not to let things get out, but they just keep marching around in your head driving you crazy until you can't hardly stand it anymore. Feeling afraid and trapped when your life changes is nothing to blame yourself for. It's natural. You wanting some space didn't kill Charlie, it didn't have anything to do with anything. If you could kill your husband just by wishing bad stuff Ray would have disintegrated years ago."

"There's a fine line. Everything is different when your husband retires." Millie was distant, absorbed in her own thoughts. "Some of my friends got divorces. They just couldn't take it. Before Charlie retired I couldn't imagine it. Not wanting your husband at home. You think it's going to be a dream come true. But then, when it happens, it's hard, everything changes."

Millie picked up a roll and buttered it. Lisa poured some Balsamic vinegar onto her salad.

"It makes you wonder how many "heart attacks" aren't really heart attacks at all?"

"You mean real murders, not errant wishes?" Lisa questioned.

"God, I know that sounds terrible. I don't even know why I said it, and certainly I didn't ever consider it, but I swear, I'm sure some women just get to the point that they can't stand it anymore and they aren't as strong as you, not strong enough to leave, so they do something else?"

"Like what?"

"I don't know, like mix up the pills, or put a pillow over their husband's face while they're laying there on the couch snoring away. They don't do autopsies you know."

"What do you mean?" Lisa wasn't quite sure where this was going.

"On retirees, they almost never do autopsies on older people who die at home any more. I guess there are just too many of them, and almost all of them have something going on health wise, so they just don't do them, unless the family asks or something. I thought they might want to do one on Charlie, but they didn't. I'm sure some murders slip by undetected," Millie said.

"You didn't, did you?" Lisa asked carefully, afraid of the answer.

"Of course not." Millie said, taken aback, "How could you think that?"

"I didn't." Lisa

"They're just things that run through your head. It doesn't make sense, does it?" Millie smiled. "How are things with Ray?" She said, changing the subject.

"Better, I'm working through it. I still get angry. Ray snapped at me and was pushing me about coming home at Charlie's visitation, outside, and I told him he should have thought about that before he started screwing his nurse."

"Did you tell him how you knew?" Millie asked, a hint of anxiety in her voice.

"No, he had no idea that I knew."

"Sometimes I wonder how they were ever doctors, neither one of them was very observant. Well, what I mean is…I mean Charlie wasn't, Ray still isn't. You know what I'm saying," Millie offered awkwardly.

"I know what you mean. But no we didn't have time to go into it that night, and I haven't brought it up again. You can kind of tell Ray is just waiting for the other shoe to fall. But, he's being extra nice while he's waiting."

"I'll bet," Millie exclaimed. "When are you going to tell him?"

"I'm not going to tell him anything about you or Charlie, if that's what you mean. My God, I can't…I needed to know…so I could control something in my own life."

"I can't tell you how hard it was, to do it. I was torn. I wished Charlie had never told me about it in the first place. Then I wouldn't have felt like I was in the middle. I had to make a choice. I didn't want to. I told Charlie to go to Ray and tell him he needed to tell you, but he wouldn't. He kept saying that I needed to mind my own business and stay out of it. He was furious with me when he found out that I'd told you. But, I had to, I would have wanted someone to tell me if it had been Charlie," Millie explained. "Even if it meant that things were over between us."

"I know it was a hard thing for you to do, and even if things work out with Ray, it was something I needed to know. To feel like…to feel like…myself, I guess."

Eleven

On Sunday morning Lisa loaded the rifles and some ammunition into the trunk of her car without mentioning it to Ray. After lunch she drove east, headed out of town.

"Where are you going?" Ray asked as they passed Bonita Lakes. "I thought we were going to the mall?"

"I thought we might do something else," she said.

"Is there something going on at the Agricultural center?"

"Nope, it's a surprise."

It clearly was. Ray still didn't know where he was when she turned on to the old Sand Flat Road.

"What's out here?" he asked.

She nodded her head forward as they came over a hill. The road dead-ended at the police training facility.

"If you're going to learn to shoot, this is the place to do it," she explained.

'What am I going to learn to shoot? I don't really need to learn how to shoot a pistol. Besides, they won't even let us on...you have to be a police officer." Ray was clearly apprehensive.

"It's fine, the range is open to anybody on the weekend. There are rifle ranges on the back. I have the rifles in the trunk."

This was the kind of thing they needed to do together, she thought. It would help them work things out in a new way. Doing things they hadn't done before. Doing things from different roles, so maybe he could learn to respect her abilities and start to see her as more of a whole person and not just as a...a...wife.

Ray had actually been a lot more receptive than she'd anticipated to her teaching him to shoot and, at first, seemed to be having fun with it. They went through everything and he did great with the little twenty-two. By the end of the first box of shells he was hitting the black ring of the twenty-five yard target with every shot.

It was the gun that her father had started her with, and it was the one that made the most sense for Ray to start with. After all, he'd never shot a gun before in his life. They should've probably just stopped there for the first day. Just let him keep working on the mechanics and getting the routines down. Shooting well. Just to build up his confidence. But he was doing so well he wanted to give the bigger gun a try, and that's when the trouble started.

Before she let him pick up the other rifle, she wanted to go back through everything one more time. How the safety worked. How to remove the bolt from the rifle. All of the stuff they'd gone through on the twenty-two. Just to be sure. There were differences between the two guns, differences that could be important.

That was when Ray's whole attitude changed. Before she got halfway through he was nodding his head like: "Come on, come on, I already know this shit." Everyone around them could see it. He might as well have just said it out loud.

When he got in a hurry to do something Ray acted like a kid with ADD or something. He was being a dick, so she just cut to the chase.

Ray leaned his forearm on the bench and aimed at the target. He'd gotten ahead of himself. His earphones sat perched on the top of his head, not touching his ears. She touched him on the shoulder to try and warn him, but he'd held up his hand.

"I know what I'm doing. We've been over it and over it and over it."

"Okay…" she said, and then watched carefully as he aimed the rifle at the twenty-five yard target. It was quite obvious that what happened when he pulled the trigger of the little rifle came as a complete surprise to him. His expression was priceless. His mouth flew open and he jerked his head around to look at her. Furious that she'd tricked him into doing something stupid.

"You forgot your hearing protection."

People around them smiled. Ray's face turned beet red.

"You did pretty good though." She offered, feeling just a little bit guilty for embarrassing him.

His bullet had hit just a little low on the bulls-eye, but it showed that he had remembered what he'd learned from shooting the twenty-two.

"Damn, that was loud." He said under his breath.

"That's why they call them high-powered rifles," she'd explained, while he was still shaking his head.

The second shot was the end of Ray shooting well at all. He aimed forever, then he closed his eyes and jerked the trigger. Dirt sprayed all over the target. He must have hit the ground in front of it by two or three feet. Since that bullet had hit low, he tried to aim higher, they couldn't see where that one hit at all. The shot after that was back into the dirt.

Ray laid the gun down on the bench and got up muttering under his breath. So, she did what made the most sense. She took the next shot. Just to make sure the gun was on target, Ray's first shot may have just been a fluke. The bullet hit the black circle in the center of the target. Then she did it twice more with the same results. So the gun was on.

After that Ray's shooting got even more erratic, sometimes hitting in front of the target, sometimes hitting the paper around the bull's eye, and sometimes flying over the target and hitting the dirt that had been piled up behind the targets to make a backstop.

Some of it was that he was anticipating the blast and recoil. The rest of it was that he was pissed off, and he damned sure wasn't going to stop shooting until he was hitting the target too. She wasn't even sure that he was aiming any more.

Thank God they ran out of ammunition. The only shells she had were reloads that her father had made, and she only had two boxes of those. She remembered an old trick that her father had used on her and her brothers when they were learning to shoot. She didn't tell Ray that they were out of bullets. Instead, she took the gun from him and closed the bolt on an empty chamber, then handed it back. When he pulled the trigger with no cartridge in the chamber the flinch was obvious.

"Okay," she said, taking the rifle and working the bolt. "Now concentrate on aiming the rifle. Don't think of anything else...okay, now gently gently, begin to squeeze the trigger."

Ray jerked the trigger and pulled the front of the rifle left with his left hand.

"Okay, work the action. Now you know that the gun's empty, squeeze gently, and don't try to jerk it. Just curl your finger in."

The firing pin dropped with a metallic clink, but the rifle stayed rock steady.

"Let's try it again," she said.

It embarrassed him, but he did it twice more.

"Alright, give me another bullet," he barked. He was pissed.

"We don't have anymore," she said.

"God damn it..." he sputtered.

Then very calmly and deliberately he started to gather all of their gear together. She tried to help, and he handed her one of the gun cases. Took the ear and eye protection back to the counter and walked to the car. Just leaving her standing there. She had to follow after him, down the line of all those other shooters.

They didn't speak in the car on the way home. They didn't speak while she packed. He helped her load the car and gave her a quick peck on the cheek and that was that. It was well past dark when she finally got the car loaded and on the road back to Oxford. He didn't call to check and see if she'd made it home.

Twelve

Manfred lay on his back, sweating in the dark. He couldn't wait to get out of the bed. He'd been looking up at the ceiling long enough. Waiting for the sun to come up, so he wouldn't have to turn the lights on. He didn't want to wake his wife or son just yet. Let them rest a while longer if they could.

He waited a few more minutes, until it got light enough for him to see the outlines of the furniture clearly to get up. There wasn't really any place to in the room to sit with Fritzy asleep on the couch, so he went to the bathroom and slipped on a shirt and a pair of pants. As he sat in a chair and pulled on his loafers he looked at the lumpy outline of his son sprawled out, a leg hanging off the couch. He'd taken his exam and spent the evening with them last night, then stayed to go to the clinic this morning. To be there for the first chemotherapy session. Manfred was touched by the boy's concern. He hoped it was unfounded. He didn't expect this to be a big deal, but then again, he had no basis for expectation. He had no frame of reference. He'd never been around this type of thing before. The only thing he had to gage it by were the things that he had been going through since he got here, and they seemed to be going fairly well, so far.

Manfred slipped out the door and walked to the elevator. It was ridiculous how much he wanted a cigarette, but he wasn't going to have one. He'd told Gret he'd quit. Not that stopping was going to do anything at this point. The cancer was already here. It was a bit late to try and prevent it now. The horse was out of the barn.

In the lobby he ordered a cup of coffee and looked longingly at the row of cigarette packages arranged neatly behind the counter, but coffee was all he got. He'd been awake most of the night thinking about different ways things could go, and the conclusion that he'd come to was that he didn't know enough to predict the outcome with any certainty at all. There was no way to sort out all the possible options that kept running through his head. No way to tell which of the things he'd been thinking about were real concerns and which ones were just fear?

His head hurt. Maybe the coffee would help. He took the bottle of pills they'd given him to take before the chemotherapy out of his pocket and laid all the pills out in a line on his napkin.

There was an oblong blue pill, five little white pills, and three pink capsules and he was suppose to swallow them all without drinking "too much water." He swallowed them dry then took a swig of the coffee instead.

"Realistic seemed to be a keyword of some type in this game. There were no assurances. There were no guarantees. The problem was, he wasn't sure what realistic even meant?" It was such a nebulous concept.

"A two-year survival, should be a realistic expectation."

"With clear scans we can realistically expect that the tumor is still confined to your chest."

"Oh yes, a return to work is certainly realistic."

None of that helped him in any way. Not even a little bit. It wasn't realistic expectations he wanted, not even hope. Manfred needed to know… know exactly what his future held. What was going to happen to him, not to some percentage out of a hundred people, to HIM. He needed to come to some conclusions. Decide where it was <u>he</u> needed to go. A major portion of the economy of the whole country of Namibia was riding on the outcome, and he had no idea how to play the odds.

He started to say a prayer, but stopped. What was he going to pray for…a sign of some sort? What if it was the wrong one? Did he really want to know what was going to happen if it wasn't what he was hoping for? If it was going to be all balled up? He should. That way he could at least plan for it.

"Make up your mind son," he said to the eye he saw reflected up at him in his coffee.

That was one of the worst things the cancer had done to him. Normally, if he didn't know how he needed to act on something, like the diamonds, he knew that if he just applied himself, he'd find a way to work it out. But with this he didn't. God didn't give him, the doctors, or anybody else, a crystal ball to let them see the future. The only way to know what was going to happen was to go through it. Do the best you could. But all the planning in the world wasn't going to save him if it wasn't in the cards. He was just going to have to trust that the doctors had an ace up their sleeves and would use it to win this hand.

Trust wasn't something Manfred was very good at. He'd made his life being distrustful. It came with the job. But he was going to have to trust his doctors. He didn't have a choice.

Gretchen had convinced him he had to take the first course of chemotherapy while he was still here in Windhoek. They could probably handle it back home after that. The doctors at home, in Ludritz, did a good job. If you got hurt they could sew you up or splint a fracture with the best of them. Gretchen worked with them every day, so she probably knew what they could or couldn't handle better than anybody else, probably better than they knew themselves.

She felt that the first time that they gave the medicine was the most complicated. If something were going to go wrong it would probably show up right at first. If it did, she wanted him to be here at the cancer center, where they'd know just what to do for him, or at least they would probably have seen something similar a time or two, and if they hadn't, no one else was going to have much of an idea of what to do either.

He'd wanted to take all of his treatment at home. But she wouldn't hear it. She was determined that he was going to do everything just so, that that would make the difference. That if everything was done just so, everything would turn out to be just fine and that within a few weeks the tumor was going to be out of their lives forever.

Manfred wasn't that optimistic. He was a realist. The odds weren't with him, and forever was a long, long time. He'd worry about forever later. Right now all he could deal with was right now. He needed to get better for right now. It was like the old joke said: How do you eat an elephant? … One bite as a time. That was how he was going to have to deal with this.

He'd made arrangements to be off of work for two weeks. If there was a hold up of some kind he didn't know what he'd do. There was no one that could really cover. His job was like a series of veils and mazes now. Someone that looked at it might think they could see something, feel like they knew where they were going, even feel like they could do it, but it was his job to be sure they didn't. Nobody else could get ready for the inspectors that were coming because no one else knew any of the details about the black market diamonds, not even where they were, and no one, except Manfred, knew enough of the history to put the whole picture together. He'd made sure of it, and that was one the things that worried him the most about work. If something happened to him there wasn't anyone else who would be able to prevent the coming storm. It would be bad for the consortium, bad for the country, and would wreck a centuries long balance of trade that was precarious in the modern world, at best.

On the other hand, mining sanctions weren't going to mean much to him if he was dead.

Today all he could do was get through this case of the nerves. Not a thing to worry about. They'd cut a hole in the right side of his chest so they could stick some tubing into a big vein there to be able to give him the drugs through. That was supposed to make it easier on him in the long run. His veins wouldn't get scarred or collapsed when they gave him the medicine. The drugs were like drain cleaner or something. Apparently they could burn your veins right up, or they could burn holes in you if they got out of the veins and ran into the tissue around them. The best he could tell, they were going to shoot a bunch of poison into his veins, and hope it killed the tumor better than it killed him.

"Isn't science wonderful?" he whispered.

Thirteen

Ray's first gun purchase was an impulse buy. It wasn't supposed to be. He'd gone to the gun store just to look and see what kinds of rifles they had. He was just trying to figure out what it was he needed. He'd read everything he could get his hands on. Weighing the pros of this one against the cons of that one. Which gun could be used on the broadest range of game. Trying to decide how much he needed to spend. But as soon as he walked into Bud's Guns all that went straight out the window.

There were too many guns to make any sense of. They had every kind of gun imaginable lined up along the wall. Every one of them was perfect for the job of shooting something.

Some were big and heavy with long fat barrels. Those were mostly varmint guns the salesman said, meant to lay still and shoot at things far away. Not so good for carrying.

"What do you plan do with it?" the salesman asked.

"I want to hunt with it…in Africa." Ray answered confidently.

"Well, what kind of gun you need kind of depends on what you plan to shoot," the man explained.

"I'd like to shoot an elephant." Ray answered without really considering all the implications of that statement.

"Let me get Bud, he'll be better to talk to on that one, but these are the guns you want to look at then." He said pointing to a rack with only six guns in it.

And that's how Ray bought his first gun. His gun, he flexed his bicep to test its heft. This was a man's gun, and it was his now, he'd filled out all of the paper work and written the check. He looked at himself holding it in the mirror with Browning written across it behind the cash register.

He didn't want to shoot deer or squirrels or birds or any of that, he thought as he drove. None of that kind of hunting proved anything. It only mattered if what you were hunting had a chance to win. Not just a chance to get away but a chance to kill you too, an elephant or a lion maybe. That was what he wanted to hunt, nothing less.

If you were going to go and hunt something that could crush you to a pulp as easily as you could kill it, you had to have a gun you could trust your life to.   Robert Ruark had even titled one of his books that, *Use Enough Gun*. Ray wanted to have a rifle of his own to shoot, one he didn't have to make excuses for, something that was specific for hunting in Africa. He wanted a gun that he could be proud of when he showed it to Fritz Dietrich.

How many people got the chance to have a professional hunter from Africa come and give them some pointers on shooting, anyway? This was going to be great, he thought as he walked around the car and opened the door to get it out of the Porsche's passenger seat, in the garage at home. It had been too long to fit in the trunk.

He looked at the big double-barrel rifle in the sunlight as he walked into the house. The deep blue of the twin tubes looked like history itself paired to the dark satin wood of the rifle's stock and forearm. It was one of the best double-rifles ever made. Bud, the owner of the gun shop had told him that. It was German. They built great rifles in Germany. That was where the Mauser, probably the greatest rifle of all time, came from.

He'd gotten a great deal on it too. They sold for over five thousand dollars new, and he'd gotten it for only thirty-five hundred, with the leather case and two boxes of cartridges thrown in to boot. That was probably another five hundred dollars worth of stuff he got for free.

Bud knew the gun's whole history. He'd sold it to its first owner. That guy only shot one box of shells with it before he decided to trade it in for something he could hunt antelope with.

It didn't have a scope, but Bud, and the salesman behind the counter, Norm, thought that he should shoot it some, to see if he still wanted a scope on it after he'd shot it a few times. Having the iron sights line up right was the most important thing, Norm had said. After all, elephants were pretty big, they had hearts the size of hubcaps, and you generally didn't shoot them from much more than a hundred yards away, so he probably wouldn't need one. He'd talk to Fritz about that more when he got here.

Ray tossed the gun up to his shoulder a few times, like they had him do at the gun shop, to see if it fit him. Each time the front blade came right up into the V of the rear. A perfect fit. His fingers wrapped around the tops of the twin tubes on both sides of the forearm. He was going to have a good grip, and shouldn't have any trouble with the recoil. He'd have to remember his hearing protection, though. His ears were pretty sensitive. As he held the gun at arms length he noticed the prints of his fingers and thumb on the blued metal of the barrels. He carried it into the kitchen and rubbed it down with a dishtowel with some oil, before slipping the rifle back into its leather case.

He pulled one of the boxes of cartridges out of the gun case and looked at the loaded bullet, the thing was almost as big as his index finger, .470 Nitro Express, he read the letters stamped on the cartridges face. It was a lot bigger than the shells for Lisa's little gun, a hell of a lot bigger.

You'd think that with a cartridge that big that the gun would kick the daylights out of you, but Norm had said something about geometry. Ray hadn't understood it very well, something about the rifle rolling up instead of kicking straight back, so you didn't feel it as much. And, the rifle weighed over ten pounds, so that would take up a lot of it too. It couldn't possibly kick any more than that light little thing of Lisa's did. He guessed he'd find out soon enough.

Fourteen

It was Saturday morning and Fritz had already been on the road for three hours. He had about two hours to give a shooting lesson here in Meridian, before he had to get back on the road to make his flight out of Jackson. He'd talked to so many people over the last few days that he could barely remember the name of the fellow he was supposed to meet. Ray...Ray...Ray...hell, he couldn't remember the guy's last name for the life of him, Martin or Munson or something. He turned off of the Interstate and headed south following the directions the rental car's navigation system gave him. He went past a mall and a park, and back out of town before the woman's voice on the GPS said, "Turn right now," at a gravel and red clay split. He hoped Pete Early had given him the right address. He didn't have much time as it was. He didn't know how much good he could do in two hours anyway.

Well, look on the bright side, he told himself. He already had the man's deposit check in his wallet. So, no matter what, whether he ever came to Africa or not, it wasn't going to be a complete waste of time. He was a thousand dollars ahead of the game no matter what. If he could teach him to shoot and get him a few good trophies there was the chance for a lot more after that. You had to play for the long haul. Another of Walt's favorites there.

When he pulled into the gravel parking lot, Fritz saw Ray "whatever-his-name-was" standing next to a blue sports car. He was holding up a double rifle broken open and looking through it at the sun. That didn't make sense, he didn't even know how to shoot and where would he get an elephant gun around here? Fritz pulled in beside him. As he stepped out of the car he saw Pete and his son headed in their direction from the range.

"Good God, what are you doing with that cannon?" Pete bellowed as they approached.

Ray Moffett's face reddened slightly before he extended his hand. "I just picked it up this morning. I thought I'd see how it fits me."

"I hope you brought a Lead Sled, or that things going to kill your shoulder," the boy, Billy, offered unasked.

"How are you? How was your trip?" Ray asked extending his hand to Fritz.

Fritz nodded as they shook hands. He took the gun out of Ray's hands and examined it.

"New gun. Maybe I should shoot it first. Make sure it's safe." He said professionally, "Unless you mind?" He turned to face Ray directly.

"That would be great." Ray was clearly relieved.

"Great, then," Fritz answered, he was the professional, and protecting the client was part of the job. As often as not, that meant protecting the clients from themselves as well. Sometimes it meant protecting their egos. This clearly fell into both of those categories.

"Have you ever shot one of those, dad?" the boy interrupted.

"I've shot a couple of doubles before, a .375 and a .416. What's that one?" Pete asked.

"A .470..." Ray started.

"Holy cow. What in the heck did you buy that for? You planning to start with elephants or something?" Billy asked in much too loud a voice.

"I got a good deal on it, so I thought I'd go ahead and get it while I had the chance." Ray answered sheepishly.

Pete stuck out his hand and took the gun from Fritz. Lifting it to his shoulder.

"Not a bad gun, at least it's got some weight to it. I'll tell you one thing though, you better always pull the rear trigger first, until you get used to it. If you pull the front trigger and don't know what you're doing the recoil will smack you and you'll end up pulling the rear trigger too, then you'll double."

"Man, that would break your shoulder wouldn't it dad?" Billy asked, delighted by the idea of something like that happening to somebody else.

"What do you mean, double?" Ray asked, directing his question more toward Fritz than Pete.

"It means both barrels go off at the same time," Billy piped. "And that has got to hurt – BIG TIME! I'd love to see that."

Pete scowled at his son as he handed the rifle back to Fritz, who broke it and rested it on his shoulder as they walked to the picnic tables in front of the hundred-yard range. Pete and Billy laid their guns on a bench then headed over to the range master's table. They came back with their arms loaded with targets, headphones, eye protection, and sandbags

Fritz walked over to a trash container and found a couple of cardboard cartons that had been used to gather up empty shotgun shells from the skeet range. He dumped the hulls into the garbage and carried the boxes back with him.

When the range master called for a cease-fire, Fritz stepped off thirty meters and sat down one of the empty boxes. Since there were only six firing lanes, it wasn't too surprising that the big elephant gun quickly became the center of attention. Everyone who had been shooting or watching, even the range master, drifted over and formed a loose semi-circle behind Fritz as he picked up the rifle and poked two of the oversized rounds into the twin chambers.

"May I fire?" Fritz asked formally. The range master nodded. Fritz went ahead and slipped on the hearing protection. He'd never have that luxury at home. A hunter had to hear to hunt. Hearing protection was a nicety of the shooting range, but shooters shot more at the range than a hunter did hunting so it was a good precaution, and it would keep his ears from ringing for the rest of the trip home.

He handled the rifle like he would have fired his old shotgun, they had similar actions, but decided he'd be well advised to listen to Pete's advice on trigger selection. Making sure the safety was on, he slid his finger over the front trigger and tested its distance from the one behind it. He moved his finger between the triggers several times with the gun up and on his shoulder before he slid the safety forward to the fire position. As soon as the sights aligned he kept his focus on his target and squeezed the back trigger. The wallop was quite a bit of a slug, but he kept his eyes on the box, it only moved slightly, but behind it a column of dirt and sand flew twenty-five feet into the air, as the huge solid tore a trench through the earth. The rifle rolled up on his shoulder and he let it come back down naturally. As soon as the sights crossed the top of the box he inched his finger forward onto the front trigger, and squeezed it towards its companion. Again the box shuddered and the dirt flew, as he absorbed the second blow of the one-two punch the big gun was built to deliver.

"That'll do," he said, as he broke the gun and pulled out the smoking cases with his fingers, an extractor gun, not an ejector he thought as he turned and noticed the swarm of admiring looks that surrounded him. "You're up next," he said handing the gun to Ray.

"That's why they call it taking a bash," Fritz explained, as he took off his hearing protection. "You know that you have to take a punch, the trick is to just let it come. Don't try to get ready for it, don't think you can wrestle the gun and keep it from happening. You just have to let it happen."

Ray put the gun to his shoulder, aimed and squeezed the back trigger, feeling the metallic vibration of the falling firing pin.

"Don't make it a habit of that." Fritz warned. The striker on the firing pins can fracture. You won't know it until you need it. Then when you pull the

78

trigger the gun won't go boom when you need it to."

"My wife had me snap the trigger on her rifle to get used to shooting without flinching." Ray explained.

"So your wife shoots?" Fritz said his eyes widening slightly. "I thought you didn't have a wife?"

"We're separated. Like I said, it's kind of complicated."

"If you're still with her enough to trust her around loaded guns you can't be too separated." Fritz said with a smile. "But she probably had you shooting a bolt gun, their springs are longer, so they don't have to be as stiff. They also have longer firing pins. These box locks don't really have firing pins, they just have strikers on short stiff springs, so they're more likely to crack. Alright, forget about the gun, focus on the box, and squeeze the trigger."

Ray did as he had been instructed and was rewarded by one of the most powerful blows to the shoulder and jaw that he had ever felt. His molars slammed together, biting the edge of his tongue and making his eyes water. His shoulder felt as if his humerus had been crushed to dust. But, he kept his face on the gun, just like he'd seen Fritz do, and let it come back down. As he reached forward with his finger he tried to grasp the forearm of the rifle as hard as he could with his left hand and the barrel pulled to that side immediately. He stopped his trigger pull and got the sights back onto the box. He tried to forget how much it was going to hurt, and only looked at the box, he forgot about the sights and gently squeezed the trigger.

Fritz, Billy, and the range master were pounding him on the back almost before the gun came down.

"Great job."

"Way to go."

"Two for two."

Ray smiled, happy not to have embarrassed himself with everybody watching. He broke the rifle, took out the shells, and laid it on the table.

"Let's give it a minute and rest a bit before we try it again." Fritz suggested as Ray removed his earmuffs. "Kills on both ends doesn't it?" He asked with a knowing smile.

"Sure does, it's harder than I thought to pretend it isn't going to hit you…" Ray started.

"It isn't the first one though, is it?" Fritz laughed. "What shows the man is the second shot."

"That was a lot harder." Ray admitted.

"But you did it though, didn't you?" Fritz said. "Still and all, let's give it a minute before we try it again, okay?"

"Okay," Ray sighed with relief.

"Do you mind if I give it a try?" Pete asked, reaching for the rifle.

"Help yourself." Ray offered.

"Hey dad, show us how to shoot it with the front trigger first." Billy suggested.

Ray watched, trying to see what the trick was, as the bigger man brushed his finger across the front trigger several times with the safety still on. Each time making sure that his finger moved to the side, away from the trigger behind it.

Pete looked intently down the sights, Ray watched as his finger came first to the rear trigger, his thumb slid the safety off, and his finger inched forward to brush the front trigger. When the gun went off, it sounded like two shots in rapid succession, two plumes of dirt flew high into the air, and Pete Early spun to the side, and fell in a lump on the ground, a trickle of blood slid down his chin as he sat clutching his shoulder and shaking his head.

Billy had gotten his wish.

Fifteen

As the sun set, the darkness grew, until the television became the only light in the room. The liquid crystals of the screen were tiny suns that transformed the color and detail of everything they illuminated. The room became softer and less focused. Until you noticed the hospital bed in the center of the room less than you noticed the small beeping and glowing devices that sat at its periphery. Tubes running from up to down. Gravity used as a medical tool with lights and gauges to tell you that, yes, gravity was still a constant. The person lying covered in hospital linens an unfocused mid-ground, almost invisible now.

Fritz leaned as far back as the recliner would go and closed his eyes. He was too tired to bother getting up to turn on the light. Gretchen would be back soon. He'd just take a nap until she returned. He teetered on the edge of sleep. Eyes blinking slower and staying closed longer with each sliding moment.

On the screen, a bright red BMW flew past a white McLaren-Mercedes. The Mercedes answered with a burst of speed and the two cars came hurtling down the straightaway neck and neck. They scrubbed off speed and set up for a sweeper to the left. Their wheels were only inches apart as they came into the turn. They were still locked together at the apex but then the red car's driver hit the gas too hard trying to pass the Mercedes coming out of the turn. When he did, the rear end started to slide sideways and the two car's wheels touched. Suddenly the BMW was airborne. The power of the spinning wheels acted like a catapult to throw the car skyward. As it flew it spiraled in a lazy arc until it was inverted directly above the Mercedes.

When it came crashing down the wheels came off first, bouncing along the track and into the following cars. Then pieces of fuselage and engine bits flew in every direction.

"Damn." Fritz muttered sleepily.

"They're both going to have a headache in the morning," a voice croaked from the dark.

Fritz jumped at the sound and spun towards the bed he'd been sitting beside.

"You're awake?" Fritz exclaimed, uncoordinated as he hurried, struggled to get himself out of the reclined chair, kicking and bucking to get it to close so he could get out..

"I guess so," Manfred answered. "Have I been asleep long?"

"A while." Fritz answered, unsure of exactly what he should say. How much he should say.

'What're you doing here anyway?"

"Keeping an eye on you, so Gretchen could go back to the hotel and get some sleep."

"Where's the boy?" Manfred asked.

"Back at school, he had to go back. He had classes. He's off tomorrow though," Fritz explained.

"What day is it?"

"It's Friday, but probably not the one you expect." Fritz answered.

"How did it get to be Friday already? It was Monday when I came in to start the chemotherapy."

"That was two weeks ago." Fritz answered cautiously. He wasn't sure what you should tell somebody who was just waking up from a coma. Where you should start from. Did you just say, "Well you've been about dead for the past two weeks."

"What are you talking about 'two weeks'? I just came in this morning. It's night now, right?" Manfred said, starting to get agitated.

Fritz took a deep breath. Maybe he should slow things down, try a little different tack. Damn he wished Gretchen were here. She'd know what to say, what to do.

"Do you remember anything?" he asked, stalling for time, hoping somebody else would walk in and take over.

Manfred shook his head from side to side tentatively.

"Are you okay? Do you need anything? Maybe I should get the nurse?" Fritz started.

"I just want to know what in the hell's going on?" Manfred growled in a voice raspy from having the tube in his throat for so long.

Fritz frowned, that was wrong. "Well you remembered coming in for the chemotherapy don't you? Let's start there. What's the last thing you remember after that?"

Manfred blinked slowly. "After that ...after that...I don't know?"

"Okay then, do you remember getting the medicine?"

"I remember, that they started the IV."

"What happened then?" Fritz prodded.

"After that it gets fuzzy. I'm not sure what's real and what's a dream. I can remember the nurse, the one who was giving me the chemotherapy. She was leaning across me. Then she was sitting on top of me and mashing down on my chest quite hard and I couldn't breathe." Manfred stopped, his breathing was fast, his eyes blinked rapidly.

Fritz looked up at the heart monitor. His brother's pulse was a hundred and eighteen. "We don't have to talk about it any more, if you don't want to.

"I have to, I guess, " Manfred said reaching for a glass of water that was sitting on the bedside table.

Fritz picked it up and held the straw for his brother to drink. Manfred took a tentative sip, and then another. He worked to get the liquid down. "My mouth is so dry, it's hard to swallow it."

"I guess it would be."

"Here, give it to me. I can't get my neck right with you holding it." Manfred took the cup and captured the straw between his lips. He drank until the cup was almost empty. "That's better."

"Anyway, the last thing I really remember is that Gret kissed me. But when she kissed me it felt like she blew in my mouth."

"I'm not sure she was kissing you."

"I know that, I'm just telling you what it felt like. I know it wasn't exactly like that, but it was what it felt like...to me. I can remember thinking, 'This isn't right.' That's what I was thinking when I looked up and saw the car crash, then I looked over and you were sitting here, so I said something...I guess she was trying to resuscitate me?" There was a question in his voice.

"Some guys'll do anything to get a girl to kiss 'em, even if they have to stop breathing." Fritz nudged his brother's arm.

"I stopped breathing? So she was doing resuscitation."

"I guess, Gret says that your heart stopped beating for a while. Your brain stopped working too, somehow all of it sent you into a coma." Fritz said.

"Did they say why?" Manfred asked seriously.

"Something about an allergic reaction to one of the medicines or something. That's why you quit breathing. I guess your heart stopped because you weren't breathing. You have to ask Gret or the doctor, I'm not sure." Fritz answered.

"But why was I unconscious. You said I was in a coma. Was that from the medicine too?"

"How in the hell would I know? I don't know anything about that sort of stuff." Fritz answered, throwing up his hands.

"I thought maybe Gretchen told you something."

"She told me some stuff, but I didn't really understand it. All I know is;

you stopped breathing, then your heart stopped, then you were unconscious." Fritz answered.

They sat there in silence for a little while. Manfred was letting it all sink in. They both stared at the TV, but neither one of them was really watching it. But, then, cars driving around didn't take all that much concentration.

"My mouth tastes like something took a shit in it?" Manfred said absently.

"Could have. You were sleeping with your mouth open. Probably a cat." Fritz answered.

"You're a fat lot of help." Manfred laughed finally. "Look in that drawer over there and see if you can find me a toothbrush."

Fritz rattled around and came up with a toothbrush, some toothpaste, and an emesis basin. Then he filled a Styrofoam cup with water from the tap.

"Help me sit up. How'd you get here, even?" Manfred asked as he dipped the toothbrush into the water. "I dood du wer ub norf," he said as he brushed. Did je dend zumbody ub fbor jou?"

"No, she called Walt while we were still in the United States. He got hold of me before I left Mississippi. I flew in a few days ago."

"You were in the United States? What were you doing out of the country?" Manfred frowned. "You could have been arrested. Those murder warrants are all still out there. You don't know if the U. S. has an extradition treaty with Zimbabwe or not."

"I didn't think they applied any more, nobody's sure if there's even a country called Zimbabwe anymore…the government's a shambles."

"You can't take that chance. If they ever get their hands on you, you won't get out of there again."

"Well its too late to worry about it now, I'm back already," Fritz flashed a mischievous grin.

"What were you doing over there anyway?"

"We started out in Las Vegas. Walt and I were at the Safari Club convention out there. After that, Walt went west out to California, and I went east to Mississippi, then drove down to Alabama and over to Florida. "

Manfred nodded trying to remember how the three states were arranged exactly.

"Walt had it set up so we stayed with former clients who'd hunted over here before."

"You stayed at their houses?"

"No, we slept in a hotel, they just had the parties at their houses." Fritz explained.

"Parties?"

"Well, they all agreed to get some of their friends together, so we could try to sell them on coming here for a hunt. You show them some film, tell them some lies…" Fritz shrugged and made a face.

Manfred's face softened, but it was clear that he still wasn't happy. "Walt should have known better. He knew… I talked to him about it. About keeping you in Namibia. They could have had you listed as a terrorist. They could have put you on a no-fly list or something."

"Well, they must not have. I made it back, and nobody stopped me at any of the airports."

"That doesn't make it okay. Besides, you're not a salesman anyway, you never sold anything in your life."

"I sold stolen guns."

"That's not what I'm talking about. You've never sold anything in the way of legitimate commerce."

"I have now. I went to six cities, did six pitches, and booked a dozen hunts."

"Did they just say they were coming, or did they have to put up some cash to do it?" Manfred asked, skeptically.

"They had to put up a thousand dollar deposit. That's twelve thousand dollars even if none of them shows up."

Manny looked at him squinting his eyes doubtfully.

"No, I'm serious," Fritz continued. "One of the fellows who put down a deposit hasn't ever even hunted before. Not anything, he hadn't even fired a gun before he signed up to come."

"You may want to be sure you don't draw that one as a hunter," Manfred suggested. "Having a fellow who has no idea of how to handle a firearm walking around behind you with a rifle sounds like a good way to get shot in the back."

"I know, I'm in no hurry for that. I went back up to Mississippi to work with him some, teach him how to shoot, just to see if he had any aptitude, you know. He did pretty well for someone who had no idea of what they were doing. Somebody talked the poor bastard into buying a double rifle. Can't shoot, and he wanted to start with a damned elephant gun, of all things."

"Well, pay attention to that one when he comes anyway. Anybody just handling a gun for the first time is going to be a little unpredictable."

"He seems to be a nice guy though. It's funny. I think he's probably the only one out of all the people I talked to that really gets what hunting is. Most of the others think it's just about shooting something." Fritz explained.

"That's how it gets when hunting isn't about eating anymore."

"I told him about the leopard. You remember, the one we treed when we were kids?"

Manny had climbed up on a branch and somehow managed to loop a chain around the rear paw of a leopard their dog had treed, up in the hills on the desert's edge. They hadn't thought it out much farther than that. They'd caught a leopard.

Then everything went wild when the leopard jumped down between them. Fritz had almost pissed himself. He was only ten, he had no idea what to do at that point. The dog was the only thing that had saved him in that first foray. Rushing between him and the leopard, knocking him out of the way.

Manny had grabbed the chain and made a loop around the trunk of the tree, then he'd taken off running as hard as he could with the leopard right behind him.

When the leopard got to the end of the chain it jerked back so hard it flipped over onto its back, jerking Manny to a stop as well. Manny only had about a meter more chain than the leopard did. All he could do was throw his weight into holding what he had, straining with all his might to keep the leopard from gaining ground. The leopard rolled and came up with its claws slashing. Inches away, but not quite there. The leopard lunged against the chain, growling, and hissing. Spitting right in Manny's face the whole time. All Manny could do was hold tight. The slightest slip and the leopard would be on him. Then, the leopard went after the chain, trying to bite the thing off, to free his rear leg. When he did, Manny jerked for all he was worth and got another foot or two of separation. After that, it was like reeling in a fish. Every time the leopard went after the chain or the dog, Manny took up the slack until, finally, he got a safe enough distance away.

Fritz had been petrified. He'd just stood there watching the dog rush in and out and his brother fight the chain. Until Manny looked over and asked, as calm as ice, "Fritz could you get the rifle and shoot him, please?" Like he was asking him to pass the salt. That was the Manny he knew. Not a man in a hospital bed. Not a man who could be killed by something as little as cancer. He had to be alright. Fritz couldn't imagine anything else.

If Manfred's face brightened as Gretchen walked through the door, hers lit up like a beacon when she saw him sitting up, and talking. She literally floated across the room, straight toward him. As she passed Fritz she greeted him with a squeeze of the shoulder and a peck on the cheek but never seemed to perceptibly slow down. She wrapped her arms around Manfred's neck and buried her face into his shoulder as she hugged him. And, for just that moment, time stopped. If only ever so briefly, the whole world stopped, and there were just two people, in a dark hospital room, holding each other for all they were worth.

Sixteen

It was Friday. Ray was on days. It had been a long week and he hadn't spoken to Lisa since she'd left after the disaster at the shooting range. He knew he should have already called and apologized for being such a jerk. But for some reason he hadn't, and it seemed like every day that went by made it harder to pick up the phone. Expanding the gap between them again, until he didn't have any idea where to start.

So, he kept flailing around trying to figure out what he needed to do to fix things and the longer he flailed, the harder it got to figure out what it was he should do. Work was the only place that made sense in his life. At least there he knew what he was supposed to be doing.

I had been a good shift, so far. He was relaxed as he moved from room to room. It had been a slow morning. He took his time looking in ears, listening to chests, and writing prescriptions. No one was too sick. After the rooms emptied out he sat down to drink a cup of coffee and read the sports page.

He knew things would pick up as the day went on so he enjoyed the time he had now to relax. On Fridays folks that had been sick all week long would decide that today was the day they needed to see a doctor. That they needed to do something about whatever it was that was bothering them before the weekend got there. But, the docs in town had figured that out too, so most of the offices closed at noon on Fridays. The Emergency Department didn't have that option.

Today the flood came early. By eleven the rooms were all full again, the newspaper folded and tossed to the back of the desk, the coffee long since grown too cold to bother with. It stayed that way the rest of the afternoon. A heart attack they'd had to shock three times was the first real emergency of the day. While Ray was getting him sent up to the CCU a twelve-year-old little girl came in with an acute asthma attack. He could hear her wheezing from down the hall and when he came into the room the first thing he saw were two terrified blue eyes and a pair of equally blue lips. That meant it was a worse attack than she'd had in a while. Her mother sat rolling the admission paper work into a tight spiral as she gave him the history. The little girl hadn't had an attack in years, and they'd just gotten a new kitten. He moved the stethoscope around her chest, checked her pulse, and ordered a breathing treatment to try and open up her constricted airways.

"Looks like Fluffy needs a new home," he whispered to the nurse that was with him as they got into the hallway. He'd tell the mother later. He sure as hell wasn't going to say anything in front of the child until they got her breathing squared away. The last thing he needed was for her to start crying. Crying would make her breathing worse than it already was and that was the last thing she needed.

Ray had them shoot a chest x-ray. It looked a little patchy in one of the bases. He decided then that if she didn't clear completely with the nebulizer treatment and a shot of epinephrine that he'd push to put her in overnight. Safer, just keep her here until they got a handle on it.

An hour later a young boy with a long history of sickle-cell disease came in with a sickling crisis. His blood cells were deforming because of their genetic instability. The misshapen cells clumped in the marrow of his legs causing him to writhe on the stretcher groaning in pain.

The boy's name was Christopher. Ray knew him and his mama pretty well. They'd been through this a half-dozen times in the last two years. He'd come in and have to be admitted to get his pain managed and the sickling under control. After a shot of pain medicine and a call to his hematologist, Christopher was on his way upstairs too.

The two admissions had kept Ray from getting lunch but, the day shift ended at three for the staff, so he'd have a few minutes while the staff reported out and did their turn over to grab a bite to eat.

He took a deep breath and walked through the door into the hospital's main hallway. He should have at least a half-hour. It would take fifteen or twenty minutes to give report, then another ten to fifteen minutes before they'd get the rooms filled up again. He might even be able to get a nap in if he ate quickly. He decided to skip the doctor's lounge and grab something in the cafeteria.

He didn't get a tray. As he made his way through the line Ray grabbed a turkey sandwich and a small salad to go. He pulled a can of diet Coke out of the cooler, and got in line at the cash register.

"Hey," a familiar voice said just behind him.

It was a voice he didn't have to hear another word to recognize. Ray swallowed hard. All of the saliva in his mouth disappeared. He forced himself to turn around to face her slowly, his heart pounded high in his chest his jaw clenched.

"Hi Anne. How have you been?" he asked.

She was dressed in scrubs. "I don't know…" Her voice was tiny.

He noticed the stethoscope around her neck.

"That will be six fifty." The girl behind the register said.

He paid and then stepped through, out of the way, so she could sit her things on the counter.

"What are you doing here? I thought you were still in Birmingham."

"I was."

"So, what are you doing here?" he asked.

"I'm coming on, I'm starting back in the E.R. tonight."

"You're back for good or just a couple of shifts?" he asked tentatively.

"Just the apple and yogurt?" The cashier interrupted.

"Yeah, that'll do it for now." Anne answered. She counted out her money and Ray fell in step beside her as they walked toward one of the tables.

She looked up at him, biting her lower lip, "I should have talked to you first. Wanda gave me my job back. You okay with that?"

There wasn't a right way to answer that question. "You're a great nurse. I…I'd…uhh. I'd love to have you back."

Involuntarily he started to reach for her hand. His hands were still full of food.

"Don't be so enthusiastic." The hurt in her eyes was obvious.

"I just wondered about it, that's all." He sat his food down at an empty table.

"Wondered what?" she asked.

"Why you were back?" He pulled a chair out for her to sit down.

"I have to go and get report, I can't sit down. I'm glad that you're okay with this," she said too rapidly, then turned and walked away.

Ray sat down, but his eyes never left her, until the door closed behind her and then he stared at the door. "Shit," he whispered.

He sat there for several minutes after she'd gone. Finally he looked down at his food and wasn't quite sure what to do with it. Then he remembered that he was taking it back to his office. He didn't have much of an appetite any more. He shoved the sandwich and diet Coke into the pockets of his white coat and tossed the salad unopened into the trashcan. His hand was shaking as he dropped it in. He shoved his hands back into his pockets with his lunch and walked out of the cafeteria.

He sat in his office, staring at the wall, until the phone rang. There were two bites gone from the sandwich and the soda sat unopened on his desk.

"Hey, there're a couple of patients in rooms waiting for you." Anne's voice came through the receiver. "Nothing too urgent. A laceration that's probably going to need a couple of stitches, a four year old with a hundred and two temp, and another kid with an earache."

"I'll be right there," he mumbled.

How was it that just hearing her voice could still make his heart pound like this? She wasn't talking to him romantically. She was just giving him a status update. Even that, made him feel like he was going to throw up. This wasn't good. He wasn't ready for this again. It felt like he couldn't take a deep breath. How in the hell could he still have these feelings after the way she'd treated him?

She hadn't even bothered to tell him she was leaving. He'd heard it from the nursing supervisor. The fucking nursing supervisor told him that the woman he'd left his wife to be with had resigned and was moving away. She hadn't returned his phone calls, no good-bye, no explanation, nothing.

Now here she was. Back again. All she had to do was walk back through the door and he was acting like some dumb love struck teen-ager. Wanting her so badly he felt like he had to physically restrain himself. He was terrified of having her anywhere near him.

It was still too dangerous. Their affair had started with a single drop of blood, just the one, just below her left eye. The whole erosive sequence of events that destroyed his marriage, his self-respect, and to a large extent his ego was tied to a simple drop of blood that had splashed onto her face and washed him away.

There had been more blood than that of course. Liters of it, spilled out of the gunshot victim all over the trauma bay. The man had come in drugged up and combative. That was probably what got him shot in the first place.

The resuscitation had been a roller coaster ride of violence and panic right up until the end. Every time they stopped the bleeding and got enough blood products and fluid into him to raise his blood pressure he'd start fighting again, and every time they got him under control, he crashed again. They had poured so much of everything into him that his entire clotting cascade activated and his blood began to clot inside his own vascular system. That used up all of the clotting factors he had left, plus all of the ones that they had given him. Then there was no way to stop the bleeding. It was called disseminated intravascular coagulopathy, and the only treatment was to give him Heparin, a drug meant to stop the blood from clotting. Sometimes it worked and sometimes it didn't, only this time it didn't.

He'd made a lot of excuses for what came next. Who could say really what the cause was, tension, adrenalin, fatigue, who knew? Who cared?

He had been standing in his office changing into a clean white coat, when Anne came into the office behind him with the papers for him to sign, to transfer the body to the funeral home. When he turned around she was too close, it was a pleasant closeness but one that created an immediate tension. Then he saw the single drop, on her cheek, just below her left eye. His response to that drop had sealed his fate. He cupped the back of her head in his left hand and pulled her close, he reached up with the edge of his thumb to wipe it away, by then it was already too late, she was against him. The kiss was inevitable by then, and the kiss was like dropping a match into a pool of gasoline.

It wasn't that he hadn't thought of Lisa, he hadn't thought of anything. It came in a rush, every touch, every kiss, defied common sense. They hadn't even bothered to lock the door. Once it started they couldn't stop. They couldn't see anything but each other. They couldn't imagine anything but what was right in front of them.

It wasn't until it was over that the first waves of guilt washed onto the shore. Anne had felt it too. There was a sadness he'd seen in her face as they kissed. Then she'd hurried out of the door.

He told himself then, as soon as she'd walked out of his office and was gone, that it would never happen again. And he'd meant it. He meant it every time he said it. As if somehow the mantra of hollow reservations could erase what had started between them.

But it didn't. She was all he could think about. He could close his eyes and remember exactly how she felt, how she smelled, her taste. It was funny that he had been the naïve one. He'd been the one to think that it was something real, real enough to ask Lisa for a separation.

Now she was back, and he wasn't sure what that meant at all.

Seventeen

Manfred was glad to be home. It had taken him another week, after he woke up, to convince the doctors in Windhoek to let him out of the hospital. They'd changed his chemotherapy around some, after that first kind almost killed him. The new kind seemed to do okay. It made him a little sick to his stomach and gave him some diarrhea, but at least he didn't stop breathing and try to die when they gave it to him.

He'd done so well that they were going to let him take the next few courses at the clinic here in Luderitz. That alone made him feel better. He'd run by the office the day after they got home. He was surprised how much he'd missed it. It was who he was. It was who he'd been his whole adult life. It was the only job he'd ever had. It had changed a little and transformed itself over the years, but basically it was the same job. Without it he wasn't sure who he'd be.

Officially, he worked for the country of Namibia, directly for the president. That was something no one knew, not his wife, not his son, not his brother, not even the people who thought he worked for them. He worked for something that was only called "the company." The company was run, on paper, as a division of the mining consortiums, but, in fact, was an arm of the government. The consortium thought he worked for them, and in some ways he did. He protected their assets as he always had, by giving them one of the most trusted security forces on the planet. After all, the mining here in Namibia represented the most precious substances on earth. It wasn't just the diamonds. Diamonds were the oldest, the thing people thought of when they thought of the riches of Africa. Uranium was the newest, it required the most security of the ores, but there was also gold and copper. Cadmium, lead, tin he watched them all, and he watched the companies that produced them to be sure that they played by the rules. He kept track of production volumes, shipment sizes, anything that was necessary to ensure the security of Namibia's natural resources. He made sure that what was being reported on revenue statements to the government actually coincided with what was being taken out of the country.

There had been problems with diversion of funds and underreporting by foreign companies early on, right after Namibia became a democracy. There was a sense of entitlement that made the international business community feel it was somehow justifiable to try to rob any black led African governments, legitimate or not. It was an old mindset that was hard to break. Manfred was the guardian in place to prevent that. He was scrupulously fair. He gave an executive no more sway than he gave a miner he caught slipping gems out to the black market. More than one mining director had found himself pulled out of his bed in the middle of the night and stuck on the first one-way flight out of the country for creative reporting.

This was Namibia. There was no right to confront your accuser, no right to a fair trial. No one offered a flight or interrogation was going to turn down the ticket. Manfred kept himself well away from the dreary practicalities of it all. He only needed to suggest Director So-and-so needed a ride home. The rest was handled by the military.

He'd built one of the most sophisticated security systems on earth, or under it for that matter. One that remained completely undetected by the outside world. They'd been able to adapt as technology advanced, money was never an object, but Manfred was well aware that technology was never enough. To do the job right required time, work, and dedication. It all came down to attention to detail. That was what had allowed him to be effective, to stay ahead of everyone else in the game. He'd built the job, but the job had also built him and he was quick to recognize when someone wasn't giving him the kind of effort he expected. A good leader knew where the weak link was, and right now the weak link was him.

He was starting to feel like he was out of the loop. He wasn't on top of his game anymore. Not since the cancer. The personal involvement was starting to wane and that was going to cause holes in the network. Holes he was going to have to find a way to patch before the cancer took too much more away from him. This was how failure started.

He picked up a cigarette and tapped it on the top of his desk without lighting it. Now that he could see the end, he wished he could start over at the beginning again and do it over. Everything had been new back then. New, and the whole world was focused on what was happening here. It was all such a big adventure then, no one knew what would happen. Manny had ended up in the middle of it all completely by accident. A boy who'd just learned as he went.

He'd just finished with his schooling and was starting his mandatory stint in the South African Defense Force, the SADF. They'd shipped him straight from training camp to the Diamond Coast. Their job was to keep the blacks and the Cubans that were trying to take over the country from gaining control of the western desert.

When America's Central Intelligence Agency leaked a Soviet communication sent to Fidel Castro on the importance of securing the control of "strategic metals" and strangling off the diamond production in South West Africa, control of the western desert became the new imperative.

While Brezhnev was publically labeling the Cubans as being out of control and lobbying for a negotiated peace in what he was already calling " the Namibian problem", it was obvious that securing a better source of high-grade Uranium was his primary strategic goal in the matter, the diamonds were just an added benefit.

It was a strange time in the world then, the United States was crippled by the Watergate hearings and the memory of their war in Viet Nam. The Soviets were still embarrassed by what had happened in Cuba, with the Bay of Pigs fiasco. Both sides were sitting at the table together smiling for the camera, signing non-proliferation treaties, and kicking and gouging each other under the table for all they were worth. Africa, the continent itself, was at stake, and the desert mining production was right in the crosshairs.

No one could have chosen a more unlikely group of defenders of the new world order. The Defense Force just took the first ten guys to come out of training camp and sent them straight to the WRC, the western regional command, with orders to establish a new mission, a desert patrol to secure the western desert. Manfred was one of those ten boys.

They'd rolled into the WRC compound on a six-by-six truck with a driver and a captain named Boren in the front. He was the newly promoted western regional commander. He'd been the owner of a shoe store, Boren's Shoes and Boots. He'd served in the reserves on and off for ten years and had been an excellent manager. His troops had always been well equipped and well fed on a minimal budget. He had an eye for a bargain and watched every dollar. This was his first command, so they sent him an American advisor to help him, a C.I.A. operative named Wilson.

Since Captain Boren wasn't sure what to have the men do, Wilson took over by default. Wilson's first priority was obtaining accurate information about who was who and what was where. He found a cartographer somewhere. A sergeant who'd had most of his right leg blown off. He wasn't able to get around in the field much but the son-of-a-gun knew how to draw a map. Wilson nicknamed him Peg, for obvious reasons.

With one leg, Peg couldn't drive the truck. So Peg rode and Wilson drove. That didn't leave a lot for the rest of them to do. They could roast under the dark canvas that covered the bed of the truck driving across the desert, or stay back at the compound. Neither Peg nor Wilson seemed to care which.

Captain Boren quickly surmised that Wilson's agenda had little to do with what was best for South West Africa or for Boren. So he'd used his supply connections to get them two more trucks and a Ford sedan with an automatic transmission for Peg to drive Wilson around in.

The captain divided the ten of them into three teams of three men to a truck and told them to head south into the restricted zone and patrol the area. The tenth man went with Wilson to settle problems. Wherever Wilson went there were always problems.

When the trucks left Swakopmund that first morning their instructions were to engage any marauding blacks they came across, and to report back on insurgent activity in the area. They drove out of town headed south but none of them had ever been allowed to drive before and they hadn't seen much from the benches in the back of the truck when Wilson was driving, so they had no idea where they were going.

They'd stopped on the road after only a mile. The nine of them got out of their trucks and stood in a kind of loose clump for a while. None of them had any idea of what the captain was talking about. They had no idea of what an insurgent looked like or where to search for them. The country was full of blacks. How were they supposed to know which ones lived there and which ones were marauding? They had no idea what they were supposed to be doing, or even where they were supposed to go to do it.

They tried looking at their maps, but the area they were supposed to patrol was just a huge blank on the southern part of the map, a dotted outline with the legend "Restricted Zone" printed in the center of it. There were sweeping grease pencil marks where Wilson had shown them what they were responsible for. The problem was that where the pencil marks were, there wasn't anything there.

"Any of you bastards have any idea where we're supposed to go?" one of the older boys asked.

Nobody said anything at first, they all just stood there and looked at each other, each man's gaze passing from face to face, each hoping that he wasn't the one that was supposed to come up with an answer.

After a few minutes Manfred spoke up. "I'm from Luderitz. We could head down to Walvis Bay first. We can take the roads wherever they go from there. Then sweep around on to Luderitz and see who we can find that can give us some help finding our way in the south. I grew up with most of the folks down there and know some of the roads and ghost towns down there."

"Ghost towns?" One of the more timid boys asked.

95

"They're just shells in the desert, ran out of water, ran out of people. We'll go down and take a look." Manfred suggested.

So that's what they did. They made notes and filled in their maps as they went and their maps took on greater and greater detail as the days went past. When they got back Wilson took them and had Peg transfer their notes to the big map in the intel shed.

Peg talked to some of the boys and put Manfred in charge of intelligence activities. From that moment on, he was the one that decided what it was they'd do each day. At first, they just rode through the desert on trucks filling in the details on the map. They'd drive from one hill to the next. They could see everything for miles from the hills.

Since nothing that they'd been taught in their training applied out here, Manfred made up his own routines. Mostly, he'd just talk to who ever they ran into. The farther they ranged the less they were able to return to the compound at nights. They started to go to a new area every evening and set up camp at a crossroad. In the morning one truck would drive north and the other truck would drive south until lunch, then they'd turn around and go back. The third truck would stay at the crossroads and monitor the traffic traveling east and west. They'd stop whoever came by and ask them if they'd seen anything interesting. Sometimes they had, most of the times they hadn't. When both trucks got back in the evening they'd drive to the next crossroad and set up camp there. After a while they got the lay of the land and found out a lot about what was going on where, and what was happening at the mines. They got to know the miners, and the desert towns as well.

The truth was, in terms of combat operations, there really wasn't anything for them to do at all. Sure, there was a lot of desert to patrol, and there were tons of diamond shipments to guard. But there weren't really any rebels or Cubans out in the Namib to fight. The desert was so vast and so unforgiving that only the bushman could hope to cross it on foot. And while you might see a bushman walking around wearing a SWAPO t-shirt once in a while, they weren't any more political than a donkey or a gemsbok. They got the shirts for free and they didn't believe in wasting anything.

Their unit got started guarding ore shipments the same way they got started with everything else, by accident. One of the mine owners met Captain Boren at a party and when he heard about the new patrols asked if they could guard the ore shipments from his mine to the shipment facility. Wilson thought that was a tremendous idea, so after that, they pretty much just guarded ore shipments, no more patrols. Soon, every mine needed soldiers to guard their shipments too. The word got back to Windhoek and their unit grew until they had six truck crews and a support staff. Manfred, as intel , was in charge of scheduling escort patrols with the mines and recording what it was that each patrol was guarding. He recorded the exact details of each shipment and submitted it at the end of each week in his intel report to the captain.

It took two trucks to guard each shipment. It took two because Manfred decided that was how many it should take. He put one in the front and one in the back. He divided the unit into three teams with two trucks in each team and they rotated between the mines. If they kept to their schedule, each team worked a specific area, getting to know the mines and towns in their area. That, unfortunately, meant that his troopers got into more trouble. It was usually fighting, gambling, girls, or some combination of the above.

The troopers had almost unlimited powers in those days, and some of the boys abused it. They got the girls because of it, and they were always in fights with the local men and boys for the same reason.

Manny was always different, he hadn't had any money growing up, so he wasn't going to waste any of it that came to him on drinks or the girls who wanted him to buy them drinks. He didn't have anything against either one, they just weren't something he was willing to throw away his money on.

Because finding out stuff was the main part of his job now, Manfred always tried to be respectful to everyone he dealt with. It helped to make them trust you, in turn, that made them want to tell you more stuff. He depended on the bushmen the most, they were the eyes and ears of the desert. He depended on the local boys, and the poor black kids to let him know what was going on in the towns. He didn't need to pretend. He really did respect the bushmen, and their ability to survive where no one else could, and he knew what it was like to be a kid and to be poor. What it was like to be bullied and have nothing but what you could get for yourself. What it meant to have a little brother to have to take care of. He saw himself and Fritz in the face of every ragged kid in every dried up desert town they passed through.

They were just kids trying to make it from one day to the next and there wasn't any reason for the troopers, that were supposed to be there to protect them, to make their lives more miserable by stealing their girls, beating them up, or taking their money at cards or dice, and he acted on those beliefs. He frequently found himself between an angry trooper and an aggrieved local and found that he could usually, if he stayed calm, smooth everything out. Because of this talent, he quickly became known as a good man who never abused his power. The locals knew they could trust him. They weren't afraid to talk to him if they had a problem, they felt like they could tell him anything, and they did.

Wilson saw it firsthand on an interrogation they did to look into the death of a Herero transport driver. Manfred asked other Hereros one set of questions, about who had problems with the driver and who had problems with the Hereros locally. Then he asked the Kavangos about the Nama, and then the Nama themselves. In the end it was about a woman, a Kavango, the wife of a Nama, a problem for both.

"God damn, son, where'd you learn to do that?" Wilson asked when it was over.

"I just asked them in a way that made sense." Manfred answered confused that Wilson was upset about the methods he'd used.

"Boy you know what you are? You're a fucking treasure that's what you are. You're a natural. You can't teach this shit, and you can't buy it. You make those bastards want to help you." Wilson explained hitting the desk for emphasis with his right hand while he smoked an unfiltered cigarette with his left.

Wilson talked to the captain about it a week later. It wasn't long before Manfred got promoted, and put in command of the other boys he worked with. At nineteen he found himself officially in charge of the twenty-five-man detachment that was guarding the largest treasure trove on the face of the earth.

Wilson told Manny to make it his business to get to know everyone around the area, not just the poor kids and the blacks. That he needed to start working from the bottom of the barrel to the top. So he did, and as a result of that, got to know just about everyone who lived in the Restricted Area. From the mine supervisors to the front office guys, black or white, everyone in the mining district ended up knowing Manfred Dietrich.

His troops trusted him too. He built a sense of pride in the unit, and the boys responded by becoming better soldiers. They became more honest men, who admitted their mistakes. It was a lesson he would use over and over in the years to come. Show men that they can become better men and quite often they would, without your having to do another thing. He also learned that the more you know what to expect of the men around you, the easier it is to predict what they're capable of. If something bad occurred, Manfred could usually predict who was involved before he ever asked the first question. That made getting the answer a lot easier.

Two months before Manfred's conscripted service ended, Wilson disappeared. Peg went with him. Manfred had been expecting it for a while. Wilson had gotten the information he'd come for, on mining production and production capabilities from the shipment records that Manfred had kept for the past year and a half. Manfred hadn't realized that he was being used until near the end and by then it was too late to do anything differently.

Wilson and Peg were both gone. Captain Boren was now Major Boren and he needed an executive officer, so Manfred was promoted to lieutenant and told to keep on with what he had been doing. By then Manfred had acquired a wealth of information and a set of skills he'd honed spying on his own country for the CIA.

When elections were finally held in 1990 and the black run SWAPO candidate Sam Nujoma was swept into the presidency, Manfred was asked by both the mines and the new government to act as a consultant on securing the restricted zone. He took both offers and found a way to combine them for the good of the country.

At work, day-in and day-out Manfred's job was to try to stay one step ahead of those people that spent all of their free time trying to come up with a way to carry off whatever they could of the company's product. He started with the diamonds, because that was where the greatest losses were. The problem with trying to keep people from stealing raw diamonds is that they're small, easily pilferable, and essentially look a lot like any other rock you might find laying around out in the desert.

Manfred saw the folly of the antiquated system of discovery and punishment that had been the mainstay of the diamond mine's security program since colonial times. By this point, people expected to be beaten if they got caught, it was something they planned on. It was no longer an effective deterrent. Historically, new security procedures were only instituted whenever a breach was discovered, but the focus was always punishment, not prevention. So he started the first proactive program to prevent smuggling.

Manfred reasoned that almost all of the attempts at smuggling out the uncut diamonds happened when the employees were leaving the mining compounds, for their "family time". So, that was where he put in the first controls.

He convinced the companies to incorporate a working uniform. The miners were supplied with coveralls that they wore to work, and that were washed in a laundry inside the compound. It gave the miners good sturdy clothes to work in and it gave them a sense of pride. Pride in themselves and pride in the company. What was more important though was that it gave him control of their personal belongings.

When the mining personnel got ready to leave the compound to go home to their families they were required to leave their work clothes at the work site to be laundered and to swap back into the street clothes they'd worn when they'd reported in for their shifts to work.

The street clothes, along with any other personal items that they had brought with them were identified with a picture "belongings" ID attached to clear plastic bags that the items were placed in. A member of the security force attached the ID with a wire tie and placed each bag in a secured storage area. Each man's clothes were safe and no man could use another man's clothes.

Workers changed clothes under the direct observation of the security staff.

He'd also set up the implementation of random searches at a checkpoint twenty- five miles from the gate, all vehicles were stopped and searched going out from the mines. The two things dramatically reduced pilferage, but there was still a steady loss. Manfred knew that there were those thieves that were wiling to hide the diamonds anywhere you could cram a rock. Every fold, every orifice was a potential hiding place. So Manfred installed fluoroscopes at the gates.

He soon found that as far as knowing what was going on, the bushmen were the best. They were smart and naturally curious. They, as far as he could tell, were completely without guile, they couldn't steal and they never lied. They did, however, love a good joke and delighted in laughing at the mistakes and minor misfortunes of others.

They loved to share and they loved to talk and teach their ways. Manfred was glad to learn. The clicks and pops that made up their language were difficult for his tongue to make at first. This resulted in quite a bit of laughter from his teachers. Discerning what each one meant was harder still, two sounds that sounded identical might mean a beetle if made a certain way, or an elephant, if made another. But he stayed with it, until he could communicate fairly well with any bushman he met.

In Namibia there were less than two million people and eighty-eight percent of them were black. But in Africa, black isn't black. Who you are is who you come from. Ovambos ruled the country and were about half of the black population, they were haughty and proud in their dealings with those who were not of the Ovambo tribe and that created resentments that could be beneficial in gathering information. Kavangos, Hereros, Damara, or Nama each had reasons to like or dislike each other. You just had to know who to ask about what, and that they all despised and were afraid of the bushmen, the San.

If you kept a San elder nearby when you asked questions, other tribes were terrified to lie to you. They were convinced that the bushman could read their minds. Fritz wasn't sure. Maybe they could. He did know that they could tell from a person's footprints, who was carrying a hidden load, and what they were carrying it in. They were natural masters of observation and they used every sense to do it. He never learned how they knew many of the things they did, but he knew enough to listen to them and to take what they told him seriously without understanding it.

It was this kind of local knowledge, coupled with the ability to make unexpected arrests that gave him a giant advantage over most of the thieves he encountered.

There was no reason to worry about complaints from the workers.

Namibian law presumed guilt, unlike England and the United States where a person is considered innocent until proven guilty. In Namibia if you were found with an uncut diamond, you had better have a bill of sale that accurately described the diamond in your possession, if you wanted to avoid prison. Security patrols and police had the right to search anyone suspected of smuggling anywhere at any time.

In a lot of ways his job was a lot like being a magician, it worked better if nobody knew how you did it. Manfred planned to keep it that way. He never talked about his work to a soul outside his team. Not about what they did, and certainly not about how they did it.

Eighteen

Ray shook his head, took a deep breath, and walked out of his office into the main hall of the Emergency Department. He was working his sixth night in a string of six nights in a row. He always liked to schedule his night shifts back to back, so he could get them out of the way all at once and be done with them. The up side of doing it that way was he got an eight-day mini-vacation when he got through. The down side was, working six nights in a row got harder every time he did it.

He saw Anne leaning into a supply cart loading bags of IV fluid into the crook of her arm. She smiled when she saw him.

"Just another day in paradise," he said sarcastically.

"You're looking rough," she observed.

The last two weeks had been a Chinese water torture of …of…nothing. They were polite to the point of absurdity, but they only spoke about work, limiting their conversation to just enough to get the job done. Neither one of them mentioning what they both knew filled the space between them. He wasn't going to be the one to bring it up. He was the injured party damn it. He was not going to be the one.

So he did stupid things, like looking at his cell phone thirty times a day in case she'd called and he'd missed it. Hoping…hoping what? Why didn't he just accept the fact that she'd chosen her husband and son over him, and pick his own marriage? Pick Lisa, before it was too late and he lost her for good. He was trying. He'd called her and apologized. Seeing Anne pushed him to do it, as some lame attempt at self-control or something. He wasn't confused this time. Lisa was the person he needed to be with. He'd be with her tomorrow. He was going to spend his time off up in Oxford. Why was he being so damned stupid today?

Anne patted his shoulder. "Well, you'd better get some coffee, if you're going to. We have a sixteen year old girl who fell out of the back of a pick-up on her way in with severe head trauma."

"She stable?" he asked, suddenly serious.

"Nope, it doesn't sound like it, but they've got her head and neck stabilized, a large bore line in, and started steroids."

"Forget the coffee, I'll never get to drink it…"

"I'm going to get the room ready," she answered.

He headed into the nursing station and was just checking the board when the ambulance pulled in. It was hard to tell what the person on the stretcher was as it rolled through the twin doors. A blood soaked dressing covered the patients face. An endo-tracheal tube poked through the bandage, connected to an AMBU bag that was the only thing keeping the patient breathing. There were air splints on both of her legs and her right arm. A Philadelphia collar immobilized her neck. And now, it was all up to him. To take the right steps, one at a time, to fix what had to be fixed as soon as possible without breaking anything else. Anne, a younger nurse, who was new to the ED, their radiology tech, a girl from the lab, and both paramedics all looked at him expectantly.

She had a tube in. Her neck was immobilized. Move to the next step.

"Keep bagging her. What're her pulses like?" he asked Anne as he finished pulling on his gloves.

"Ninety-six on the monitor, good oxygen saturation." One of the EMTs answered.

Anne was already moving to the right arm and sliding her fingers under the splint. "Good pulses here." She said before moving to the feet.

Ray pulled the dressing away from the girl's face. Her long blonde hair was caked with clotted blood. He could see immediately that her facial bones had been fractured. He couldn't be sure because of the matted hair but there looked like there was deformity of her forehead and skull as well. He slid his hands over her skull and it felt like a baggie full of jigsaw puzzle pieces. Her skull had broken like an egg. That was probably the only reason she was still alive. Swelling inside an intact skull was a disaster. The skull was a hard case. It was meant to protect the brain, but it also meant that there wasn't any extra room inside there for the brain to swell. If that happened, it was like squeezing a tube of toothpaste and all that soft brain tissue got squeezed out of the only hole big enough for it to go through, and down into the upper spinal canal. When that happened important things got crimped and when they crimped the whole system shut down. That was a problem she wasn't going to have.

"What in the hell happened?" He asked the paramedic standing next to him.

"The driver said that she was riding in the back of the pick-up. They had a couple of kids up front and three girls in the back. She was leaning up trying to holler something into the cab through the window, and they hit a bump. Somehow she fell and spun, and the rear wheel of the truck went right over her head. The car behind 'em ran over her legs."

"You have good pulses in both feet. But they both have significant crush injury below the knees." Anne announced.

Ray was shining a flashlight into the girl's eyes. "The pupil on the right's blown." He announced. Ray unfastened the collar and gently worked his fingers along the back of the girl's neck. "There's a deformity here, too. I think her neck's broken at C three or four. Let's get a cross table lateral x-ray of that, AP views of the arm and legs, and a portable chest x-ray before we put her in the CT scanner. She already has steroids on board. Let's draw a trauma panel, blood gasses, a blood alcohol, and a tox screen to look for any other drugs she has in her system. Anne, get me whoever's on call for neurosurgery."

With that the first rush was done. Now all he could do was wait. He picked up the chart and sat down with it to write until Anne got the neurosurgeon on the line. He heard her retch and suddenly the room filled with the stench of regurgitated beer.

"Log-roll her, Log-roll her for crap's sake. Her neck's broken," he ordered the young nurse that had instinctively reached to turn the patient's head. Already he'd dropped the chart and was on his feet. "She has a tube in her airway already. That's going to protect the airway. She's not going to drown or anything, but let's see if we can get an NG tube into her stomach. I'll have to do it blind. He grabbed the large tube out of the plastic pack that the Lab tech had already peeled open for him, and proceeded to slide it in through the girl's nose. It wouldn't go. He grabbed a light and a fiber optic scope and looked through the eyepiece as he advanced it into the same nostril.

"Her whole central face is broken away. It's a LaForte's four or five. There's no way to get through this side."

He checked her color and looked at the monitor, her blood pressure and pulse were both going up. She was building up pressure in her head. He could get the scope down past the larynx and into the upper esophagus on the other side, so he passed a guide wire through the scope and then fed the tube over it, then down into the stomach. He pushed some air in through the tube with a syringe and listened to her stomach to be sure the tube was in the right place. Somehow, while he had been doing this, the nurses had cleaned her up some.

"Doctor Wilson's on line three." Anne called in to him.

That was how the night started, and it went downhill from there. Next there was the boy on a dirt bike that tried to jump a swimming pool and went through a plate glass window. His blood alcohol content was 0.12 which was over the limit but not enough to explain why he would race a motorcycle up his driveway, run up a two by eight plank at fifty miles an hour and not figure that he wouldn't be able to stop before he wound up in the living room. He looked like he'd lost a fight with a saber-tooth tiger. He ended up with a hundred and twenty stitches in his hands, arms, his face, and his legs before it was all closed up.

Then a depressed woman tried to commit suicide by taking an overdose of her sleeping pills. That didn't seem to be working quite as fast as she wanted. So she doused herself with lighter fluid and set herself on fire. Which must have hurt a lot more than she expected, because she jumped out of a second story window to put herself out. Ray wasn't sure if she was lucky or not that it was only a second floor window, because she broke both of her heels, and didn't manage to put the fire out. Her neighbors had seen her crawling across the lawn in flames and rushed over with blankets and a fire extinguisher. They managed to put her out, but not before she ended up with third-degree burns over most of the upper half of her body. That started a placement nightmare. Nobody wanted to admit her. Everyone was pushing for a psychiatric consult first. He ended up transferring her to a burn unit, which was where she needed to be anyway. She might survive, but she was facing hell and a burn unit was the only real chance that she had.

While he was writing up her chart, he felt soft hands rubbing his shoulder and turned to catch a glimpse of Anne's scrub shirt out of the corner of his eye. They were the only two people in the nursing station.

"I just talked to them in ICU, that seventeen year old girl's still alive, they put her into a drug induced coma and have her on Mannitol to try and control the swelling of her brain," she said.

"Well that's something, her skull was shattered. She has pieces of bone in her brain matter. I guess they'll get them out if she survives the swelling." Ray said. It was the first time since she'd reappeared that Ray was able to be this close to her without some of his neurons shorting out, shutting down his speech center.

"I'd forgotten how good you were." She said softly, still rubbing his shoulders.

Now his brain started shorting out. "Thanks," was about all he could manage. He looked back down at his chart. Realized that he was just staring at it with no idea what so ever of what he intended to write, and sat it down on the desk in front of him.

"Why?" he asked softly.

"I guess that it's only when it's this bad that you..." she started.

"No. Why didn't you tell me anything? Why'd you just disappear?"

"We both had families." She explained, in a low voice. Taking her hands away from his shoulders.

"You still had a family. I'd already wrecked mine..." He stopped as Susan Goetz, one of the other nurses came out of an exam room with a chart and headed in his direction.

"It's Millie Lee." Susan said.

Ray stood up immediately and took the chart, "motor vehicle accident" was listed as the chief complaint.

"Is she okay?" He asked, his concern obvious.

"I think she'd just scared. She says that a car crossed the centerline and she had to swerve to keep from hitting it. She ran down the embankment and hit a pole." Susan explained.

"Come on. Let's go take a look," he said as he walked down the hall, the chart still in his hand. Both nurses followed him.

"My Gosh Millie, what happened?" he asked as he walked in the door.

Nineteen

Fritz sat quietly looking at his sister-in-law. Her thoughts were a million miles away. This was the first time that the two of them had been alone together, since the diagnosis. Manfred had sent them down to get some breakfast, while he got his blood work drawn and got hooked up to the machines that shot the chemotherapy into his veins. He said it didn't hurt, that the port was so easy to hit he never really felt anything when they did it. This was his fourth round, so he must have gotten used to it some.

This was his first treatment back at the cancer center since the allergic reaction. He'd gotten the last two treatments at home. The doctor's here were still calling the shots though. They just plugged him in at home and gave him whatever the doctors here said. It was time for the first set of scans to see if things were working, if the tumor was shrinking. Fritz figured this one must be a pretty big deal, because whatever it was, Gretchen was nervous as a cat.

"You still here?" Fritz asked her.

"Hmmm.?" She said looking up.

"Didn't mean to startle you."

"I didn't mean to be bad company," she answered.

He reached across the table and patted her shoulder. "It's going to be just fine. I know it is."

"I wish you did know that, for sure," she answered.

"I do," he said firmly, trying to sound like he did.

"I guess that's why you drove down?" She said with a wry smile and squeezed the hand he still had resting on her shoulder. "So you could be here for the celebration. I appreciate it though. I appreciate you being here."

He took his hand away from her shoulder and looked around the room. "I have to worry about you three. You're the only family I have. "

She looked at him gently.

"He's tough. He's going to do just fine," he emphasized fine.

She nodded, and looked down at her uneaten plate of eggs.

"When did he lose his hair?" Fritz asked, changing the subject.

"He lost some of it at first. Then one morning he came in and it was gone. He'd just shaved it all off. Said he didn't want to look like he had the mange."

"That's the way he'd do it." Fritz laughed.

Gretchen took a drink of her tea, long since grown cold. When she looked up he could see the tears forming in the corners of her eyes. She smiled anyway. "That's Manny to a T. Do the logical thing. He's so much stronger than I am, than I can be…"

Looking at her he felt a deep sadness. She was trying to be brave, but was letting him see the cracks. It had an unsettling effect on him, one that given the circumstances was entirely wrong. It made him realize that he still loved her. She may have been the only woman he ever really had, and he wanted to do everything in his power to protect her.

Their history had been a complicated one. He had loved her since grade school, when he hadn't had much else to love. That was when a walk along a dry street just before sundown constituted a date. But, her father was a doctor, and Fritz was a wild boy, with an alcoholic mother and no father. So that was that. He saw her once in a while after she'd gone away for school and they exchanged letters. Passionate declarations of love at first, Romeo and Juliette, us against the world, and they'd believed it for a while. But the letters got further and further apart over time, until there weren't any more. He found another girlfriend and she found someone of her own. He couldn't say which one of them quit writing first. She went to nursing school and he'd gone in the Defense Force, and then she'd married Manny.

Manny was enough older than they were that he didn't really remember her. He'd already gone, first to school and then to his own military service, when all of that had been going on. For Manny, the first time he'd ever laid eyes on her was when he saw her at the clinic in Luderitz. She was back from nursing school and was working as a nurse in her father's clinic.

Fritz had just gotten back from his first term of service and Manny had been working at the mines for a while. The two brothers were both living in their mother's house then. They owned an old fishing boat that Fritz was doing some commercial fishing with, to earn a little money, and Manny helped out whenever he was home.

Manny had come up with an infected arm after he'd cut his forearm while gutting a mackerel, on the boat. It didn't seem like much at first, it was deep and it bled a lot, but there wasn't any spurting blood so he hadn't gotten an artery, and he could move all of his fingers, so he hadn't cut any of the tendons or ligaments. They'd tied a towel around it on the way into port. By the time they got to the dock it had stopped bleeding. So, of course, they thought it would be fine.

Within a few days it was pretty apparent that that might not have been the best idea. Manny's arm started to swell and turn red. It was clearly infected, so they'd poured some iodine and hydrogen peroxide into the wound assuming that that would clear things up.

It didn't help. That night Manny's arm swelled more. He started to run a fever with shaking chills, and he was having trouble moving his fingers. The next day he went in to see the doctor to see about some antibiotics, and ended up getting admitted for sepsis instead. Fritz had been out on the boat at the time so he hadn't been there to say anything about knowing Gretchen. Fritz knew that Manny had fallen for one of the nurses, but it wasn't until after she'd said yes that Fritz knew it was Gretchen that his brother was going to marry.

The next thing he knew, she was living in their house and everything felt too stiff. There were too many things floating around unsaid. He couldn't ever relax, because he was afraid what might slip out, so Fritz spent most of his time on the boat. He never told Manny about anything and he guessed that Gretchen hadn't either, because, Manny kept after him, trying to convinced him to come home.

Fritz responded by fishing. He ran the boat every day. He paid for his fuel with the fish he caught. It was pretty good money and he didn't mind the work. Manny would come along when he was home from the mines. Fritz started spending more time up and down the coast. He had to go where the fish were. He'd come back home when Manny was off and they'd fish the local waters together, just like old times. Those nights he'd stay at the house, but in the evening he was careful to spend most of his time in his room.

As time passed, Manfred stopped fishing. He wanted to spend the time he had at home. He was becoming domestic. Within three months Gretchen was pregnant.

Fritz fished on alone, and the timing of their visits home became less and less coincident. Manny came and went with the requirements of his work, and Fritz followed the catch.

Slowly, inexorably Fritz found that he was alone. Finally, there came a night, he decided to go. He was away that night, up near the Skeleton Coast. He had anchored in a deep harbor just below the rocky shallows, like he often did when he slept on the boat. He thought about it all night sitting on the aft deck looking out across the black ripples of the endless dunes and he knew there wasn't anything else to do. She and Manny were happy. She loved Manny. Manny loved her. Manny was stable, Fritz wasn't. Gretchen deserved to be happy. She deserved a stable life. Fritz knew he had to go. They needed to build their family together. He couldn't stand to watch from the outside any more, so that was that.

The next morning, while Gretchen was at work, he went back to the house and got his things together. Then he went to the bank and withdrew all of the money he'd saved to pay off the boat. He kept just enough to get him where he was going. The rest he used to pay off the loan that he and Manny had taken out to fix up the house a few years before. He sold the boat to a broker and left the money and the bank receipt for the loan payment on the kitchen table, along with a note that said that he had gotten a phone call about a job he'd been looking into, and then he took off. It took him the width of the country before he felt like things were back to normal again. He'd had to go back to the Caprivi to do it.

That was the beginning of his gunrunning years. The defense force was a lost cause. There was no sense going back into that and there wasn't any use lolling around in some daydream of idealistic loyalty. Almost all of the country's population was black, their right to vote was coming...it was inevitable. You couldn't be sure of all the changes that that would bring. But one thing was pretty well certain, once they were in charge hey weren't going to tolerate an army whose entire purpose was the superssion of the black population. It was only a matter of time. The best you'd be able to reasonably hope for would be to be sent home without your gun to try to find a paycheck doing something else.

What would make a difference in the coming change wasn't guns, it was going to be money. Now that didn't mean that you couldn't use guns, but as far as Fritz could see, the best way to use guns was going to be to find a way to turn them into money.

Fritz's knowledge of the bush served him well. The years that he'd spent chasing around after the black market as a trooper had showed him how hard it was to catch even the sloppiest gunrunner. The ones did get caught were usually by accident...accidents or bad judgment.

So, what he'd once fought, he now became. And he did it in a new way, focused on profit. He started by eliminating the weapons that were on hand. He followed tracks, he scanned trails, and he found every cache he could. And like a good citizen, he took the troopers straight to them. This was called "creating a demand." Then, he'd help transport the captured weapons back to camp. Often he'd get paid a reward on the front end, if the haul was big enough.

He'd come back later, when he knew most of the soldiers were out on patrol, and haul the same weapons away for destruction. He'd con the guards. He'd sign the papers, and nobody was the wiser. The trick was that you had to space things out between units and make sure that the weapons disappeared, so that the same units weren't seeing the same guns show back up again.

110

As soon as he got a load, he'd haul them straight out of the country with a caravan of mules, by using the relatively new country of Zimbabwe as a freeway. He sold them to a black intermediary in Angola, who'd sell them back to the terros, in return for ivory or black rhino horns. The terros killed the rhino and elephants for meat. The horn and ivory had no value to them. Fritz would drop off the guns and pick up the ivory and horns to bring back on the returning mule caravan. He had a black market buyer that paid top dollar for them back in the city.

Things worked great for a few years. Until March 21, 1990, that was the day Namibia became an independent country and Southwest Africa was no more. All governmental ties with South Africa were officially cut. Everything Fritz feared would happen when that day came turned out to be true. Sam Nujoma, the president of the terros, was elected president of the new government. The first thing he did was to send the defense force home, with no guns and no pay.

With no customers and no friends to turn a blind eye, to his border crossings, the transit from Angola to Zimbabwe became more problematic. After a firefight that cost him an entire shipment of ivory, and very nearly his life, Fritz decided that it was time for him to settle down. So, he took what money he'd saved and bought a farm in Zimbabwe. He knew that Zimbabwe wasn't stable yet, but Fritz truly believed that with enough work he could do fine wherever he was. That turned out to be a somewhat optimistic viewpoint.

Twenty

Ray got off at seven the next morning. It was Wednesday, so Jim, his yardman, was there. Jim was just getting the riding mower out of the garage when Ray pulled up. Ray waved as he got out of the car.

Jim cut the engine. "Want me to wash the car til you get to sleep?"

"Sure," Ray said as he tossed him the keys.

Ray took a shower and got into bed. He couldn't turn it off. The night's scenes rolled through his head. He got back up. He turned on the television and flipped the channels. After a while he settled on a special on Guadalcanal on the History Channel. About the time his eyes closed in the recliner the lawn mower fired up. He tried to sleep, but the roar of the lawn mower gave way to the whine of the weedeater and even the droning of the announcers on "War Week" couldn't put him to sleep. When the steady hum of the leaf blower finally came through the windows it was late afternoon. By then he was hungry so he ran by Squealers for a couple of Delights, pulled pork topped with cole slaw and hot barbecue sauce. He picked up an extra sandwich for Jim. It was seven that night before he finally got to sleep.

He woke up at eight the next morning feeling jetlagged, but he wasn't able to get back to sleep. He had plenty of time to sort through the mail and get packed before he hit the road. Lisa wasn't off until four. He was halfway through his second cup of coffee when his cell phone rang. It was a number he didn't recognize.

"Hello," he answered.

"Hey," Anne's voice said over the phone.

He drew in a deep breath.

"Are you there?" she asked.

"Yeah…I'm here."

There was a short silence before she spoke again. "I just wanted to check on you. You looked a pretty beat by the time you got off."

"Yeah, I'm better…I slept…I'm okay. I'm just packing to go and spend the week with Lisa." He answered.

"So, things are good…with Lisa," she asked hesitantly.

"Yeah. They're good."

"That's good." Anne echoed.

"We're trying to get things worked out."

"I hope you can. I've felt bad, about what you said the other night…I was wrong…"

"We were both wrong." Ray said.

"No. About not calling you…I should at least have had the courage to tell you face to face…I just want you to know that I'm sorry. I didn't mean to hurt you."

"It's okay, I appreciate you telling me now." Ray answered.

"I just wanted you to know that you weren't the only one…that had things turned upside down."

"Moving must have been hard, at least you had Josh and Davey." Ray said, referring to her husband and her son.

"Look," Anne said, suddenly chipper. "You go and enjoy your week off with your wife. I just felt bad…so…look…I've got to go. We can talk when you get back. The phone disconnected before he could say goodbye.

He played the conversation over and over again in his head the whole drive to Oxford. Even when he got to Lisa's apartment he couldn't put it out of his mind.

"So, what have you been up to? You seem a little preoccupied." Lisa asked as she poured them both a glass of pinot grigio.

"Just the same old stuff…" Ray started, but he didn't know where to go from there. How did just talking with Anne make it feel strange to be with Lisa? He felt guilty and evasive, even though there was nothing to feel guilty about.

Everything was turning into a mess again. They weren't even over the fight they'd had the last time they were together and now he felt like he had something to hide, and he wasn't exactly sure what it was supposed to be hiding.

"I'm still feeling kind of thick-headed from being on nights all week. Hey, that reminds me, I saw Millie in the E.R. last night."

"Last night, is she okay?"

"No, not last night, the night before. The last night I worked. She had an accident, ran off of the road, but she was fine, just a few bumps and bruises,"

"Thank goodness she didn't break anything," Lisa started.

"Well, she broke her thumb." Ray said, as an afterthought.

"Her thumb? That's a funny thing to break in a car wreck."

"I guess she saw it coming and stiffened up. Her arms were out straight and locked when she hit the pole. The force of her body coming forward drove her thumbs into the steering wheel." He demonstrated the mechanics of the injury with his own right arm.

"On the right?" Lisa asked.

"No the direction of the force wasn't lateral, it was straight forward." Ray explained.

"No I was talking about which thumb, silly."

"Oh, it was the left one," he answered.

"At least that's good." Lisa said.

"It still hurts the same, but at least she can write, and play tennis. Those were her words, not mine." Ray paraphrased.

"I'll have to call her, and see how she's doing." Lisa said.

Shit, Ray thought. He should never have brought Millie up. Damn it, why didn't he think about things more before he said them?

He tried to remember if Millie had ever seen Anne, or not. He thought about it. He felt like he had Alzheimer's or something. He couldn't remember.

"What's wrong?" Lisa asked.

"Just thinking about Millie and the accident," he answered as he clicked the remote to turn on the television.

Susan was the nurse that took care of her? He remembered Susan telling him Millie was there. He followed her into the room, but there wasn't any way to know if she'd seen Anne or not, while she'd been there.

He was pretty sure Millie knew about what had happened. She had to know about the affair. Charlie would have told her. Hell, everybody knew about it after Lisa had left. Shit, shit, shit.

"How'd she wreck?" Lisa asked, taking the remote and turning down the volume.

Ray let the blue tide pouring out of the television wash over him, pretending to be interested in what the anchors were talking about. They went to a clip. A woman stood looking at the camera, her hair a mess, a smoking trailer in the background.

"We was just lucky to get out o dat thing. It'd been cold and we went to sleep with tha heater on," the woman said.

"That's part of what's bothering me," Ray answered, switching to the news on Channel Five. "She said that she'd had to swerve to miss a car that crossed the line."

"You sound like you don't believe her." Lisa said.

"It was just that the police said that the witnesses didn't see any other cars. The guy who called 9-1-1 said that she was driving along in the right lane and she suddenly swerved back and forth a few times and seemed to lose control. Then she just ran down the bank, into the ditch. Apparently she tried to drive back out, too, but there was water and too much mud down there for her to get enough traction to get back out."

He took in a deep breath and blew it out through his mouth, relaxing back into the cushions of the sofa.

He looked back at the TV, on Channel Five Sports the Ole Miss quarterback was talking about why he was going into the National Football League instead of coming back to play for his senior season next year.

"I want to get the chance to play in the NFL. I've had a great couple of seasons here, and my knee is as strong as ever.

That meant, "I got my knee hurt in the State game, and I need to get as much money as I can now, before someone knocks my leg off," Ray interpreted.

"Who can blame him?" Lisa said, taking another sip of her wine.

Ray flipped the channel changer to Channel Seven, "...after this message we'll be back with tomorrow's weather, with Alice Meadows." A voice said over the picture of an attractive blonde is a business-like gray skirt and a tight sweater pointing at a weather map.

They should just go to dinner. They could have a nice night together, and then he could get some more sleep. He'd be able to think straighter in the morning. He was making a mountain out of a molehill. He was just tired. He wasn't thinking straight for a bunch of reasons.

"What do you think happened?" Lisa's voice jerked him back into the world around him.

"I don't know. I don't know what to think...she'd had some drinks..."

"You didn't have them draw a blood alcohol did you?" Lisa asked.

"I should have, but I didn't, so I don't know. She didn't...she wasn't obviously intoxicated." Ray explained. "I guess I still should have."

"No you shouldn't." Lisa said sharply. "She's got enough going on without that."

"But what if she has a problem. She doesn't need to be on the road..."

"How long have you known Millie?" Lisa asked.

"That doesn't mean anything Lisa. She just lost her husband. Maybe she's been trying to numb the pain..." He started, but then he fell silent, squinting his eyes a little. "I don't think she has a drinking problem...that wasn't really the issue, but there are some other things about it that bother me."

"What sort of things?"

"It's nothing really...nothing I can say for sure." Ray started.

"Well then tell me what you think it is?" Lisa asked, impatiently.

"The thing that stays in the back of my head...what worries me...is that there are a lot of studies that show that more than half of all single-car accidents are really some kind of a suicide attempt. You know, there's no way to know for sure, but a lot of times you wonder how a wreck like that could have happened. Did they have a heart attack? Did they fall asleep? How did they hit the only tree in a ten mile stretch?"

"You don't really think that, do you?"

"I don't know. I have to think about it. She was driving down a straight road. Nobody saw the other car. She just lost her husband. How did she just end up in a ditch? I think it's something that we at least have to consider." Ray explained.

Lisa sat for a few moments, watching, as the TV blared a beer commercial. "SEE FOR YOURSELF. JUST WHAT YOU NEED TO MAKE YOUR NEXT TAILGATE THE BEST EVER…"

"I need to talk to her," she announced in her most determined voice. "I need to talk to her myself."

This was Lisa, the clinician, the psychologist. Determined to help a friend who might be in trouble. Ray quickly started to wonder if it was actually him that was suicidal. Perhaps he had some sort of perverse death wish. He wasn't even sure if Millie knew who Anne was or if she had seen her or not, and now he was just about making sure that if she did know, that it was going to have to come up. How could he say all of that stuff and not know that it was going to lead to some sort of long, in-depth conversation with Millie? What was he, some kind of stupid asshole?

It turned out that on a couple of things, Ray had been dead on target. By the next morning he really did have a completely different outlook on everything. He'd also gotten the answers to several of his questions from the night before. Number one, yes, Millie did know who Anne was. Number two, no, Millie was not suicidal and number three, yes, a stupid asshole probably the least objectionable thing he appeared to be.

Twenty-One

Manfred had already been in Windhoek for five days. The chemotherapy had taken the first few days, and the scans they'd done to see how the chemotherapy was working took another. Now after all of this, they were being sent on to see some new kind of doctor, one that specialized in treating cancer with radiation.

Manfred didn't know if they were being sent there, because the scans were good news or because the scans were bad news. Nobody had talked to them about what was happening with the scans at all. The only thing they knew was that they had to wait until they talked to him to see where they went from here.

The new doc's name was Patterson. His office was in the basement of the cancer center. Which made sense. Being in the basement would have saved the hospital a lot on construction costs. Less need for shielding, nothing to worry about radiating but dirt, and who cared if you radiated a bunch of worms? He'd used enough x-ray equipment in his job to know a little about that sort of stuff, but the machines that they were using here had to be a thousand times more powerful than the little units that they'd used for screening at the mines. They were even more powerful than the industrial x-rays that they used to look for stress fractures in the pipes or mine supports.

He and Gretchen held hands as they stepped into the elevator, Fritzy was at school and Fritz was doing whatever it was he did between trips to the city. He was bringing a group of hunters in to the airport later in the afternoon, and was going to try and meet them for dinner after that.

He looked at his wife, and squeezed her hand as he pushed the button labeled B.

When they got to the front desk the receptionist handed them another pile of papers.

"We already did these upstairs," he told her.

"We need you to do them for our office," was the only answer he got.

They sat in the exam room and Gretchen filled out the stack of paperwork, most of them looked like the same forms that they'd already filled out at the other doctor's offices.

"Why can't they just share these things?"

"Every office has different things they're looking for," she explained as she made the check marks on one of the forms.

"No they don't. These are the same questions that we answered upstairs."

"A lot of them are." She said, laying down her pen and brushing the back of his hand. "Don't lose your temper over something this little. Besides, it gives us something to do while we wait."

"I don't want something to do. I just want to know what the stupid damned scans show. Why do they have to make such an ordeal out of everything…" The opening of the exam room door cut him off mid-tirade.

"Mr. Dietrich? I'm Doctor Patterson." The man in the white coat said as he walked through the door with an outstretched hand.

Manfred stood and extended his hand. "Nice to meet you. This is my wife Gretchen."

"Let's sit down." The doctor said pulling his stool so that he sat across the examination table from them with his back against the wall. He placed the chart on the table between them, opened it, and flipped the pages, looking for what it was that he wanted. "I've gone through your case, and I've just reviewed the stupid damned scans you were referring to when I walked in." He looked up and smiled.

Manfred looked back sheepishly, and Gretchen looked at the floor and smiled, trying to hide her amusement, but failed miserably.

"I agree whole heartedly. Let's get straight to the point." Doctor Patterson said, putting his finger on the page in front of him and pursing his lips as he re-read the reports.

Manfred held his breath. The silence was killing him. He wanted to scream. It was like standing in front of a firing squad and waiting to hear the word "FIRE." He suddenly wished for the familiar comfort of the paper work, instead of this. They were past "READY" and the doctor had just said "AIM."

The doctor began speaking, but Manfred missed the first part of it. All he could hear in his mind was "F…I…R……."

"…marked reduction in the size of the left upper lobe mass, with resolution of the previously seen hilar adenopathy." The doctor read the radiology report out loud.

It sounded like that had to be good news Manfred thought. He looked over at Gretchen and she was smiling her head off, so he was pretty sure it was.

"I think your wife gets the gist of what I'm saying." The doctor said smiling. "Let me put it into a little plainer language. Most of the disease is gone. But…" he continued, raising a finger. "There is still some tumor left. Which means that we still have more work to do. That's why you're here."

Manfred breathed out for the first time since the doctor started talking. The doctor went on explaining about the radiation and how they gave it and the side effects you could expect during treatment and when you could expect them, but Manfred really didn't hear much of it. He just nodded his head and enjoyed the feeling of air moving in and out of his lungs. Gret was paying attention and they were going to get to watch a movie about it anyway. Mostly, what he got out of it was that he was going to have to stay in the city for the next seven weeks to get the treatments.

That was one of the first things that he was going to need to take care of he thought, as the doctor was explaining what esophogitis was to Gretchen, I have to make some arrangements to work here for the time that I'm going to be on treatment. With the treatments taking seven weeks it was going to be easier to arrange than it would be for something shorter. He had to work during the treatments, still hadn't figured out what he was going to be able to do to physically hide or disguise the diamonds. He had delayed as much as possible in allowing the inspections but the pressure from the government in Zimbabwe was growing.

He'd already had several frank conversations with the president and his advisors, about how things would need to be handled in the future depending on the various ways that things could work out. They would support him in every way they could, he knew that, but part of his job was to prepare for contingencies just like this, and just because it was him that was the subject at hand, it was no less critical to have put into place a plan of action for each of the possible outcomes.

The plan that he'd written was quite specific. He'd written most of it before he'd ever thought of it as anything more than an abstract theoretical consideration. It was rigid, it was fair, and it was designed to watch out for the interests of the government and the consortium.

As soon as it was apparent that he would not be cured he would be taken out of a position of any responsibility. This was to prevent his own fatalism from affecting the outcome of the investigations.

"Now if everything goes like we hope and we get a good response in your chest, we will need to come back in six to eight weeks and look at giving you a few treatments to your brain." Doctor Patterson continued with his explanation.

"To my brain, I wasn't aware of anything that showed any tumor in my brain." Manfred said, suddenly completely focused on what it was that the doctor was saying. That was another aspect of the contingency plan. If there were any question of an impairment of his judgment or abilities he would be required to step down immediately. There was no recourse for that one.

It had caused him some concern after the coma earlier. Luckily, the doctors had certified him as sane and sound after he woke up. So that took care of that.

"No there isn't any, but remember when I said that this is the kind of tumor that likes to travel around?"

Manfred nodded, although he didn't recall that part of the conversation at all.

"That the chemotherapy will take care of any of the tiny bits of tumor that may have spread to any other parts of your body?"

Manfred nodded again. He did remember some of that.

"There's only one place that the chemotherapy can't get to, and that's your brain. There's something called the 'blood-brain barrier.' It's made to keep toxic things, like chemotherapy, from getting inside our brains and making us crazy…well, crazier than we are normally." He smiled at his joke and waited to be sure Manfred was understanding what he was saying. "So, even if we get rid of the tumor in your chest entirely, there's still a chance that the cancer can recur, or, come back. But, we do all we can and hope for the best, but there's nothing we can do to eliminate all of the risk. But, the chance of tumor cells hiding in your brain is a risk we can do something about. If we don't do anything about it there's a thirty-five percent chance that the tumor will show up there later…in your brain. Because that was the only place we weren't able to protect."

That was what had killed Gretchen's father. Not the tumor in his lungs. The tumor spreading to his brain, was what had done him in.

"We can reduce that risk to eleven percent by doing ten or twelve treatments to your brain, to eradicate any microscopic disease that may still be hiding there."

"Well certainly we want to do that, if it will reduce the risk." Gretchen said emphatically.

"What are the side effects of that?" Manfred asked.

"Very few really, it's a relatively low dose of radiation, but we have to get rid of the tumor in your chest first, it doesn't do any good really, unless we have control there. I'm just mentioning it so we can come back and revisit it when the time's right," the doctor went on.

"How would we know if the tumor had spread to my brain already?" Manfred asked.

"Well we don't see any evidence of it, no clinical signs or symptoms that tell us that it has, and the MRI we did of your head when you were first diagnosed was fine, and the CT scan they got in the hospital when you were unconscious after your first treatment didn't show anything to worry about."

"Then why would we treat my brain?" Manfred asked.

"We don't have to. That's your choice of course, but it cuts the rate from thirty-five percent to ten to twelve percent. That's pretty significant."

"We are going to treat it, if we get to that point." Gretchen said, firmly.

"I'm not saying that. I just want to understand," Manfred started, looking at his wife unhappily, to try to get her to hush a minute and let him speak. Then he turned his attention back to the doctor. "If there isn't any evidence that there's a tumor there?"

The doctor raised his hands palms up. "There are limits to what we can see. God doesn't give us a crystal ball. A CT scan can only see collections of about a million cells, there may be a smaller colony, say twenty-thousand cells that is resting there, we can't see it, the chemotherapy can't get to it. Someday it will make itself known."

"How? How will it make itself known? What do I need to look for?" Manfred asked.

"There are a lot of things to look for, headache, visual changes, paralysis, difficulty speaking, agitation, any of these things, really anything that's different could be a symptom that there's a problem." As the doctor explained a touch of concern crossed his face. "Is there something that you're worried about Mr. Dietrich? If you're having any symptoms we can always repeat the scans, just to be sure."

"No, I just wanted to know what to look for, just in case. I don't want to wait if there is something that comes up." Manfred explained.

The doctor's smile returned and as he stood he reached over and patted Manfred's shoulder. "Well, we'll keep an eye on you under treatment. You just let us know if something comes up and we can get right on it. Alright then, we can start the planning on your chest on Monday."

The nurse took them to another room and they sat and watched the movie, some of it was interesting, but it was hard for Manfred to pay as much attention to it as he should have. He was too busy worrying about a tumor growing inside his brain.

Twenty-Two

God, she had been such an idiot. Professionally, it was obvious. A couple living in separate cities and seeing each other only at irregular intervals had almost no chance of working through the kinds of issues that resulted from infidelity. Why did she think that the same expectations didn't necessarily apply to her? How had she let herself get to the point that she actually believed that things were going to work out? That somehow she and Ray were going to magically resolve all of their problems and get it right this time. Those were completely unrealistic expectations. She could see that. It was just that everything had been going so well since the funeral. She'd really started to believe they could do it.

If she looked at it professionally, there was no reason for her to be sitting here on her couch putting herself through this emotional roller coaster ride again. But knowing it wasn't reasonable didn't stop the tears. Reasonable or not, it still hurt.

She'd been waiting for a month, for them to have this week together. She'd planned it, she'd worried about it, she'd even mustered up her courage and decided that this was going to be their chance to try and really work out the things that were keeping her from being able to feel like they were a couple again, so much for plans.

Their special week, the seven days that were going to let them start all over again, had ended up lasting less than seven hours. All of her fears, everything that had been nagging her in the back of her head had, in one phone call, turned out to be true and blown all of her plans to dust.

"You selfish bastard," she muttered.

It still hurt. Of course it hurt, but she was mad too. What infuriated her the most was that he was so...so... What? Stupid? When she'd asked him if what Millie had told her was true, he'd said, "But nothing's happened." Like that made everything okay.

Millie had seen the little bitch standing behind him, rubbing his

122

shoulders when they'd wheeled the stretcher into the ER. She was rubbing his shoulders in front of everyone and Ray expected that anyone could believe that nothing had happened?

Lisa felt her eyes stinging, and realized she was crying again. He'd let her start to fall back in love with him, had made love to her like it meant something again, and "she" was back the whole time.

His failure to grasp the depth of his betrayal was beyond her comprehension. She could only shake her head in disbelief. "Nothing's happened? Nothing's happened? How can you sit there and say nothing's happened?" She'd asked.

"Because nothing has."

"You mean, this time…or again…or yet?" she spat.

"Not, yet! You make it sound like it's inevitable or something. She just came back to work." He explained, just like it actually made some sense for that to have happened.

"How many hospitals are there in Mississippi?" She'd asked calmly.

"I don't know. What difference does that make?" He'd asked.

"Are you being deliberately dense? You know damned good and well, what I'm getting at," she'd screamed.

He'd sighed and shook his head, exasperated that she'd wanted an answer. Like he was the victim and she was putting him through some sort of unreasonable inquisition, or something.

"Why in the hell is she working in your ER, for you, every day?"

"Night." He'd answered.

"God damn it, what difference does that make?" She'd exploded. "Stop pretending you're an idiot. If you're going to pretend, at least do me the favor of pretending you have some respect for my intellegence."

"I was just saying, she came back on nights. The hospital didn't even ask me before they hired her. What was I supposed to do?" He threw up his hands.

"For starters, you could have mentioned it." She accused. "For another, stop trying to convince me that the hospital just hired your private masseuse back against your will!"

"How am I supposed to know what to do? When we split up. We went all of the way to the point that we got separated, and you knew all along what was going on, you knew about Anne then and you never bothered to mention it. How was I supposed to know that you wanted me to mention something now?"

It was the last thing that he said with any emotion. After that, it was like he just deflated. He just wasn't even there any more. He withdrew into some kind of emotionless shell.

To try and get through it, she'd grabbed his cell phone. She'd looked under his recent calls and saw a number without a name.

"Is this her phone number?" She'd demanded. "Is it?"

Ray shrugged, so she pushed it. She'd watched his face as she held the phone towards him at arm's length.

A woman's voice that she didn't recognize was saying, "Ray...Ray is that you?"

"Tell her that you'll be there tonight." Lisa demanded handing him the phone.

He took the phone and hung up without saying anything. Then he'd looked at her sadly and said, "Lisa, it's not like that."

She should never have given it to him. She should have kept it. She should've shouted into it. She should have said, "No, this is his wife!" But she hadn't, she'd just handed it to him, like the little coward she was. Why hadn't she screamed at her? Why hadn't she thrown the phone right in Ray's face with her still on it asking for him? But no, instead of actually doing something, she'd just said, "Get out!" Then sat down on the couch and watched as he got his things, and went to the door

"Ray, wait." She'd said before he could open it.

He'd looked at her expectantly.

"If you've ever loved me, I need you to do something for me."

"What?"

"Have enough decency to stay away from me and let me live my life without you ripping my guts out over and over and over again. That's all I'm asking from you ever again, just go away...and stay away. That's all I'm asking."

And he had. That was what hurt the worst. He hadn't even fought for her, hadn't argued, hadn't begged her to forgive him, he'd just left. The unfaithful bastard had just gotten in that ridiculous car of his and left.

She'd listened to the exhaust note as it faded, and knew that it was taking what was left of her marriage and her husband out of her life. Shrinking them to nothingness as the sound disappeared into the distance.

When it was gone, she kept trying to hear it coming back. Listening for it. Sitting there until it was dark. Eventually she got up and tried to go to bed. Sleep was not there.

She'd lain as still as she could in the dark. As if she was afraid of waking the husband that was no longer there, until she could see the first reddish rays of light coming into the window. Then, finally, she could get up and make coffee.

Now she was an hour late for work and she still hadn't even had a shower yet. She had to get control and make herself function. She couldn't let herself fall apart again, like she had the last time. It had been a private meltdown.

She'd never shown it. Never let anyone know.

Once Millie had told her, the signs were everywhere. Blaring in neon perfusion; "ANOTHER WOMAN." She'd sat in that house for two days, like she was catatonic. Ray had come and gone like nothing was happening. Too absorbed in his affair to notice that she still even existed at all. After two days of catatonia, she had taken the job here in Oxford, and knew when she did it, what was coming. It didn't take long either, until Ray asked her for the separation she knew he wanted.

What could have made her think that they could fix all that? He dumped her, "she" dumped him, and then he came back to her. How screwed up was that?

Lisa felt like a total fool. That was what they were trying to base a relationship on? Sure they'd had children, sure they'd had a past life, but that was the key phrase, wasn't it? "A past life." And now "she" had come back.

Lisa smelled the coffee beginning to burn and got up off of the couch where she'd been sitting, paralyzed, for the last two hours and walked into the kitchen. Normally she would've turned off the coffee maker and been gone an hour ago. There was a thick oily tar congealing on the bottom of the glass carafe, which was just beginning to smoke. She grabbed the stinking mess and carried it to the sink. She should've known better than to stick hot glass into cold water, but without thinking, she did just that. It wasn't until she heard the PING and saw the crack spreading across the glass bottom that she realized what she'd done.

"Fuck," she screamed, in the empty apartment. She hated that word, it made her cringe if she heard one of her students say it, but it was how she felt right now. She couldn't help it. Fuck Ray, fuck her, fuck that little bitch Ray was screwing, and fuck this fucking coffee pot.

Now the stupid thing was broken and she was going to have to try to find a new one. She had to have coffee. Just because she was having a nervous breakdown didn't mean she didn't need her coffee.

Lisa threw the cracked pot into the trashcan as hard as she could and was gratified when it shattered into a million pieces. It made her want to throw more things. She wanted to open the kitchen cabinets and throw everything that was in them, even the crystal wine glasses that had been Ray's mother's, especially the crystal wine glasses that had been Ray's mother's, but she didn't have time. She still might do it, but it wasn't going to be this morning. She was already late, and now she was going to be later.

Lisa looked at herself in the mirror as she dried her hair. No wonder he wanted a younger woman. Her boobs looked like they'd dropped a quarter, and were trying to see where it went. She was a fifty-year-old woman with a fifty-year-old body. How was she supposed to compete with a woman who was fifteen years younger?

You'd have thought that she'd have the routine down better by now. Your husband screws around you have this set response. It wasn't like she hadn't been through it before. Why was she letting this destroy her again? In some ways it was worse this time. She didn't know why.

Twenty-Three

Fritz was pleasantly surprised by the invitation to have lunch alone with his brother, although he would have preferred to wait until a little later in the day. Until his hangover had passed. But he was happy that Manny felt like doing it none the less. A healthy appetite was always a good sign. Besides, it was Manny, he wouldn't need to pretend he wasn't hung over.

The restaurant was on a little back street he barely remembered, but he found it without much difficulty. Manny was already sitting at a table looking at the menu when he arrived.

"Hey boy," he said as he sat down across the table from his brother.

"I appreciated last night. It was nice of you to make it a party. I know Gret really appreciated it too." Manfred said warmly.

"I never pass up a chance for a steak." Fritz said, dismissively. An attractive, young, Nama woman appeared at their table, with a note pad and pencil. "You'd better start me off with a Bloody Mary this morning," he said.

Manfred raised his eyebrows. "Hair of the dog?"

"Wine always gives me a headache." Fritz said, his smile fainter than usual.

"Probably the third bottle was the bad one." Manfred observed.

"Probably so, but it was a party. Better bring me a strong tea, too," Fritz added before the girl left.

They sat in silence for a few minutes, as they tended to do when they were alone together, and watched as the waitress returned and sat down the steaming pot and two cups, then hurried off to get the Bloody Mary.

Fritz opened the pot's lid and looked in. "You may want to pour yours now, I'm going to let mine get a bit stronger than usual."

Manfred went ahead and poured himself a cup, leaving room for a bit of milk. Then he added two spoons full of sugar, stirred that carefully, and finally poured in the milk.

As Fritz checked the tea again the waitress brought his Bloody Mary.

He turned it up and drank it down before he poured the tea.

Finally, after they'd both gotten their tea the way they wanted it, Manfred looked up from his cup. "That's one of the things I wanted to talk to you about."

"What part?" Fritz asked, confused.

"The party part, I guess." Manfred said.

Fritz looked at him blankly and Manfred continued.

"There are a lot of things...a lot of things to consider. But, to cut to the chase, and I really don't know how to do this..." Manfred stopped, trying to find the right words to explain it, looked at his brother, and frowned.

"Just spit it out then." Fritz suggested.

"I guess, what I'm getting at is, that, I need you to help me."

"Why do you think I'm here? Whatever you need, all you have to do is ask." Fritz answered.

"This isn't like that. I don't want you to feel like you have to do this. It's a terrible thing to have to ask anyone to do..." Manfred started.

"What could be so terrible?" Fritz chuckled. "What do I have to do? Kill somebody or something?"

"Probably," Manfred said. He stroked his chin for a moment, thinking it over. "As much as I'd hate it, that's the only way I can see for things to work out."

"Why do you need someone killed?" Fritz asked, suddenly serious.

"It's the only way for you to get into the restricted zone...to get the diamonds...and to get rid of the problems of yours, from the deaths in Zimbabwe." Manfred said simply.

Their server was approaching the table and Manfred made a slight nod in her direction. Fritz immediately recognized the intent of the gesture and kept his thoughts to himself for the moment.

After they'd ordered their lunches and the woman had headed to the kitchen, Manfred resumed his explanation. "Look, I know what you're thinking, but I've spent the last twenty-four hours thinking this thing out. I don't have all of the details worked out yet, but I'll tell you what I'm thinking."

Fritz leaned over the table attentively and nodded for his brother to go on.

"You remember what it was like for us? You know, growing up?" Manfred asked.

"Of course," Fritz answered.

"We missed a lot of things, a lot because we didn't have money, we only had each other... I don't want that for my son." Manfred explained.

"You don't have to worry about any of that. Gret isn't going to turn into an alcoholic like Lilly did, besides you aren't going to die, we're going to beat this thing." Fritz reassured his brother.

"I might beat it for a year, or even two, but the chances that I'm going to beat it for good are only about twenty percent. I've been looking at the statistics on the Internet ever since I was diagnosed. The odds are against me… and what's going to happen to the two of them when I'm gone? I won't have a chance to do this later. If I wait until it's too late. If I wait until the cancer spreads to my brain. There won't be a chance anymore."

"Manny, you shouldn't talk this way."

"I have to. I don't have a choice. I have to be realistic. You and I…we suffered because no one took the time to do it."

"You could be one of the twenty percent." Fritz insisted.

"And what if I'm not." Manfred continued. "I'm going to risk throwing away my wife and son's future for a twenty percent chance of success. You know better than to take a bet like that."

"So what are you saying? You think they'll be better off …"

Manfred cut him off mid-sentence. "If what? If they have money? Of course they'll be better off, but it'll only work if they have enough money to get out of here. There's no future here for Fritzy, you know that as well as I do. Think of all the things that have happened in our lifetime, do you think it's going to get any better in his?"

Fritz shook his head sadly. His brother's assessment was certainly pessimistic, but it was also certainly true.

"I'll do what I can to help them. You know you can depend on that." Fritz offered weakly.

"And I know that. But we need to be realistic. If you gave them every dollar you made it wouldn't be enough to send the boy to college in Europe, certainly not enough to let Gret move there with him. I do know you'd try… but if I'm not here, the connections that I have, the people I'd hoped would help him…well they won't be much good, will they? It has to be something I can depend on…you understand?…it has to be money in the bank. Enough money."

Fritz could see what his brother was getting at. "How much, what are you thinking about?"

"It doesn't make sense to go small. There has to be enough profit so that everyone keeps their mouth shut." Manfred answered.

"How much then?"

"Around a hundred million." Manfred said nonchalantly, a professional assessment, nothing more.

Fritz swallowed hard, and was happy to see the serving girl approaching with their food. It would give him a few minutes at least to collect his thoughts.

Manfred saw her too, before Fritz could even indicate her approach. "Ahh, wonderful. Our food's arrived. We can talk later about the silly details," he said with a smile.

There wasn't anybody in the world that knew more about protecting diamonds than his brother, Fritz thought. It made sense that there wouldn't be anybody who would be better at stealing them and not getting caught. But getting that many uncut diamonds out of Namibia would take something that bordered on magic.

The girl sat down the two plates of food. The lunches were generous, and smelled delicious. Fritz's nose did not let him down. The meat was as tasty as any he'd had in a good while, and there was plenty of hot mustard to put on it.

They should be having a few beers, he thought, a few glasses of beer and kidding with one another about soccer or racing or anything. That's what they should be doing right now. A nice meal just didn't seem like to right place to be bogged down in discussions of cancer, and dying, and murder, and theft. Fritz took in a deep breath and sighed. Hell, he'd put his life on the line for money before, he sure as hell, wasn't going to shy away from it if it was going to help his brother, the brother that had spent most of his life taking care of him.

"Do you ever regret what happened in Zimbabwe?" Manfred asked as he speared a boiled potato with his fork.

"It's not something to regret. There wasn't any choice." Fritz answered.

"You lost everything, your money, your farm, you'd have lost your life if they had their way. Don't you ever wish you could get it back?"

"No, there's no sense in it." Fritz answered.

"There's a way. It'll take care of what we both want." Manfred said quietly.

"It'll make you well?" Fritz asked, pointedly.

"That's up to God. What we have to take care of is what's up to us. You know they found diamonds in Zimbabwe?" Manfred continued.

"In Marange. But I don't see how that helps us. I can't go back there. Well, I could, but it wouldn't be that healthy to do so."

"But you don't have to. The diamonds from Zimbabwe have come here instead." Manfred said with a smile. "For years we've owned the EPO, the exclusive prospecting order in Marange, under the Kimberlitic name, up until 2006. Do you know what the Kimberly Process is?"

Fritz shook his head no.

"To make it simple, they're the governing body for the international diamond trade. They don't have the right to hand out punishment or anything. But, make no mistake about it, what they say goes. If they cut you, you can't sell diamonds in any legitimate market in the world."

"That would essentially shut down the country." Fritz said.

"Exactly. Anyway, in 2006 they awarded the EPO, the one that we held, to a British company. But, before they could get a rock out of the ground, your buddy Mugabe formed a company of his own, the ZMDC, the Zimbabwe Mining Development Corporation and kicked them out of the country. That's when everything went to shit."

"Kind of like his farming reform?"

"A little less bloody. I think only eighty people got killed in this one. Anyway, instead of one organized mining operation producing the diamonds, suddenly there were ten thousand native miners digging stones out of the ground. They were essentially slave labor. They were supposed to sell everything they dug to the government. But, in 2007 their economy crashed, and all of a sudden the Zimbabwe dollar wasn't worth using to wipe your ass. What do you think became of the diamonds when that happened?"

"Black market?" Fritz replied.

"Black market's right. Well that was a problem for us. We couldn't have that many stones flooding into the market or prices would crash. Diamonds are only worth so much because we limit the supply. So we had to do something." Manfred poured himself some more tea, and concentrated on getting the milk and sugar straight. When he finished, he looked back up at Fritz. "So, we bought them. For almost nothing."

"So now you sell them off a little at a time?" Fritz asked.

"We can't sell them at all. Remember the Kimberly Process, all diamonds have to be certified as having been acquired through legitimate sources to be eligible for sale in the raw diamond market, without the certificate they can't even be sold if they've been polished, so they can't ever enter the marketplace without that certificate of origin?"

Fritz nodded.

"They met here in Namibia last month. They were supposed to be meeting to suspend Zimbabwe. If that had happened like it was supposed to, that would have forced them to sell through us again. It would have allowed us to market the diamonds. Because we would have been generating the certificates of origin for everything coming out of there. But, for some reason, the World Trade Organization didn't do what everyone expected. Instead, they put them on a probationary status for the next twelve months, which leaves them an active member of the Process. It also prevents us from selling any of the diamonds until this gets resolved. In fact, Zimbabwe got wind that someone was buying up all of the black market diamonds, and have filed suit to have all of the diamonds that can be identified returned. So we can't even admit that we may or may not have purchased some of the diamonds, because that would launch a full-scale investigation. The only option is denial."

Manfred looked at him expectantly. Fritz felt like a fool, but he still didn't understand what his brother was getting at. "What does the World Trade Organization have to do with what the Kimberly people decide?"

"They're part and parcel. The whole thing came out of the United Nations in 2003. Conflict diamonds, blood diamonds, whatever they've decide to call them today, they were set up to stop them from being able to be sold." Manfred explained patiently.

"But if they can sell them, can't you sell them too, just certify that they're good." Fritz offered.

"Because we can't. All of the diamonds that we've been buying up since 2006 are in limbo."

"How could they know? Why don't you just say you dug them here?" Fritz persisted. "How can they tell one rock from another?"

"Trace mineral analysis. It can tell just about which section of a mine a raw diamond comes from. Any of them that showed up on the marketplace would start a commotion." Manfred explained.

"So how many are there?"

"Over two hundred million dollars worth. Of course, we didn't spend a fraction of that for them. So prior to the complaint by Zimbabwe we weren't in any hurry to do anything with them. We could afford to bide our time. Once the complaint was registered they became a liability. So I hid them. No one, except for the director of security, which would be me, will have any idea of where they are for the next twelve months. They can't be sold. They can't be acknowledged. They can't even be talked about internally."

"Somebody has to know they're there." Fritz started.

"Of course they do, but there isn't any way they can admit it. That favors us. But there's something even bigger than that."

"And that is?" Fritz asked.

"Bierstadt testified at the Process meeting that we didn't have them. There's no way to undo that." Manfred said, extending his hands palms up. "We have them right here."

"So why steal them at all? Why not try a blackmail type thing? We could use an intermediary. Hell we could get Bink to do it. It would save us both a lot of trouble, and there wouldn't be any reason for anyone to get hurt?" Fritz suggested.

"It doesn't work like that. No, they wouldn't be quite so nice about it at home. They can still control everything inside of Namibia and South Africa, and someone would certainly get hurt, in fact, within a day or two, we would all three turn up dead. I would die of my cancer, Bink would be killed in a robbery, and you would find yourself being handed over to the government of Zimbabwe, along with some of the diamonds to prove you stole them. You're already wanted for the murder of five or so policemen, whatever the number was they came up with. So, you wouldn't have to worry about a trial." Manfred explained.

"Then how does knowing any of this help us?" Fritz asked.

"Because they can't even try to look for the diamonds once we get them out of the country. Unless, of course, we were stupid enough to run to South Africa, which most thieves would," Manfred said. "They would either go south or try to get them out of the country on a boat or a plane, and in either case they'd be caught."

"Then how do <u>we</u> do it?" Fritz asked.

Manfred raised a finger, and their conversation fell silent, as the girl brought their check. Manfred paid, as usual, and they made their way out the door and on to the quiet side street.

Manfred was the first to resume their conversation. "In the details of what we should do, there are still some things that I need to work out. There are very few people that we can trust in something like this, but I do have a few ideas. All the security is designed to pick up movement of contraband where people go. So the answer is to go where they can't."

"You mean across the desert?" Fritz asked.

"Yes and no, the final answer is the water. I finally figured that out. There must be two components to the plan, the desert and the water. The problem is that you can't go out of any of the ports. They're watched too. The best way to avoid detection is to go north, through the desert, then to the sea up along the Skeleton Coast. They won't expect anyone to launch from there."

The Skeleton Coast was two hundred kilometers of jagged rocks and strong currents dotted with the decaying hulks of two hundred years worth of wrecked ships. It was a sailor's nightmare.

"If we have a boat stashed, and skirt the coast it can be done. We've both done it, at some time or another. Trying to keep away from the Fish and Game when we'd caught too many fish. Same thing, bigger catch."

"There's no way anyone could get through the Namib up there, there aren't even roads." Fritz sputtered.

"There's no way a white man can get through there, but a bushman can."

"Even if I made it along the coast up through there where am I going to...Angola?" Fritz started, the volume of his voice rising.

Manfred interrupted him by squeezing his arm, and said quietly as they crossed the street, "you're not going to Angola."

"Where then?" Fritz asked, still agitated. "Up the entire length of the western coast of the continent? To Gibraltar?"

"Just up the coast. Cross the border. Then you turn west."

"Into the Atlantic? And where am I heading then? The next port in that direction is Brazil?" The conversation was doing nothing to help his hangover.

"Not so far. You remember where the old Boers were sent into exile, where the Brits sent Napoleon? You're going to Saint Helena." Manfred explained.

"In a fishing boat?"

"I don't suppose it matters what size boat we steal. We just have to make sure you have a dingy, and that you come into the back side of the island away from the port. Don't anchor, let the boat drift away, or better still, set the throttle and jump overboard, then swim to the dingy and let the boat plow out into the middle of the Atlantic. If somebody finds it they won't have any idea how it got there. Once you're on the island, it's a British colony. You shouldn't have any trouble getting to England from there. A few forged papers, get you set up with a British or an American passport and you're all set."

Fritz looked at his brother dubiously.

"Once you're there you're home free. I have friends there. Friends that owe me a lot." Manfred continued, ignoring the look. "The island's a part of Great Britain, once you make the island they can't come after you. Even if they found out that the diamonds were missing, they couldn't say anything about it for fear of getting slapped with some very stiff sanctions, for lying to the Process members." He winked at his brother. "For the next year, at least, these diamonds, they don't exist. That gives us twelve months. I could be dead by then…hell, if my plan works, you should be dead by then."

Fritz furrowed his brow.

Manfred smiled. "Officially dead. Your body will be carousing around in the United States or Europe with a new identity and more money than you could possibly spend, but poor Fritz Dietrich will be no more. A tragedy mourned by all."

"Let's try to make sure it's only on paper." Fritz suggested.

"When the time comes, I'll tell Gretchen about the money that our uncle put back for us when he sold the old man's bank. And there it will be, sitting in the same Scottish bank that our grandfather owned, enough money to take care of them for the rest of their lives, enough to buy them a new start after I'm gone.

And they'll have a legacy to go with it. The legacy our mother lost when she got sent off to Africa. They'll have the five hundred year history of the

Russell clan, really the only thing that's left of our family that's worth a damned, they'll have the name, and once that's supplemented by some funds deposited by you, funds that Gret and Fritzy will think have been sitting there untouched for the past twenty years compounding interest, they'll have the start they need to fit in."

"…and if you're cured?" Fritz asked.

"I'll have a year or so to figure that one out. There'll be a year before anyone can even start to look and see what I've done."

Twenty-Four

Ray flipped open his laptop and moved the cursor to his saved mail file. South African Air, that was the one he was looking for. He double clicked and opened the file. His itinerary opened on the screen. He flew out in two weeks, Meridian to Atlanta then to Miami on Delta. From Miami he flew to Cape Town on South African Air, with an overnight layover there, then into Windhoek the next day. It seemed simple enough. The flight arrangements were really the least of his worries. He'd flown before. It was the hunt he was worried about. Reading was great and it had helped some, but there was no substitute for experience.

Pete Early had been a lot of help to him. Pete turned out to be an okay guy. They'd run into each other several times at the shooting range. The big rifle doubling on him had knocked out a lot of the bluster and they got along well. He was going back to Africa this spring too, so he let Ray tag along with him as he made arrangements and took him through the whole process. Pete got him hooked up with a receiving agent down in New Orleans to go to the airport and do all of the paperwork for when he brought his trophies back into the United States. He helped him come up with an equipment list so that he'd have some idea of what to pack. He even ended up helping him get rid of that damned double rifle. He'd taken it to the range a couple of times, but his hands shook so much he couldn't pull the trigger. He couldn't have hit an elephant at ten yards, much less an antelope at a hundred.

Bud, at Bud's Guns, wouldn't buy it back for cash of course, so he'd ended up having to trade it in on another pretty expensive rifle. This one came with a scope on it. It was a Blaser K-95. It was the lightest gun he'd ever held. It was a break open single shot in .308. It wasn't any elephant gun, but he probably didn't need to start on something as big as an elephant anyway.

He'd been spending a lot of time at the range since he got the new gun, trying to get ready. With the Blaser he knew that he was going to need to hit whatever he shot at right the first time. That's kind of the way it worked with a single shot. He'd worked a lot with Lisa's twenty-two, too. One of the things that surprised him was that with practice he found that he could reload and shoot the Blaser almost as fast as he could cycle the Winchester, if he had his spare rounds in the shell holder on his belt. He was able to keep his eyes on the target better with the Blaser too, even though he had to break it open. He'd drop the front and the scope down and keep looking at what he was trying to shoot, drop in a new cartridge with his left hand and flip the barrel back up, and he was ready to shoot again without ever moving his right hand or the butt of the rifle.

He guessed that the twenty-two and the other two guns were among the things that he was going to have to pack up and send to Lisa, if she didn't change her mind about the divorce. She'd called him last week and told him that she'd gone ahead and had her lawyer file divorce papers in Meridian, so it would speed things up.

That had been a depressing conversation. Hell, the whole thing was depressing. Nothing he could say got through to her.

It was like she'd never dealt with the affair in the first place, and now it didn't matter that nothing had happened since the two of them had started getting back together. She could only focus on the fact that he'd had the affair in the first place. The fact that Anne even existed infuriated her. Now she was damned and determined to make everything legal, and in her words, "start my own life."

What had she been doing up there at Ole Miss up to this point? She'd been living her own life, he wasn't there imposing on her freedom, and if she wasn't, it didn't have anything to do with the fact that they weren't legally divorced. These were probably thoughts that he should have kept to himself. Saying them hadn't helped much. Now she wasn't answering her phone at all when he called her.

He looked back at the computer screen. Okay, so he had his airline tickets. He checked to be sure he had his reservations at the Kalahari Sands Hotel and Casino for his first and last nights there in Namibia. They were confirmed and he printed them along with the airline tickets out and put them with his passport into his travel case to carry onto the plane for the flight. Then he e-mailed both the airline and the hotel confirmations to himself, just in case he lost them. He'd be able to pull them up on his cell phone if he ended up needing a back up for the printed copies.

Fritz's boss would issue him his license once he got there. He had forty rounds of ammunition. He looked at the two shell boxes lying on the carpet next to the gun case that came with the Blaser. It was funny to look at the case and think that the rifle could even fit into it. It was dwarfed by the duffle bag beside it. The little rifle could be taken down into two pieces so the rifle case was only a little longer than a briefcase. He'd have to pack the shells in the duffel bag, that's why the rifle couldn't go in there. The shells couldn't be in the same case with the rifle, airline regulations. A sensible safety precaution, he thought. He filled out his Import/Export forms so he could bring his gun back into the country when he came back. He put them into the case with the rifle.

He looked at the pile of stuff waiting to be put into the duffel bag. All of them, most of them new, were scattered across the floor, arranged in what he thought were reasonable groups. He looked at the different piles and tried to think of what it was that he might be missing. He picked up the checklist and looked at it as he checked to be sure that each item was there. As far as he could tell, he had everything that Pete had suggested. He'd even put together a medical kit with everything a self-respecting ER doc would need if something happened in the bush, away from help. He couldn't think of anything else. He was as ready as he was going to get.

And if Lisa got her way, he'd have a divorce decree he could pack in there with all of the other stuff to take with him before he left. Life was strange. This wasn't what he'd envisioned when he said he wanted to change his life.

He shut down the computer and stood up from the desk that he and Lisa had shared for over twenty years, walked through the house that they'd shared for the last twelve years, and then past the bed he'd slept alone in for the past year.

He was filled with a sense of emptiness mostly. It was a feeling that was really beyond sadness. It was like someone had cut off one of his arms or his leg or something. Something that was part of him wasn't there any more. People got by with one arm, and he'd get by without Lisa, but neither were options he would select by choice. It was something you had to endure, not something that you chose to do. He sighed and stepped into the shower they'd shared the last time she was here, and stuck his face into the stream of water. What the hell, he had to get ready for work.

The steaming water felt good and he stayed under it breathing through his mouth for a long time. He was steam cleaning his lungs, it was a shame he couldn't steam clean his brain. It would be a lot easier if he could. He could wash away the stupid thoughts and memories that had been torturing him for the past few weeks, but what would he wash away. He wouldn't wash away the good memories he had of the times he and Lisa'd had together. Even if it was easier to face the divorce without them, he wasn't willing to give them up. Maybe if he could wash away the memories of Anne he wouldn't feel so guilty about how everything had ended up turning out for her.

Her story had come out a little at a time. It started during the slow times at work, in public places when no one else was in earshot. As they talked about what had happened, she started to share the details of the disintegration of her own marriage, and their relationship changed. They'd never talked before. They'd only had sex. Everything they said or did was designed to lead to the same conclusion. There wasn't any complexity. There wasn't any depth of shared experience. It was lust. She'd been an exciting thing to him, not a person. Now she was something entirely different, different in a way that ate a hole in his soul.

She'd confessed to her husband about the affair, after he'd asked Lisa for a separation. There was no way something like that was going to stay quiet in a town as small as Meridian. No way he wasn't going to find out, so she'd told him herself and asked him to forgive her.

That was the beginning of the end of her marriage too. Not quickly and quietly like his had ended, but slowly, and violently, and in front of her son. The rhythm of her life became dominated by cycles of violence. Cycles fed by jealousy, mistrust, abuse, and more violence, and each time it went around it got worse. Escalating until she ended up in the Emergency Room in Birmingham with a cut up face, where the force of her husband's knuckles had torn her flesh, and a broken arm.

He tried not to remember the hollow, distant stare she'd had as she gazed into the distance as she related all of the details. How that as she drove home she'd looked into the mirror and saw all of the faces of all the other battered women she'd seen come into Emergency Rooms over the years. The women that had come in over and over, always thinking that if they just hung on things would get worked out, until finally they came in dead. How she'd looked at her son in the car seat behind her and knew then and there it was over. She'd never gone home.

Now she was staying with her parents, trying to hold things together for she and her son. There was no infatuation left in her. She'd had enough problems with getting a restraining order and going through her own divorce. She didn't need to be in the middle of his. As they'd talked he'd realized that there was something that had been broken besides her arm, something that made her fragile and guarded now.

Ray felt nauseated when he pictured her laying there on the gurney, with her son curled beside her, crying. Bleeding while she told him that everything was going to be all right.

He blew out his breath and scrubbed at his face with the washcloth. Life was so damned tricky. Disaster was around every turn. He saw the results of it every day at work. A guy starts a chain saw. He's used one his whole life, but today he hits a knot or a nail, the saw jumps, and he loses his arm. He spends the rest of his life getting over it. A doctor screws his nurse, the spouses find out, they jump, and everyone spends the rest of their lives trying to get over having their hearts cut out, even an innocent kid.   That wasn't so much to feel guilty about, was it?

"Crap," he said, as he stepped out of the shower. He wasn't the innocent victim here. He was the chainsaw.

Twenty-Five

Fritz woke up in the pitch black of darkness in the jungle. At first he wasn't sure of what woke him. Looking around he realized that the entire camp was pitch black. Something or someone had knocked out the generators. Then there was a concussion that shook the bunk he was laying on so hard he was afraid he was going to be shaken right out of it. Dust filled the air. He couldn't see it, but he felt it, as it fell from the rafters onto his face and filled his nose and mouth when he tried to breathe.

Then the flash came. The white light of it blinded him, and he couldn't see anything. His night vision was gone. With the second explosion he rolled out of the bed and onto the dirt floor. There were the smells of fresh dirt, cordite, and blood mingling in the dark. They'd finally come. He knew they would, and he knew he had to get out, before they got a range on the building, whatever building it was he was in.

He swept his hands back and forth under the bed and pulled his rifle and a rucksack toward him. He moved his toes and felt the earth move between them. He needed boots. His hands darted back under the bed as the next concussion hit him and smashed his forehead into the side rail of the bunk. He could feel the blood as it began trickling down his forehead. Streaming straight down until it hit his eyebrow and following that, flowing down the side of his face.

He began to hear the chatter of small arms fire, moving closer and closer. Frantically, he swept his arms. Finally his hand struck the first boot, he searched wildly for the second. A bullet tore into the top of the bunk above him. He felt the sharp strike in the wood of the side rail against his back, before the mattress' stuffing rained down.

He grabbed his boots but he didn't have time to put them on now. He had to get out of the building before someone punched a rocket into it, or shot lower. He tried to grab his gear, but he couldn't get the gun up with the pack and boots in his hands.

Biting onto the boots strings with his teeth, he could taste a mixture of dirt and sweat on top of the waxy taste of the strings. With his hands freed of the boots, he threw his rucksack over his right shoulder. Then he grabbed the assault rifle and began to crawl across the dirt floor toward the door.

Within minutes he could taste his own blood in his mouth. It was streaming down from his forehead, and collected on the boot strings. It was and always would be the taste of his fear.

He made it to the door as the next rocket hit, much closer this time. Dirt, dust, and smoke roiled into the doorway. Again, the flash blinded him, and he squeezed his eyes shut tightly to try and preserve as much of his night vision as he still could. A machine gun started, and the door beside him began to disintegrate, the wood splintering and stabbing into the tops of his arms and the back of his neck.

He brought the rifle up and set the front sight on the stuttering muzzle flash of the bucking machine gun, and pulled the trigger. The muzzle flash stopped, and he ran, his feet bare moving over the splintered wood, but he hardly felt it.

He skirted around the impact site of the last rocket, as he did the building he had just escaped from exploded. He dove behind a low wall, hitting the ground hard and wrenching his shoulder. He felt a stab of pain in his arm as he covered his head with his arms. Then the clay, thatch and splintered timbers of the bunkhouse fell down around him.

His mouth was dry and the skin of his lip ripped away as he snatched the shoelaces out of his mouth. No time to lace them. He took a quick double wrap around his ankle and tied the first boot.

He was shoving his foot into the second boot when he saw the man, a large man directing fighters by waving his hand and gesturing with a machete. The fires that burned around them illuminated his face. He was a white man with a mustache, a Cuban. Fritz dropped the boot and spun raising his rifle as the man ran toward him. He was too close and the machete was coming too fast.

Fritz ducked and threw the barrel of the rifle up to protect his head. He saw the blade of the machete strike the gun, before he felt his arms begin to collapse with the force. He hadn't had enough time to get the gun up and the machete forced the rifle barrel back down and the blade struck the left side of his skull. He felt a dull whack, but not the pain he'd expected. The machete had hit hard. Not hard enough to kill him, but hard enough to wedge itself in the bone.

Fritz pushed the rifle's barrel forward, under the man's chin, and pulled the trigger. He saw the red halo that surrounded the man's face as the back of his skull was blown away. He saw the eyes widen and the hand lose its grip and fall away from the machete. Slowly, slowly the man began to fall backward.

AHHHHH, AAAAHHHHH, AAAAHHH he screamed into the darkness. His heart was pounding in his throat, his body drenched in a cold sweat. His fingers traced the knotted scar on the left side of his scalp. Slowly, he began to realize where he was. He threw aside the blankets and got to his feet.

Fritz's hands shook as he walked to the window. He held them up and looked at them, balling them into fists to stop their trembling. He hadn't had it for years, and now it was back.

The dream had really happened. It was part of a memory he had from the war, when he was seventeen. It was his first experience in the Caprivi Strip.

The Caprivi was an anomaly in a desert country like Namibia, a lush tropical finger that stuck out along the Zambezi River from the countries northeastern border. He was a kid raised on the costal desert. Overnight he found himself sent to fight in a jungle. He didn't know anything about jungles. It was his second night. They'd just drawn their equipment. For a costal boy, the jungle was a horror. You couldn't see anything to get a fix on where you were. It was the end of being a kid.

The attack, which seemed to Fritz to have lasted for hours, was over in forty minutes, in that period of time the terros had launched thirty rockets, killing ten of the kids that had been sent up with him.

Bink had appeared out of the darkness and somehow he'd gotten the rest of the surviving kids to gather around him. By sheer force of will, he got the boys that were left, regrouped in the dark and spread them out, two at a time, to form at first a defensive perimeter, then a slowly expanding circle of fire. A battle crazed cheerleader, screaming for them to sustain fire.

"Stop hiding. Shoot. God damn it, if you want to live, keep shooting." He'd screamed a thousand times into the darkness.

And the boys listened, and the return fire grew less and less, until the cries and shouts of the wounded were all that was left.

They stayed there firing all night. Holding their position until the morning. When it was finally light, they'd killed fifty-eight terros, and wounded a lot more than that. There was no way to know how many, but there were too many blood trails going into the bush to count.

They'd survived the largest scale assault in the history of the "struggle for independence." That was what they called it after SWAPO won the election. The Cubans were there now, with an unlimited supply of Russian weapons. The war, changed after that night, it became South West Africa's version of Vietnam.

Fritz had never had the dream while he was still in the bush. It had waited to stalk him until he was sleeping on a mattress, under a roof, away from the war. For the first few years, he could only get free of it by sleeping outdoors. It came back night after night in the city, until he'd finally give in and spend time alone in the bush.

Fritz walked across the room away from the window and got himself a beer and a bottle of Scotch, then got himself a glass from the cabinet. That was how he'd eventually learned to deal with the dream, a little something to settle his nerves and then back to sleep. That usually did the trick, but sometimes it would come back. Then he'd just stay up the rest of the night.

It wasn't like he was going to fall asleep quickly without the alcohol anyway. His brain wouldn't stop. It kept on sifting through all of the things that his brother had gone over with him in the last few days. That was one thing you could say for Manny, he'd thought everything through very carefully, focusing on every detail. He knew how he was going to move the diamonds and to where. He was planning to hide them inside a section of PVC piping that was being used to do a job near the storage facility. But not any pipe, a specific piece of pipe with one end sealed and with a hole just big enough to stick a fire extinguisher hose through. He would leave the pipe in his truck, until he brought out the diamonds stuffed in canvas bags. He'd gather up sections of the scrap pieces of pipe to throw in on top of the filled pipe as camouflage. Then he'd run one of the usual patrol routes out to a small area near the perimeter, between two recently developed dunes that obscured the view of the security cameras, shove a short range battery operated homing device into one of the sacks of diamonds, push one of the sacks hard down into the pipe, shove a carefully fan-cut fire extinguisher hose through the hole in the other end of the pipe and then squeeze the handle of the fire extinguisher, shooting the diamonds, one sack at a time, over the perimeter fence. Then all somebody had to do was use a hand held receiver and find the diamonds. The only problem was, that to do it they had to avoid the roads. That meant that to get to them, they had to do it across one of the fiercest deserts on the face of the planet, on foot, at night, and show up pretty damned close to where the diamonds were for the homing device to work. A standard long-range device of any kind, especially one that operated with a radio beacon would get picked up on the electronic surveillance that the company operated to keep track of things.

This was where the bushmen came in. They were probably the only people on the face of the earth that could do it. But somebody had to go with them. They could penetrate the impenetrable, but there was no chance you were going to teach them to operate a locating device correctly. You might as well give them a coconut instead of a receiver for all the good it would do them. And that was what was going to end up costing someone their life. So Fritz could assume their identity long enough to get into and back out of the restricted zone. He'd need it later too, to get out of Saint Helena and into England. Manfred was emphatic. They couldn't afford to have some tourist running around shouting about a stolen passport. It could take a week for him to get the diamonds into and back out of England. He was going to have to have a stable cover. They also needed a body, so that they could declare Fritz dead. That would get rid of the murder charges against him and he wouldn't have to worry about getting accidently picked up and returned to Zimbabwe to face them if something went wrong.

They would have to find someone that didn't have a family, somebody with no wife or kids at home to start looking for him if he didn't get home on time. Somebody that no one would notice was missing for a couple of weeks. Unfortunately, the only guy that fit that description that Fritz knew of was the only one he knew anything about at all. Hell, he actually liked him, the guy with the double-gun.

Twenty-Six

Ray looked out at the South African Air plane that was sitting outside of the terminal window at the Miami airport. It was huge. He didn't think he'd ever seen a bigger plane. He watched the service crew through the window of his gate as they scurried around underneath it.

"You guys do a good job." He said silently. This was going to be a long flight with almost all of it over water. He and three hundred and eighty other people needed everything to work right for the next sixteen or so hours.

They called his boarding group near the last. His seat was in the front but not in First Class. They boarded the plane from the rear, forward. He'd requested an outside bulkhead seat. They were the seats with the most legroom. Pete had told him that. He was sitting on the window side. That would allow him to lean against the wall when it was time to get some sleep. He'd figured that one out for himself. He had sleeping pills, earplugs, and a buckwheat husk pillow to help out too.

He sat down and looked at the card he'd pulled out of the pouch on the bulkhead where a seat back would have been. The plane was an Airbus 330-600 the card said. He was looking at the cabin layout when a couple in their mid-sixties approached the seats next to him. The wife took the center, next to Ray. She nodded as she sat down. The man pulled their carry-on suitcases. He placed their coats in the overhead compartment, but struggled to fit their second suitcase in. The bins were already full. No matter how hard he pushed he couldn't fit the other suitcase into it. There wasn't a seat in front of them to shove his bag under and the woman behind him had already put her stuff under the seat he was sitting in.

That brought a stewardess who immediately took the bag, explaining that she'd store it in the luggage compartment. Ray tried to ignore it all, until he realized that she was talking to him too. She was pointing at the travel bag he had sitting on the floor in front of him. Everything he needed for the flight was in there. The last thing he needed was it being hauled away, so he couldn't get to it if he needed something.

"Can't I put it behind my legs?" Ray asked.

"No sir, all bags must be securely stowed for take-off and landing," she was friendly, but it was clear that there wasn't any use trying to argue.

"Can we try to fit it into the storage bin?" Ray asked.

She could see his reluctance. That started a brief enjoyable show, as the stewardess struggled hands above her head, just in front of Ray's knees. She was really very pretty as she wedged and pushed the bag until it fit into the compartment.

"You can always get it down after we get in the air, if you need it," she reassured him.

He smiled and nodded hoping she could come back and get it down for him later. In three hours he'd be divorced.

He was watching as she leaned forward to speak to a teenager playing a video game across the aisle. He let his mind wander a bit but was jerked back to reality when the old man bumped into his wife as he sat down. That knocked her sideways, she in turn hit Ray, and Ray's head hit the window. More jostling as the man fastened his seatbelt. Not much in the way of shoulder room. The wife spoke to her husband sharply and he began an elaborate explanation in what Ray thought was German.

He looked at the things that he'd taken out of the bag before the stewardess had taken it. He was holding his i-pod and his divorce decree. Why in the hell had he kept that out instead of his Kindle?

He shoved it into the pouch on the bulkhead in front of him and left it there for the first twenty minutes of the flight. Long enough to get bored with the lecture he was listening to on the i-pod. He pulled out the in-flight magazine and the divorce decree fell out in the process. When he picked it up his first impulse was to shove it back into the pouch but he didn't. He held it in his hand for a few moments. He might as well look at it. He turned back the cover sheet. A faint odor hit his nose. He looked around at his seatmate. He tried to inhale softly through his nose, so that it wasn't obvious that he was trying to detect where the odor was coming from. The smell seemed to be coming from her direction, but who knew?

He went back to his reading and threw back the first page. Once again the pungent odor hit him, this time he noticed his seatmate trying inconspicuously to smell the air around her. He held the document closer to his face and sniffed it openly. The damned thing even smelled bad. It smelled kind of musty and damp with overtones of pizza and cigars. Then he realized what it was. It smelled just like, Bert, his attorney.

The guy weighed over four hundred pounds. Even the slightest exertion produced torrents of perspiration. That got compounded by the fact that Bert was a hugger, a back slapper, an arm around the shoulder kind of guy and he was so big you couldn't get away from him once he got one of those huge arms around you. Ray always tried not to get too close to him.

Ray had never seen him smoke but he remembered a humidor on his desk. So, that's probably where the smoke smell came from, the pizza smell wasn't hard to figure out.

Lisa's lawyer had been one of their former neighbors, Jim Smiley. It was kind of a misnomer. In the fifteen years Ray had known him, he had never seen Jim smile. The closest he ever came was a slight movement of the corners of his mouth and a quick nod of the head. Ray'd never really liked him much. The divorce hadn't done much to change his opinion of Jim one way or the other.

Since Lisa'd refused to talk to him and wouldn't answer his calls it made the negotiations difficult. After he called her a few times to try to work things out, he got a legal notice from Jim warning that he was not to continue to try to contact her, and that all matters would need to be handled through legal council.

The lawyer's had hammered everything out after that. He hadn't paid much attention. He didn't want to think about it. He didn't want to fight about it. Hell, he didn't want to get divorced at all.

He pictured the two of them having to work together, Jim with his precise attention to rules and regulations, Bert sweating all over everything, and slapping him on the back. The contrast was hilarious, and Ray chuckled quietly thinking about it. The best revenge he could have ever gotten on Jim was to make him have to spend time with Bert.

The woman in the next seat looked over at him and smiled. He put the earphones into his ears and turned on some music on his i-pod. He wondered how long the batteries would last. They probably wouldn't make it through the whole flight. It didn't matter. He'd buy a pair of the airline's headphones to listen to the movies later anyway.

Ray rolled the decree into a tube and shoved it in the space between the seat and the wall beside him. It had only taken a week or two and it was done, everything finalized. He'd tried to sign all of the papers without reading them.

Bert was dumfounded, "You don't want to go through it together to make sure it's what you want? We haven't really gone over any of it. You're gonna have to live with this thing." Bert admonished, throwing a very damp arm over Ray's shoulder.

"You've read it. I'm sure it's fine." Ray answered, trying not to breathe too much. All he wanted was to get the hell out of there.

"Do you want me to go over it?" Bert asked, clearly perturbed.

"Can you just hit the high points?" Ray pleaded. So he did.

It wasn't too demanding, Lisa hadn't asked for much. Her personal items from the house and her car were about the only things she asked for specifically. She already had her car, and she and their son would get her personal stuff out of the house while he was gone. They'd already split the retirement money and before she left, he wrote her a check for her equity in the house. The lawyer's had had an independent realtor estimate what it was worth. It had cost him a good part of his stock portfolio to do it, but it was fair, and he hadn't had to take out another mortgage.

The judge thought all of this was a splendid arrangement too, and signed everything without ever making them show up in court. Sine die.

It became official at midnight. He'd be somewhere over the middle of the Atlantic when that happened. He guessed that he'd be divorced before she would, as he'd be three or four time zones ahead of her by then. He wasn't sure that that gave him any particular advantage.

One good thing you could say for wallowing in self-pity, it sure made the time fly. He glanced at his watch when he saw the stewardesses begin to move around the cabin with their carts and saw that an hour and a half had already gone by. If he jumped right into guilt and self-recrimination after dinner, they should be in Cape Town before he knew it.

Another advantage of being on the bulkhead row that Ray hadn't thought about was that they got to be the first ones to get their food. The stewardess from before leaned toward him and asked him something, her accent sounded wonderful, but he had no idea what she'd said.

"Excuse me?"

"Would you like zee chicken or zee steak?" She repeated.

"Oh, the steak, " he answered.

"…and a red wine?" she asked, handing him his tray.

"No, white…well I guess the red with steak?"

She leaned forward and handed him a bottle of each and winked. "To make up for the bag."

The effect was devastating, but short-lived. She immediately turned her attention to the couple.

Dinner held a couple of pleasant surprises. The first was dinner. It was really very good. It was airline food, but it was good airline food. Another was the wine, they were South African, of course, and they were both excellent.

The flight droned on, he watched a movie about a baseball player who was a jerk to everyone around him. Then he got paralyzed in an automobile accident, and all of the people he had been horrible to ended up having to take care of him. A clearly orchestrated tear-jerker, and if that wasn't depressing enough the second movie was about a couple going through a divorce. He looked at his watch. He himself was divorced now. He didn't need to watch a movie about it. He was living it. The only difference was, that he was pretty sure that unless the plane crashed, his divorce wasn't going to end up with a happy ending for anybody in the next two hours. If the plane did crash, at least there would be a happy ending for Lisa. He hadn't changed the beneficiary on his insurance policies yet, so she'd still get the four million dollar annuity, and the two million in term insurance that they'd taken out to help pay for the house and for the kids education. She'd be single, with a six million dollar bonus.

He decided to go to sleep, and took one of the sleeping pills. He put in the earphones, spread a blanket over himself, and then stretched out, propping his head in the corner between the seatback and his pillow, which was against the window. He drifted off briefly, but woke up with a cold, stiff neck. He tried to roll up on his side some to get away from the window, but he couldn't recline the seat enough to get it so it didn't hurt his back. The couple beside him were going through their own contortions, she laying her head on him, he leaning against her. The three of them wiggled and squirmed like a trio of worms for the next hour. Occasionally, one of them would drop off to sleep, only to be roused back when another of them shifted position. In the midst of this Ray had an idea. It turned out to work pretty well. The couple spread out across the three seats, with the armrests raised, and Ray laid down on the floor where their feet had been, using his bag for a pillow. They were all sleeping away soundly when the second shift stewardesses came on and conducted their routine cabin check.

"I'm sorry sir, but safety regulations don't permit passengers to sleep on the floor. Sir...sir, are you awake..." Ray heard from far away and coming from above him somewhere. Opening his eyes he was looking at only seat legs and people's feet. It was kind of hard to tell what was going on. It took him a minute to get oriented to where he was. In the meantime he felt someone shaking his shoulder, he hoped it was the pretty one with the French accent. It wasn't. It was a rather large woman who was shaking him quite briskly now. He took the earphones out of his ears.

"Sir, we really can't allow you to sleep on the floor," she insisted.

"It's really more comfortable for everyone," he replied, groggily.

"For safety reasons," she continued.

"What could be safer than sleeping on the floor. There's nowhere to fall."

"For one thing, your feet are sticking out into the aisle. People could trip over them." An air of officiousness crept into her words.

"I'm sorry. I'll tuck them in," he offered.

"That isn't allowed. I'm sorry sir, but you have to resume your place in your seat."

"Oh shit," he sighed as he tried to straighten up. His back was as stiff as a board. He had to crawl into the aisle on his hands and knees and then grab the armrest to pull himself up. Maybe sleeping on the floor wasn't the best idea. His seatmates were awake, of course and arranged themselves back into their own seats, as the stewardess resumed her rounds.

He needed to walk some, his back was killing him, so he headed to the lavatory, taking time to stretch and bend along the way. He massaged the crick in his neck with one hand as he urinated. He looked into the mirror to confirm that he looked as bad as he felt, washed his hands, and then splashed water on his face and wetted his hair to try to calm it down. It had been rubbing up against the seat bottom and his bag and was sticking up in every possible direction.

He felt like a voyeur as he walked around the darkened plane. It was like peeking into people's bedroom windows as they slept. There were people in just about every different position, trying a hundred different ways to get comfortable. There were a few that were still awake, reading, or watching TV shows on the screens on the seatbacks in front of them, but there weren't many of them. Some nodded or waved as he walked past. One thing was for sure though. There weren't any people sleeping on the floor.

The curtain was drawn so he couldn't see what was going on in First Class. They didn't want the masses to disturb the elite as they slumbered reclining in their travel beds he supposed. He found a stewardess and got a bottle of water before he headed back to try and get some more sleep. When he got back to his seat he took another sleeping pill and settled back. His mind started to drift, he shifted fitfully, never sure if he were just thinking weird thoughts or dreaming. Finally, the sun rose and the breakfast service began. He couldn't ever remember being more grateful for overcooked scrambled eggs and limp bacon in his life.

He was looking out the window at some boats when he got his first view of Africa. It was breathtaking. The first thing he noticed were the colors, the brilliant blue of the ocean against the craggy green mountains, and in the middle, Cape Town sat in a natural bowl, open to the water and surrounded by the great green mountains.

He thought he could see the Cape of Good Hope, and opened his travel book as the plane inched closer with exquisite slowness, to try and see if he was right. It was really Cape Point, but it was still beautiful from the air, and he couldn't wait to stand on it. Mostly he wanted to just stand on the ground anywhere, anything that would get him off of this damned plane.

His travel agent had arranged for him to stay at a bed and breakfast tonight. He had a six a.m. flight to Windhoek in the morning. He planned to take the cable car up to the top of Table Mountain this afternoon and then wander around the waterfront after that. He was going to make an early evening of it. He'd get to bed early and ward off the jet lag and the effects of sleeping in the airplane seat overnight. It was going to feel great to lie down in a bed, to actually lie down and stretch out without an armrest, or a bulkhead, or a seatmate to prevent him from getting into a comfortable position. He stretched as they came in over the land. He couldn't wait. He was feeling especially old today.

Ray got his luggage off of the baggage cart and headed out of the terminal to find a taxi. It took him several minutes to explain to the driver where he wanted to go, and even then he wasn't sure the driver understood him. He showed him the address but that didn't seem to make any difference either. Finally a policeman who was walking by looked at the address and explained to the driver where to go. After that, they drove in silence between the shacks that had sprung up around the airport, shanties of cardboard and plywood crowded up to the perimeter fence. Beyond them he could see the houses and buildings of the city bowl. There were a sequence of accentuated contrasts that he was forced to reconcile as they drove. Grey tired men, and women in brightly colored cloth. The competing beauties of the city and the spectacular wild mountains that surrounded it. They passed blocks that looked like he could have arrived somewhere a hundred years in the past. Then turning a corner they were surrounded by fashionable shops filled with the most modern merchandise, and quickly back to a depth of the poverty more profound than he had ever seen before. These weren't the poor of America with their cell phones, flash cars, and obesity. These were the emaciated and dried up poor that hadn't eaten or had enough to drink in years.

They stopped in front of a pink confection of a house with a sign that identified it as Mosant House in the front yard. By the time he carried his bag up the steps to the house from the road his back was killing him. Maybe he would just lie down for a few minutes. Maybe table Mountain could wait until the trip back. He carried his bags to his room and laid down on a feather mattress that felt like a cloud. He heard the laughing chatter of women outside his window and looked out to see three black women carrying huge bundles of laundry up the hill balanced on their heads. They were laughing and chatting as they went. One of them had a baby wrapped against her with a yellow cloth. The green of the vegetation and the blue of the sky set off their brightly colored clothing with their impossibly black faces and white smiles. No he was not in America, that was clear. He laid back and let himself drift off to sleep

Twenty-Seven

Ray saw Fritz waving an arm at him as he came through the gate, and lifted his own in return.

"How was your trip?" Fritz asked as they shook hands.

"Long. I thought we flew straight here, but there was some change and we ended up sitting in Johannesburg for five hours until they could get another plane." Ray answered.

"I guessed that might be what happened. I called before I came, to see when you'd get here. It worked out well. I've got two other hunters coming in on another plane out of Jo-burg, on the next flight in. They should be here by the time I get you checked-in and get back here. Let's get your gear." They walked to an open area where the bags were being wheeled up on a cart. Several passengers unwilling to wait for the cart to be unloaded walked over and began pulling their things off of it. Ray could see his duffel on the bottom of the pile. There were several longer gun cases laid together on the bottom of the trolley as well.

From where he was standing Ray could see the shorter half-case that his rifle was in. It was at the top of the pile of bags, resting on two suitcases. He watched aghast as a woman snatched one of the suitcases away. He winced and gritted his teeth as it hit the ground. All of the time he'd spent at home getting it zeroed was pretty much wasted at this point.

"I hope you have a range," he said, looking over at Fritz disgusted.

"That was yours then? It shouldn't bother the iron sights," he added.

"It's got a scope on it," Ray answered, as he retrieved the case off of the ground. "Maybe it stayed zeroed." He said holding up the case as Fritz joined him.

"This was probably a love tap compared to the wringing out the baggage handlers give it on the way over here." He paused for a moment and cocked his head. "You scoped a .470? I hope you brought along some sutures, to sew up your eye when you shoot it."

Ray laughed thinking about trying to shoot the .470 with a scope. "No, I got rid of that. I couldn't shoot it...even without a scope on it."

"You did okay. A lot better than poor old Early did, huh?" Fritz said slapping Ray on the back and taking the gun case as Ray reached for the duffel that was, as he suspected, the last bag off of the cart. "Selling it was a lot smarter than buying it, I suppose. I'm afraid your gun dealer saw you coming. I'm sure he took it back for a little less than you paid."

"I ended up trading it on another gun." Ray said a little sheepishly.

Fritz looked at the writing on the case. "A Blaser's a good gun, it looks like you didn't do too badly on the trade. We'll do a quick sighting in first thing when we get to camp anyway. Just to be sure it's still on."

They gathered up Ray's gear and walked through the doorway, into a smaller room with metal tables. Fritz got him the right forms and opened the gun case. He got the forms that had been placed in it when he left the U.S. and put the forms together. He wrote down the local contact information and handed them to Ray.

'Just get your passport, and the shells out. They have to verify that the cartridge head stamp matches the caliber listed on the barrel of the gun, and that you've only brought the two boxes of shells." He waited while Ray found the two boxes in his duffel bag, and then handed him the papers. "Go ahead and fill out the rest of the forms and we can get in line for the inspector."

Ray fished in his travel case for his pen and started to fill out the forms on the steel tabletop. It vibrated and shook every time another passenger threw a gun case or a travel bag onto it. His handwriting looked like he had Parkinson's disease. He made his way to the bottom of the first form quickly until he reached the part where they asked for emergency contact information. Who was he supposed to put? He looked quickly at Fritz.

"A problem?" Fritz asked.

"Not really, just trying to figure out who to write down."

"Just stick down who you'd want us to call if you fell out of the truck and broke your leg or something." Fritz suggested.

"I just don't know about putting down my ex-wife, she won't even talk to me."

"Yeah, I have that effect on women too. I can just hear the call, 'No... no, don't wake him up just go ahead and put him down, he wouldn't want to suffer with a broken leg.'" Fritz pantomimed in a falsetto, smiling. Then added seriously, "Just put down one of your kids then.'

"I guess my son, Mark is the logical choice, and he's a medical student. He's so busy though it could be a while before he called back."

"He'll be fine. You just need to put down any number. That's all they require is some number."

Ray filled out the address and phone number for Mark's apartment. He didn't remember his cell phone number. He took out his cell phone and punched the button, but the phone was dead. Damn he should have charged it last night in Cape Town, instead of just falling straight to sleep. He wrote down his own cell phone number, just to fill in the blank.

He copied most of the information on the second sheet directly from the papers he'd filled out in Miami. It was a Declaration of Import for a firearm, and the first line cautioned that the firearm could not be sold or transferred without official approval. After his name and passport number he had to list the gun type, make, serial number, and caliber. Finally he had to sign the declaration stating that he had brought no more than forty rounds of ammunition appropriate for that gun into the country with him.

When he finished writing, Fritz led the way through yet another door. The room wasn't much bigger than a closet, and inside it was a very large black man in a short-sleeved green uniform shirt sitting on a high-backed swivel chair. His eyes were exquisitely bored. He was behind a wooden counter rubbed smooth as glass by thousands of gun cases being pushed across it over the years. There wasn't a bit of varnish remaining. His big hand grabbed the rifle's fore-end out of the case and held it up to the light. From his pants pocket he produced a magnifying glass and looked closely at the imprint on the barrel, then he picked up the boxes of shells and looked at first one and then the other before nodding his head.

"Three oh eight." he said.

Ray was pretty sure it was a statement and not a question, but he answered anyway. "Yes sir."

"You know that you may not use these on dangerous game. They may be used only on the smaller game and the antelope."

" I know the rules, and I'll see to that." Fritz assured the man.

"Do you have another gun?" The official asked handing the shells back across the counter to Ray.

"No sir," Ray shook his head as he spoke.

The big man turned his face towards Fritz and smiled, "Good luck. I hope you're a good guide. You have a hunter with only one shot and a splinter for a gun." He hefted the fore-end and put it back into the case. Then sprung into a flurry of action, stamping all of the papers and Ray's passport with a series of hard fast jabs of the wrist.

When he had stamped everything at least once he pushed the pile of papers and the rifle across the wooden counter. "Enjoy your hunt in Namibia," he said, and with that, they were through.

Fritz took the papers and the passport and stuck them into the gun case and turned the latch before handing the key back to Ray. "That's how you want to keep them while we're in camp. Locked in the case. So they can't get lost. It's not likely we're going to find them later if they fall out of your pocket or backpack in the brush. Keep the key with you. Even if you lose that we can pry the latches off with a crowbar if we have to, but it can be hell to get new paperwork."

Fritz carried the gun case and Ray struggled with the oversize duffel bag and his travel case as they walked out of the air terminal. The first thing that he saw as he walked out of the door reminded Ray how well his profession was thought of in other parts of the world.

Directly in front of the door was a generous parking spot with a large red cross in its center and the words, RESERVED and DOCTORS ONLY painted on each end in large red letters. You didn't see that in Miami, or even in Meridian for that matter any more.

"Wait here." Fritz said and headed across the parking lot to get the truck and pulled it into the "doctor's only" spot. "You're a doctor aren't you? It should be fine then," he said as he got out of the cab. He stowed the bags in the back of the open bed, displacing a ragged looking dog that was covered with scars. Ray had no idea what kind of dog it was, it had short legs with a broad chest and a huge set of jaws set into a head that looked about twice as big as it should have. Looking at it Ray made sure to hand his bags to Fritz to sit back there. He had no desire what so ever to start off his hunt with only one hand. The dog didn't pay much attention to any of it. In fact, that dog may have been the only thing that Ray had ever seen in his whole life that looked more bored than the gun importation inspector had been.

Fritz looked at his watch, "I can get you to the hotel and get back before the next two get here if you want, get a shower and a nap, then we'll get some dinner?"

"Sounds like a plan to me." Ray nodded.

Windhoek was kind of a surprise to Ray. It was a lot bigger and more modern than he expected. He wasn't really sure what he expected. It was just that this wasn't it. They pulled up in front of a hotel that would have looked at home about anywhere, and the bellman walked over to the back of the truck. About then things took an unexpected turn. At least Ray didn't expect it. Looking over at the smile on Fritz's face it was pretty obvious that he had some idea of what was going to happen. The dog that looked like he had been too bored to move came to abrupt and vicious life, barking, growling, snapping, and charging all at the same time when the black face looked over the tailgate. The bellman seeing a rocket propelled set of teeth closing in on him jumped back

156

and lost his footing, falling backwards. The dog, which, from its initial reaction, Ray fully expected to come over the tailgate and tear the bellman to shreds, had stopped, front legs resting of the tailgate. Its tail was wagging and as they came around the back, it looked for all the world like it had a big goofy smile spread across its ugly oversized face.

"You know not to do that." Fritz scolded half-heartedly. "Alright, get down Rex, and let me get those suitcases." He grabbed the duffel bag out of the back. Ray made no move to help. "You must be new?" Fritz said turning to hand the bag to the bellman who was just getting back to his feet.

"Yes sir," the bellman answered taking the duffel.

"Well, I'll be back in about an hour. Probably best to let me get the other two bags out for you." Fritz offered. He reached back into the truck bed and handed the gun case and travel bag over to Ray. "Remember where we put your paperwork." He said to Ray and shook his hand before getting back into the truck. "I'll be back in about an hour." He added before driving away.

Ray followed the bellman in through the sliding glass doors and was immediately engulfed by the cacophony of sound pouring out of the door of the casino and into the lobby. It was a mixture of the music coming from a band on a small stage that he could see through the door, the voices of the gamblers trying to be heard over the music, and pinging and tinkling sounds of the slots. It sounded like the casino at home in Philadelphia. He liked the slots. Maybe he'd play a little after he checked in.

The more he thought about it the better it sounded, so as soon as he got to the room, he tossed his duffel onto the bed, along with his travel case and sat the gun case of the floor beside it, then he locked the door behind him and headed down to the lobby.

For all of the noise coming from it, there weren't many people on the gaming floor. There was a cluster around the craps table, and they were the ones making most of the noise. He didn't play craps. Well, he'd played, but he may as well have just set his money on fire and saved himself the time. Roulette was worse he thought as he made his way past the nearly empty roulette table. He headed straight to the slots, the most mindless of all games of chance, stick in your cash and pull the crank. Win or lose it had nothing to do with you.

He was surprised that there were machines in one corner designed to take U.S. dollars, so he stuck in three twenties and settled down at one of them. He noticed several thin black women in short skirts, lounging around, slowly feeding coins into the machines they were draped on. One of them looked at him and winked. The last thing he wanted was to deal with a bunch of prostitutes, so he focused on his machine, and set about his war of attrition... lose, lose, lose, win small, lose a lot, win bigger. He was about ten dollars ahead when a thin arm wrapped around his neck and a hand moved up his thigh to his crotch.

"Are you here alone." A young blonde with a rough face and heavy eye shadow, pressed herself along his side. It produced an involuntary reaction that her hand detected and began to squeeze gently.

Ray reached down and detached her hand.

"I'm sorry, I'm married." He lied.

"Is she here? You liked it. We both know you did. What she doesn't know won't hurt her." The girl said in a soft voice.

"Alright, move along for now girl." Fritz said as he walked up behind them. "He'll be back later, he'll find you if he wants you then."

"I might not be here later," she answered squeezing Ray's shoulder.

"Where in the hell else are you going to be? If you're not here when he gets here, you'll be back down in twenty minutes or so." He turned to Ray. "You ready for dinner, the other two are ready to go?"

Ray took that as his cue to extricate himself. "Okay, thanks, see ya," he mumbled as he got up and made his way toward the door.

"I'll see you later," the girl said and blew him a kiss.

"Hope you don't mind," Fritz said as they went through the door. "You looked a bit uncomfortable."

"More than a bit, thanks."

"You ready to eat? I lied in there. The others aren't quite ready yet. They should be down in a few minutes."

Ray patted his pockets and realized that he'd left his passport upstairs. "I'll tell you what, if I have a minute let me run upstairs real quick."

"Sure, I'll wait here for the others." Fritz agreed.

Ray was still a little flustered when he got in the room, so he wasn't thinking as clearly as he would normally.

He looked through his travel case and couldn't find his passport. He checked his pockets again and then went back through the bag.

"Damn, that whore stole my passport." He spat and started towards the door furiously. He'd have to tell Fritz. Then he remembered what Fritz shouted at him as he drove off this afternoon. It was in his gun case. He took a deep breath and relaxed, he'd been panicking for no reason.

He looked down beside the bed. Then, he walked around to the other side. He got down on his hands and knees and looked under the bed. His panic attack was back full force now, and growing quickly. He looked in his closet. Then in the bathroom, he even pulled back the shower curtain and looked in the tub. He looked up at the light fixture. He knew it didn't make sense, but he had to find it. He'd just signed a bunch of official papers in two countries, and he hadn't even been here an hour and he'd lost his gun.

His mind was racing as he made his way back to the lobby. He spotted Fritz standing with two other men, they were both dressed in tans and greens.

"Hey, Ray, I'd like you to meet…" Fritz started.

"My gun's gone." Ray blurted.

"What do you mean your gun's gone?" Fritz asked squinting his eyes.

"My gun has been taken and so has my passport. When I went up, when I first got here, I put it beside the bed. Then I went down to the casino. When I went back upstairs just now, and it's not in my room."

"Let's go and look then. Maybe you just misplaced it," one of the men said.

"Maybe the bellman put it under the bed or something." The other one offered.

The four men made their way back upstairs and went through the same search process that Ray had just gone through.

"I'll tell you what." Fritz said. "You fellows go down and ask the man at the front desk if he knows anything about it, if he says he doesn't get him to call the bellhop," he looked at Ray. "You remember the new one, the one the dog scared? If neither of them have an answer bring them back up here. I'll stay up here until you get back."

The three men did as they were told and were in the middle of explaining everything to the desk clerk, each of the spectators offering their opinion as to what might have happened, when Fritz walked up behind them carrying the gun case. The bellman followed two steps behind him looking at the ground.

"Where was it?" Ray almost shouted.

"I knew he stole it." One of the men said.

"It was inside of the duffel." Fritz answered.

"I am so sorry for your trouble," the bellman started his explanation. "I returned to your room when I realized that I still had the second copy of your key." He held up one of the modern plastic key cards. "When you didn't answer the door, I thought I would leave it on the dresser, and I tripped on your gun case. I didn't want anything to happen to it so I put it into the duffel. I am sorry."

"No harm done. I should have looked there myself." Ray said, his relief palpable. "You scared the stew out of me though."

"Again, I can't tell you how sorry I am."

"I tell you what." Fritz said putting the gun case on the check-in counter. "Have security store this until I call for it in the morning. Be sure to give Dr. Moffet a receipt for it, and put it in the safe until morning."

As the clerk made out the receipt Ray found the key in his pocket and retrieved his passport out of the gun case.

Fritz watched as Ray put the passport into his shirt pocket.

"After all the excitement you've had this afternoon. I think it's time for a drink." Fritz declared.

Twenty-Eight

Yesterday had been a total disaster. The stupid boy had taken the gun case too soon. If he'd waited until Fritz had taken them to dinner there would have been plenty of time to get things copied and substitutes back into place before anyone noticed. He'd had a courier in the lobby and his man in the American embassy standing by to make the new documents. But what had happened? A goat fuck is what. They'd had to scramble to get the case back to Fritz. All they got was a few photocopies. He didn't know what they were going to be able to do with just that. Then after they'd returned the case, the doctor had pocketed his passport before he turned the gun case back over to security.

Manfred slammed his fist down of the arm of the chair he was sitting in. His temper was getting worse every day. So was the fatigue. Doing the chemotherapy had been hard, but doing it and the radiation at the same time felt like it was going to kill him. He'd told Doctor Patterson about it.

"Curing cancer isn't really any trick." The doctor had answered. "The trick is to do it without killing the patient. Sometimes it feels like we come close. But your weight is good, your skin looks good, your blood counts are all good, and you're breathing fine, so for now we push on."

So Manfred would push on, hoping he didn't push off before he got everything arranged for his family. There wasn't much time left. The World Trade people were coming next month. He was sitting here getting poisoned, and they were coming to look into what were turning into growing allegations out of Zimbabwe that half of the diamonds being mined there were disappearing west across the border and into Namibia. They'd asked to do surface trace mineral analysis on random batches of their choosing. He had to come up with some way to keep them from doing that on the illegal stones, and still let them test whatever they asked to. He didn't know how he was going to do it.

Under the terms of the Process, the inspectors had to be granted access to any of the storage areas they asked to see. Because it was impossible for him to predict which of the lots of diamonds that they were going to ask to test, he had to assume that they'd take some samples from each lot. The problem wasn't the diamonds he planned to divert with Fritz to sell in Europe, it was all of the rest of them. They were actually the much larger component, poorer quality, too much bulk to be worth the trouble of smuggling, for too small a return. Something had to be done about them as well. There was nothing he could think of that would suffice if the inspectors had unlimited access. Even if he scattered the illegal diamonds around and hid them among the other gems, the ones that they had mined legally there in Namibia or those that they'd recovered from marine sources, there was still a high probability that the inspection team would still stumble on one of the illegal stones.

If he hid them in a batch, maybe just shoved them in the back of a shaft somewhere, that might work, but it would have to be in one of the unused areas where no one would come across them by accident. A big part of the problem with that was that his own security apparatus made it nearly impossible to do without attracting attention. Everything was set up to ensure a one-way flow of the stones. Any movement backwards would raise suspicions. There was video surveillance in every main corridor and most of the secondary corridors. The other problem was that the inspectors could talk to anyone they wanted to. If there was too much commotion, if anything disrupted the normal routine, there was no way to predict who might mention something that was different recently. He couldn't take that risk, because he couldn't caution them. Couldn't even let on that the inspectors were coming. Scheisse. He'd be back to work in ten days. That left him a very small window to get the diamonds he needed out of the storage facility, identify and bundle the diamonds that they were after, and then come up with a way to safely hide the rest of them from the inspectors. He'd discussed possibilities of hiding potential problem stones with the President at length, but theoretically, without details, a sort of "what if" exercise and the President's instructions were direct and perfectly clear. Under no circumstances were the U.N. inspectors to find undocumented diamonds, period.

"I need to go home, I need to think clearly, and I need my wife," he said to the bag of drugs that was dripping into him.

He had been here alone for the last week and that did nothing to improve his disposition. He didn't know how Gretchen had done it for so many years. When he wasn't home he was at work, living in an artificial world removed from her, their son, their house, everything. So that made it easier for him. But being at loose ends without her and without the distractions of work was not just harder, it was miserable. It left him unhappy and agitated. He had no idea how she'd lived her life for so long with him just drifting in and out of it. Sometimes he was there, sometimes he wasn't and when he was gone she couldn't go with him, and when he was there he couldn't tell her much about what he'd done while he'd been gone. But she'd coped with it. She'd survived and thrived even in those conditions, like one of those plants you saw sometimes in the middle of the desert. How did they get there? How did they manage to live there? Who knew? They just did. Making it through the hard times, thriving in the good. Wasn't that what they all did? What was the alternative? To lay down and die, to quit, forfeit, to disappear? How many of those kinds of plants were there? The ones that had died off.

Who knew? They weren't there to see any more, so they couldn't be counted. There was something in that. Something that should be important, but he couldn't figure out what. What was it? They weren't there any more so they couldn't be counted? He was so tired. He couldn't get it straight. Maybe that's all that life was really about? Being there today to be counted. Maybe that was all he could hope for, all he could ask God for. To pass through the hard times, one at a time and be there to be counted.

Let me get through this shift. Let me make it through this chemotherapy. Don't let Doctor Patterson kill me today. Let me see my wife again, let me lie with her one more time, let me take care of her needs, let me thrive in this good time, until the next hard time comes. Maybe that was the only thing that any of us could hope for. At least until the hope was gone, and then to lie down knowing that you'd been counted and accepting that when you could be counted no more that you had finally made it through the hardest time, and that you'd done it well.

"Screw that," he told the bag of dripping fluid. He didn't have time for morbid mumbo jumbo. He had diamonds to steal, diamonds to hide, diamonds to protect, and he had to ball it all up together so no one could ever figure out what it was that he'd done. He just had to figure out how.

Twenty-Nine

The four of them rode in silence to the edge of the city. Ray still had a headache. He woke up with one. Maybe a bit too much wine at dinner last night.

He couldn't say for sure, but from the amount of coffee consumed at breakfast and the lack of conversation across the board, it seemed reasonable to conclude that the others were having the same problem. Fritz was the only one who appeared unfazed by it, smiling and happy while he loaded all of their gear into the back of the truck.

It was a four-wheel drive Toyota crew cab, but it was clearly a safari truck. It was rigged to hunt. The bed was open, but a ladder led up over the back of the cab to a shooting platform with benches for two people and a platform for a third person to stand on. There was also a seat welded to the front bumper behind a V-shaped brush guard. All in all you could have fit eight people in or on the thing somewhere.

The four that were riding along down the highway right now were all on the inside, and two of them were asleep. He was sitting up front in the passenger seat next to Fritz and his two new companions were in the back snoring. They were cousins from Oklahoma, named Bill Majors and Skip Compton and this was their first time in Africa too. They were loud and boisterous and seemed to have a penchant for getting one another into trouble. If last night was any indication, he was going to have a great time hunting with them.

It had started out with the ribs. When Bill ordered a rack of ribs the waiter had told him that if he could finish the whole thing that his bill for dinner was on the house. Well, that should have told them something, but Skip had started in on how if Bill couldn't eat a little ole rack of ribs he'd buy drinks all around for the rest of the night.

"You may want to see the ribs before you make too many promises." Fritz warned. But Skip was having too good of a time with it, and went on and on louder and louder until almost every table around them was in on the bet.

164

Then the ribs showed up.

These weren't any baby-back ribs from Mississippi or Oklahoma sitting on that great big platter. It was half a grown Kudu's ribcage. The whole hemi-thorax, it looked like something out of the Flintstones, brontosaurus ribs or something, they were three feet high and about the same long.

Skip started sputtering and trying to crawfish on his bets, but nobody was having it, especially Bill. God knows what the tab was. He put it on his credit card. But, in the end, everybody had had a little more than they meant to, because, hell it was free, and it was just the way guys were.

"Last night was pretty funny." Ray said across the cab.

"Not if you were Skip." Fritz answered smiling. "I told him to wait till he saw the ribs before he started betting everyone."

"Skip, my butt. He didn't have to try to eat all of those damned ribs, my stomach's still hurting." Bill said from behind closed eyes. "We may have to stop in a while, too, if those things don't stop rumbling around in my guts."

"Let me know. There are plenty of bushes." Fritz offered.

"Hey Fritz, what you all keep for pets? Kangaroos?" Skip asked apparently arisen from the dead.

"You've got the wrong continent. Head due east." Bill offered.

"I'm serious, kind of, why do the people have fences taller than their houses, around their yards?"

Fritz looked in the rearview mirror at Skip for a moment before answering, "Well, I guess the main reason is that they don't want the children to get eaten."

Skip raised his eyebrows, "The idea of needing a seven or eight foot fence to keep your kids safe is kind of hard to get your head around, if you're from Oklahoma. Why do they have to be so tall?"

"Two reasons," Fritz said, and then paused for a few beats to enhance the drama. "Lions...and leopards."

"How in the hell high can they jump?" Bill asked, incredulously.

"Leopards, about six-and-a-half to seven feet, lions maybe a little less." Fritz answered. The other three men in the car exchanged looks with one another, not sure what to believe.

Skip broke the silence. "You're shitting us right?"

Fritz shook his head no.

"God damn..." Bill whispered.

"So, how high is the fence around where we'll be sleeping?" Ray asked.

Fritz looked at him and winked. "Depends on where you want to sleep. Skip and Bill here wanted the true African experience so I've got you two outfitted in a thatch hut up off of the pan, on the side of a hill, but there aren't that many trees around, so we don't really have to worry too much about leopards jumping down on you. You'll hear the lions coming up the hill. Ray, I've got you in the back of the garage, in the compound, so you'll miss out on a lot of the adventure but you'll sleep a little better being inside the fence."

"Wait a minute now…" Skip started.

"How many bunks you got in the garage there?" Bill cut in.

When Fritz started to laugh the cousins knew they'd been had.

"Scared your butt." Skip punched Bill.

"You were gonna say the same thing." Bill protested.

"Like hell, I was just a little concerned about the mosquitoes on the pan like that…"

"You're all in the compound. Eight foot fence." Fritz reassured them, "…but we've got some cats inside too."

"Yeah, well, I don't worry much about house cats." Bill said, trying to recover.

"Who wants a beer?" Fritz asked as they pulled into a small village.

They drove by the bodegas and small groups of peddlers sitting on blankets, selling wooden carvings and souvenirs.

"Do we have time to go over there and shop for a few things?" Ray asked as they got out of the truck and headed into a cinder block building with a dirt floor.

"Why don't we come back down if we have an off day or something," Fritz suggested. "We still have to get the guns sighted in before dark. Bill and Skip have two apiece. That makes five. It could take a while if one of them's off by much."

Ray nodded, knowing that if one of the guns were going to be off it was probably his, after the fall it took at the airport. He took a quick picture of the outside of the bar and then followed the other three men into the cool of the darkness.

"Hey Bink, let us get four for the road, and four in a bag." Fritz ordered.

"Oh God, another flock of lambs to the slaughter. Watch out boys he'll skin you bare. This one's an outlaw. He'll have you shooting jackals at trophy prices if you don't watch him." The big man behind the counter laughed as he fished the beers out of the bottom of a barrel of water. No ice, just water. He handed one to each of them and stuffed four more into a woven wool sack and handed it to Fritz.

"You have a rest room?" Bill asked.

"He tried to eat the rack of ribs at Perry's last night." Fritz explained.

"Through there," Bink gestured in the rough direction of another door with his thumb.

Bill took a swig of his beer and sat it on the bar before he headed out the door. He wasn't gone long, his head reappeared almost as soon as it had gone through. "There's just a dirt street back here."

"There's a barrel in the tin shack there. Sorry that's all we got." Bink explained.

Bill was suddenly conflicted, he was clearly weighing the options, hesitating in the doorway, unsure how much he really needed to go, then decided in favor of the barrel and disappeared again.

Bink grabbed Fritz's arm and shook it. "The truth is he's a pretty good one. Taught him everything he knows. You boys are in for a good hunt. You know what you're looking for?"

"Kudu and gemsbok are what I'm after." Skip said, without hesitation.

"And what about you?" He turned to Ray.

Ray took a sip of his beer and thought then looked at Fritz. "I guess we'll see what's best. I started with the idea of hunting elephant, but that's kind of something for the future, maybe next trip. For now I guess we should see what's what."

"Get your feet under you first, huh?" Bink nodded.

"Something like that…"

The back door flew open and Bill came through it bent over, with his pants around his knees. He was holding on to them for dear life with one hand and keeping the other over his head to ward off the blows an amazingly old woman was raining down on him with a broom.

Bink looked at Fritz and shook his head. "Wrong door."

Bink and Fritz both moved to separate the two.

"Now Lolie, he didn't mean any harm, Just got a little mixed up is all." Bink soothed as he grabbed the broom handle and held it.

"You keep them out of my kitchen. He tried to sit on my pot."

"Just an honest mistake." Bill said finally able to get his pants up, and hastily working at the snap.

Lolie made a renewed effort to snatch her broom away from Bink, but the big man was too strong.

"I'm going to take care of it." Bink said nodding solemnly to the old woman.

"You boys get on out of here." He said winking at them. "And you," he said harshly, pointing at Bill. "Keep your pants on in an old lady's kitchen."

Fritz grabbed the bag and herded them to the door. Bink miscalculated and let go of the broom too soon and the old woman tried one final charge. He grabbed her around the waist and picked her up. "Calm down old mother."

The hunters escaped to the security of the truck before two of the three of them dissolved into laughter.

"Damn, even the old ladies are dangerous around here." Bill grumbled. "Hell, I didn't know what door to go through…"

That made the other two laugh twice as hard, his cousin laying on Bill's shoulder and pounding his back.

"Oh lord…oh lord…I can't wait to tell Helen and Sue about this." Skip was gasping for enough air to speak.

"Now there's no need in bringing this up to our wives." Bill started seriously. Clearly he was seeing a lifetime of ridicule.

Skip fell backward now and rolled against the door.

"I suspect you're screwed on this one." Fritz offered, and started the truck.

Bill frowned and turned his face to look out of the window away from his helpless cousin.

"When are we coming back here to shop?" Bill asked.

Ray hit his head on the dashboard laughing. He ended up with a lump on his head that was still throbbing an hour later when they pulled up to the gate of the hunting camp. Damn metal dashboard.

Fritz got out and motioned to Ray to follow him. He showed him how the latch worked and drug the heavy gate through the dust of the road to open it.

"Pull it to behind us," he said as he turned back and headed to the truck.

Ray stood on the far side of the gate as the truck moved through it. There was no sense giving Rex a reason to get upset. As the truck passed he could see that the dog knew it was home. It stood with its front paws on the tailgate, tail wagging and barked into his face, just for good measure. Once the truck was far enough past him to feel safe, he lifted on the rail and dragged it behind him, it stuttered some on the edges of the tire ruts and raised a small red cloud behind it. He had to lift harder and clanged the rail as he pulled it all the way shut and slid the latch to. As soon as the gate shut Rex came out of the truck. Ray flattened himself against the fence, and considered unlatching the gate and slipping back out of it, but Rex was a dog revived. No longer bored or lethargic but ran in circles around the truck wagging and barking. Still Ray kept a close eye on him as he came around the back of the truck and almost walked headlong into an adult cheetah, standing under a bush beside the truck. He could hear Fritz saying something to him, but he was having trouble concentrating. His entire being was focused on the cheetah that began to walk toward him with a low rumble in its chest. Oh hell, it was growling. His mind raced as his body stood perfectly still. Cheetahs could sprint at sixty-miles-per-hour, obviously there was no use running. Could he make it onto the truck?

The sinewy body swayed as it moved. It could obviously jump into the truck if it wanted to. He forced his mind to focus on what Fritz was saying as he came around the back of the truck and walked past him, straight at the cheetah.

"I see you've met Sally...Hey Sally...hey girl." He said holding his hand out to the animal.

"Is...is she growling?" Ray asked, still concerned.

Fritz knelt and the big cat pressed her muzzle against his face. "No that's how she purrs, it sounds like gravel doesn't it. She was raised here from a cub. Her mother had been poisoned. Fed her goat's milk with a bottle. She thinks I'm her mum. Come here and kneel down slowly so she can get used to you."

Ray did as he was told and was rewarded with a bowed head for him to pat. He scratched behind Sally's ear and the rumble deepened.

Fritz nodded his approval, "Seems she likes you."

The feeling was something he couldn't describe, he felt honored to be allowed to be so close to something so magnificent. Ray felt an immediate affection for the cat. He continued to scratch her head and she in turn licked at his other hand, as Bill and Skip made their way out of the truck and knelt beside him. With all of that attention directed in one place it apparently seemed like the place to be for Rex too. Who bounded into the center of the group. The transformation was mercurial, suddenly the big purring housecat with gentle eyes and a sandpaper tongue was a swirling vortex of teeth and claws and it was obvious where the profusion of scars on the dogs back had come from. He whirled, snapped twice in the cats face and received a smack on the ear with an open claw. They became a yowling and snarling dust ball, rolled into the bush and then tore away toward the house.

"They always play like that." Fritz said matter-of-factly and got back into the drivers seat.

The three hunters were left to look at each other incredulously.

"I hope to hell she don't play like that with one of my legs if I go out to take a leak at night." Skip said shaking his head.

"You better hope it's only your leg she decides to go after." Ray offered. They all frowned thinking about it.

It was going to be a little harder to see that big pussycat side of her, knowing that before you could do anything about it she could turn a big hunk of your hide into confetti.

"Shoowee," was the only thing that any of them could think to offer.

Thirty

Like most things, divorce was overrated. It had apparently turned Lisa into a pseudo-schizophrenic. It was like she had two people living inside her head all of the time now. It had been that way ever since she'd called Millie. A new spiteful Lisa appeared out of somewhere and took over her life. Old Lisa was still here. It was just that she wasn't in control anymore. All she could do was go along for the ride and offer a running commentary, which New Lisa never listened to.

"Yaay I'm free." New Lisa crowed when the divorce decree was final.

"Now what am I supposed to do?" Old Lisa wondered.

"We should go on a date."

"A date? I haven't been on a date in thirty years."

"All the more reason we should do it. Bob Taylor asked if I wanted to go to the Carmichael lecture with him."

"The Carmichael lecture's next week. There's no way I can get in shape soon enough for that."

"Why do I have to get in shape?"

"In case he sees me naked."

"Naked. What am I thinking? I'm not that kind of person, I'm not some slut that sleeps with someone on a casual date."

"Bob has been flirting with me for the last six months, and I like it. I like him."

Damn this new Lisa to hell. She'd said yes to Bob and now, this was what it came to. A drink after the lecture, a kiss after the drink, a hand on her thigh, awkward fumbling, lying on her back looking at the ceiling, with him thrusting inside her, trying not to cry and faking an orgasm at the same time, so she didn't hurt his feelings. When it was over she left as soon as he fell asleep, and came home to sit among the boxes in her bedroom.

This truly was the end of her marriage. She had pushed so hard through all of the divorce, pushed Ray away. She'd let her anger wash over her and carry her along because she knew she was right.

170

Now she wasn't so sure, and now he was gone, and she was sitting on the carpet looking through piles of old pictures. It was two in the morning, and all she had to show for most of her life was a stack of cardboard boxes filled with ghosts. All that she had left of the life they'd spent together.

She took another picture from the shoebox that she was holding on her lap, and looked at the two of them younger and thinner in clothes that were ridiculous. She had no idea how she had gotten her hair so big, she couldn't do it now if she had to. She missed those people, the people that they had been then. She didn't know why, but she wanted to tell Ray that. That she'd loved him once and probably she still did, but there was no way to call him. She probably wouldn't have anyway, but the fact that she couldn't made her want to. Made her feel like she needed to, and that made her feel worse.

How could she be so stupid about everything? Now Bob was in the middle of things. Her husband had gone off to a place that could kill him, as unprepared as anyone could possibly be. Because she wouldn't talk to him, she didn't even know what it was that he planned to do there or how long he intended to stay. She didn't know any of the things that she could have known if she had stopped being so self-righteous, if she had just been civil, if she just hadn't been such a bitch to him. And what was she doing? Screwing a stranger. They hadn't even used a condom. His semen was still inside her. She could feel it and it made her sick. All she could think about was Ray dying without knowing she still loved him. It was all so overwhelming. She put the shoebox down, took another drink of wine, and let herself cry a little more.

She opened another box and picked up the jewelry box she'd left behind when she'd gone. She took out her mother's pearls. How could she have left them behind? She opened a small drawer. Watches that hadn't been wound in twenty years sat lifeless inside. She held up her first engagement ring, so small. It couldn't fit on her pinky now. A little stone, it was tiny compared to the ring that he'd given her for their fifteenth anniversary. It had meant the world to her when he handed it to her that night. She squeezed the ring in the palm of her right hand and covered it with her left. She let her hands fall into her lap, still clutching the ring. Now it was nothing but dust, a tiny rock that had outlived its purpose, would outlive her. She fell sideways onto a pillow and lay there motionless. Don't diamonds always outlive love? Isn't that what they're supposed to do? "A diamond is forever." Where would hers go from here? Where had it been?

It came out of the Wesselton hole in Kimberley in 1978. But it had lain there long before. It had been there in 1866 when a fifteen-year-old boy found a shiny rock on a riverbank that he played with as a toy until his mother gave it to a friend. The toy became known as the Eureka diamond, twenty-four carats that even turned the head of Queen Victoria. It had still lain there six hundred feet under the earth three years later when a shepherd boy traded what would be the Star of South Africa to a rancher for five hundred sheep, three oxen and a horse.

Her little stone might still be there, a chip off a larger stone if not for a cook. That was what had led them to dig there. An 83-carat diamond a cook found sticking out of the side of a hill in the middle of nowhere. The cook for the Red Cap Party found it. The Red Caps were a bunch of prospectors out of Colesberg who were traveling across the Vooruitzigt farm that belonged to the De Beers brothers. The cook wasn't much of a cook. He pissed off his boss and got sent out to dig as punishment for his culinary failings. On his way to dig he tripped on a stone and ended up changing the face of southern Africa.

Africa became the diamond center of the world. By 1914 fifty thousand miners had fought the earth with picks and shovels to rescue the treasures below. They dug into the hill until the hill was gone, then they kept on digging until they dug a hole that took up forty-two acres and was seven hundred and ninety feet deep- "The Big Hole." The largest hand dug excavation in the world. They dug and they dug and they dug to dig out a mere six thousand pounds of raw diamonds. That came out to a hundred and fifty pounds a year looking at it one way and only two ounces per miner looking at it another. Either way, it was enough to keep them digging. Looking for the next Hope, the next Eureka, the next Star.

The diamonds were xenocrysts, tiny inclusions formed in the heat and pressure at the earths core that were carried up hidden in the magma that had flowed upward and formed a volcanic cone that jutted down thirty six hundred feet beneath the surface, like a giant carrot.

A town grew up to support the miners. Miners from across the continent were flooding into the diamond fields. They called it the new rush. The name stuck and so they just capitalized it, and New Rush it was.

The Boers thought it was theirs, but the British government had different ideas. They placed it under their protection, just to keep it safe, and they were going to have some elections too. Just to be sure everybody was happy with it. But they couldn't. In London, poor Lord Kimberley couldn't even consider having any elections, because he couldn't spell or pronounce any of the names in the place. After all, the Boers were so mixed up who could expect an intelligible language. They were Dutch, German, Flemish, French, Scandinavian, Portuguese, Greek, Spanish, Polish, Scot, Irish, and English mongrels.

To help Lord Kimberley out the British administrators decided to name the capitol Kimberley. So while most of the locals still thought they lived in New Rush, at least they could pronounce the new name in London. The locals were overjoyed. The Diamond Field newspaper said it well, "we went to sleep in New Rush and waked up in Kimberley, and so our dream was gone." The fifty thousand miners were consolidated and De Beers ended up the last man standing, soon they owned the world, at least in terms of diamonds, and everybody worked for them, or they didn't work.

The diamond fields became the killing fields and the Boers lost. There would be no independence for diamonds, and for their trouble the Boers got scorched earth and concentration camps for all. Which was particularly good news for the Boer women and children who got to die by the tens of thousands of starvation and disease. So other men could show other women how much they loved them for the next one hundred and forty years.

Kimberley, kimberlite, Kimberlitic, the Kimberley Process, and Lisa's memories, there were diamonds inside them all.

Thirty-One

The sighting in had gone better than Fritz had anticipated. The doctor was a whiz with the single shot. He'd obviously been working a lot since Fritz had seen him last in Florida. Aim, cock, shoot, aim, cock, shoot and he had two bullseyes at a hundred yards. Fritz had never seen one of the single-shot Blasers like that before, but for such a light little gun the thing shot like a charm. The two from Oklahoma were big time deer hunters and both of them knew their way around a rifle. Three hunters, sighting in five guns with only fifteen rounds fired was as good an outcome as any professional hunter could ask for.

Now was the time to see how they did in the field. It was still dark, and cold enough to need a jacket and gloves. He grabbed his hunt bag, checked his rifle, and walked to the truck to stow them in the cab.

Ray was the one he was worried about since he'd never hunted before. Josh, the other guide, was leaning on the hood of his truck smoking a cigarette. His face glowed red as he inhaled.

"Those things'll kill you." Fritz warned.

"They'll have to stand in line." The old man answered. "I hear we got three?"

"Yeah. You take the single today, we can swap tomorrow." The way they had always handled three hunters, if two of them weren't married to one another or something, was to alternate them as back-up. If the primary hunter got his trophy early and they could get a second hunt in that day, fine, the back-up got to hunt in the afternoon. If not that guy hunted one-on-one the next day. Just to get a chance to see how Ray handled things, Fritz wanted to keep him with him at least for the next two days. To do that, he was going to have to stick him as back-up this morning. Didn't need him getting killed before Manfred got a chance to get everything squared away. Fritz hoped that he could convince his brother that there was a way to avoid killing Ray. He liked him a lot. He'd do what he had to. He just hoped that he didn't have to.

"Morning boys," he said as he walked into the kitchen and grabbed a couple pieces of bacon with his fingers and ate them both in two bites. As he expected the Oklahomans looked a little tired. "You boys sleep okay?"

"Damned lizards jumping out of the walls all night." Bill groused.

"They're not anything to worry about, but be sure you shake out your shoes in the morning before you shove your foot in there, just to be sure." Fritz warned.

"Well they scare the bejesus out of you if they jump on you in the dark." Skip added.

"That's why I told you to be sure and draw the nets, that and the bugs. Thatch is what people have built houses out of here since before any white men ever set foot on the place, but it does have a bunch of places for stuff to hide, so use the nets. You'll sleep a lot better." Fritz advised them. He turned to Ray. "How about you?"

"No problems in the garage, tin and screens, seemed to work for me, that and the toddy before bed. I slept like a log." Ray answered.

"Good, You're back-up for the first hunt Ray, we'll work on a few things. Bill you're my primary hunter today, we're going to work the val, with Bao. He's a bushman. Skip you're hunting with Josh, you have two trackers, Christian, he's Ovambo, and his grandson Chris, short for Christian the third. You're going to work the high ground. It's pretty thick up there so that's why you have the two. If you blow the shot, you'll be tracking the rest of the day. That can happen even with a good shot, so take your time and focus on your shot placement. Finish your breakfast and I'll see you at the trucks in about thirty minutes, we want to get where we're going by first light.

It was nice to be driving. The heater was on. Ray and Bill had both climbed up into the hunting chairs for the drive out. They'd be freezing up there. Bao leaned against the door and chewed on a stick, with his feet shoved right up against the heater to try and suck as much of the heat as possible into his bones. Who knew what the stick was, probably some bushman remedy to kill the worms or something. Bao had come with him when he came to work for Walt, some kind of deal that Manny had worked out. But he had to admit that the little bushman was a godsend, he could find game in a sand pit. All of the other trackers and skinners stayed away from him. He spooked them. In the morning he was just there, and in the evening it was the same, he was just gone. Nobody had any idea of where he went to or where he stayed. He worked hard, always showed up, and only worked with Fritz. They had tried to get him to go out with one of the other guides once, he shook his head no, and then they got on the truck and nobody could find him, so they didn't try that again. He never said much, he could understand what was said, Fritz thought. He communicated like bushmen always had, clicks and pops and pointing and pantomime, and it worked for him. They had a rhythm, like a team, or a band, or something.

As the light came up they started to see the grey shapes ghosting through the brush that he was looking for. Their spiral horns still black in the growing light. He drifted the truck to a stop and cut off the engine. Bao was out before it came to a complete halt, carrying the only weapon Fritz had ever seen him carry, a crooked stick, sharpened on one end, that he used for just about everything from pointing to eating. He walked along the road analyzing the tracks of what had crossed.

"Kudu," Fritz whispered to the two hunters. They sat hunched in their jackets with their arms wrapped around themselves. "Let's try to get on them."

Bill and Ray made their way down as quietly as they could with numb hands and feet. They thumped and bumped as they gathered their gear.

"Shhhhh….they're close," Fritz warned. They'd both sit in the cab tomorrow morning, Fritz thought with a smile. A heater was a wonderful thing.

Bao squatted on his haunches in the center of the road and pointed to a splayed track, then raised his arms beside his head, to indicate horns. Fritz pointed to another track five feet further down and Bao shook his head and put his hands close together.

"That one's small, he thinks this is the one to go after." Fritz said to Bill. "We'll go like this, I'll follow Bao. Bill you stay about ten feet behind me, I'll motion you up to look if we stop, but don't come until I tell you to. We don't want them to know we're here. We can follow a long time quiet, if he spots us he's gone. Ray keep your gun open and the barrel down, you stay another ten to twenty feet behind Bill."

They got their first look forty-five minutes later, Bao stopped dead, frozen in his tracks and Fritz saw it at once, moving through the brush to their right. It was a good buck, a nice spiral, a broad V, and good length. Fritz motioned Bill up and pointed. Ray eased up as well, until Fritz held up a hand to stop him. No one moved, no one breathed as Bill eased up to take a look. The bull shambled forward out of sight beyond a large thorn tree, then eased down into a rock cut. Bill moved silently and followed, Bao right beside him.

Fritz motioned for Ray to move toward him, when he closed the distance Fritz whispered, "Keep me in sight. Don't get left behind. Walk on the sides of your feet and let your weight roll inward. Try not to step on sticks, or trip over anything."

Fritz kept on the tracks of Bill's boots until he could see his back. Bill was squatted down and motionless. Bao's hand rested on his shoulder holding

176

him from moving forward. The bull must be stopped looking back, he thought, and then he saw that Bao was not looking forward, he was looking down. Fritz followed his gaze until he saw the snake. A puff adder as big as his forearm was slowly moving between Bill's feet. Bill didn't know it was there. Fritz looked back at Ray and motioned for him to stop, Ray saw the snake too. His eyes were as big as saucers. Fritz could see him shift the gun, unsure of what to do. That wasn't the answer. He shook his head and put his finger to his lips, before he moved up gingerly beside Bill.

"Stay still, he's looking back at you. Stay perfectly still." He said and brought up his binoculars. He held them up for a moment but never took his eyes off of the snake. Bao had let go of his charge and was very slowly bringing the point of his stick, so that it was positioned just behind the snake's head, then he jabbed, pinning the snake to the ground. The snake reacted instantly, whipping its body against the inside of Bill's thigh. Bill, to his great credit didn't scream, but came down with the rifle's butt pinning the snake's fat body to the ground. The four men sat silently, staring until the snake was dead. Bao pulled the stick slowly towards him, dragging the snake out from under Bill without ever releasing the head. When it was clear, he withdrew the stick and wiped the blood from its point with a leaf.

"Do you want to stand up?" Fritz said in a normal voice.

"Yes." Bill mouthed.

"You can speak up, the kudu left a while ago." Fritz answered.

"I thought you said he was looking back?" Bill said as he stood up with shaking knees.

"I said that so you wouldn't move." Fritz explained.

"Can I scream now then?" Bill asked as he shook his hands to shake out the cramps from pushing down so hard with the rifle.

"You can if you want."

Bill turned to Bao, who had taken a small loop of twine and tightened it on the snake's mouth, then handed it to Bill.

"Thank you, there's no way I can pay you back for what you did." Bill said wrapping a big arm around the little man.

Bao gathered his fingers and put them to his mouth and made a chewing motion.

"He says you can let him eat the snake." Fritz translated.

Ray moved into the group to look at the size of the snake and Bill held him up. Holding him by the twine the snake hung down below the men's knees.

"That scared the hell out of me, and I was twenty feet away." Ray said. "I didn't know whether to shoot or not."

"If you'd have shot and missed, Bill was bit, and that was if you didn't hit him, he could have been both. If you'd have shot and hit the snake and not Bill, he'd still have been picking hunks of rock and snake parts out of his balls for the rest of the hunt." Fritz laughed.

"Thanks for not shooting." Bill said, deadpan.

"You want to stop now and eat?" Fritz asked. Knowing it was useless to try to get either one of them to relax for a while.

Bill looked up at the sun, which was almost straight above their heads by now. "What time is it?"

Fritz opened his pack and removed a stack of biltong sandwiches from its interior. "Eleven-thirty, may as well eat now, we can get another stalk in after lunch." He pulled out the four stacked cups, each one a different color and sat them on a flat rock, then he opened a Seven-up, he divided it equally between the cups, and topped them off with water from his canteen. "It helps to cut the dust," he said, handing the first cup to Ray. "Red-Ray, blue-Bill, I always give the yellow one to Bao, since he's kind of yellow, and the orange is mine." He recited as he handed them out.

They sat on the rocks and ate and talked about the snake, it was recounted from every viewpoint, except Bao's. He concentrated on coiling the snake into as tight a circle as he could. When he was finished he tied it with the twine and then tied that to the knotted rope around his waist that served as his belt.

"Is he really going to eat that?" Ray asked.

"I guess so, I've never been to his house for supper, but I have no doubts that's what he intends to do." Fritz replied. "You want the hide don't you Bill? Take it home as a keepsake."

"Sure, I'll hang it down the wall beside the fireplace."

"We'll have them skin it when we get back, then Bao can have the rest for supper. All right, let's see what we can find before it gets dark?" Fritz said gathering the remains of their lunch and folding the wax paper, he nested the cups, and they were done. Nothing remained except a small pool of the snake's blood as evidence that they'd ever been there.

They hunted their way back to the car. Twice they cut the trail of a bull crossing their path, but neither one was big enough to spend time on. They were almost back to the car when he saw it, the same bull that they had been on to that morning. If not the same one, one that was just as good.

"See the shine? In the sun their horns look bright white, from the way they reflect the light. Gun barrels are the same way, that's why I've been so hard on you about keeping your barrels down, instead of carrying them up on the sling like you do. He's about four hundred yards. We need to cut that in half. Can you make a two hundred yard shot?" He asked Bill.

Bill nodded.

"Okay Ray, stay up here on the hill and use your glasses to keep an eye on things. Watch him, but watch us too. I'll climb up the back of an anthill, and you signal which way he's going."

Ray nodded too.

They would have to move quickly. It was going to be dark soon. Twice Ray redirected their path, and then there he was, less than a hundred yards away. Bill had seen him too and his rifle was already up. Fritz nodded, the rifle barked, the kudu fell, and it was a very good day. That was what made the difference on the hunt, no one hurt and a good animal to take home. That was the best day.

They took pictures quickly in the fading light. Posing the trophy, getting the best angle to maximize the appearance of the horns, then Fritz headed to gather the truck while Bao gutted the buck. He'd keep a lot of the entrails for himself. It would be a good dinner at his camp tonight, his wife and children would be very happy indeed. The four of them got the buck into the back with the come-along, and they were headed home, for a drink, some dinner, and the telling of the day's tales. Nobody was going to top the tale of the snake. The hunters crowded into the cab, Bao sat in the back skinning out the snake as they drove. Fritz wasn't sure how he kept from cutting his fingers off, but every time he looked in the mirror that was what he saw, Bao working away, grinning from ear to ear.

They pulled into the compound late, the other truck was already at the skinning shed and the skinners had a carcass down to bare meat.

"Looks like Skip got one too." Ray said as they approached.

"That's not a kudu. It looks like a waterbuck." Fritz corrected, "Kind of the same color hide, but look at the difference in the shape of the horns, no big spiral, much straighter, see?"

Ray nodded.

"Hey Skip, we got my kudu…and a puff adder." Bill shouted out of the window as they came to a stop. Fritz stopped and let his hunters out. "Grab your gear, and I'll back this thing under the rack."

The skinners were hard at work, blood to their elbows, they had the waterbuck caped, skinned and quartered quickly. They were a good crew. The hunters stood, drinks in hand, watching as he backed up, and they put the spreader bar between the kudu's back legs. They hooked it to the winch and took up the slack. As the tension raised the animals back end up off of the bed, Fritz pulled forward to let the carcass swing down and be in a good working position for the skinners to start removing the hide. The crew knew what was coming and grabbed the horns to keep them from hitting. Another grabbed a front leg to stop any spinning motion. He felt it start to slide and looked in the mirror just in time to see all hell break loose, there were skinners screaming, there were skinners running, two of them were already up in the back of the truck. By the time he got out of the truck, there wasn't a worker left in the skinning shed, just the hunters and Bao. And Bao was shaking silently holding his ribs, almost bent double.

"You dirty little bastard." Josh shouted from inside the shed, then the old guide walked out and tried to pick up the blood-covered remains of the skinned puff adder, it was so slippery that he couldn't get a grip on it. "Who in the hell put that damned thing in there? Scaring my whole damned crew to death."

"Sorry, I didn't think about it being a problem." Bill answered.

"Didn't think it would be a problem?" Josh shouted, his face reddening. He paused then added, "How did you get it in there, you were in the cab?"

"We stuck it in there, after we got loaded up." Ray nodded. "We didn't want it bleeding all over the seats."

"Sorry, Josh." Fritz said, and then looked at his two hunters disapprovingly. "You've got to watch them every minute." He looked around for Bao, but he, and the snake were already gone.

Thirty-Two

The next morning Ray started the day as the solo hunter with Fritz. Skip and Bill were together, hunting with Josh. Fritz had decided that they should trade the sparser vegetation that they'd faced yesterday, for the thicker thorn-bush of the hills. It made for tougher hunting conditions but there were better trophies up there.

They walked steadily uphill after leaving the truck, and caught only fleeting glimpses of animals they jumped in the dense vegetation. Ray wasn't sure how he was going to get a shot at anything. They were walking in single-file. It was like walking in a tunnel. Bao went first, moving thorns to the side with his stick. Fritz was next and seemed impervious to the hooked thorns that grabbed at Rays legs and arms with every step. Ray was last, struggling to keep up. The thorns made it nearly impossible to make steady progress. They'd hook into the skin of the backs of his hands and arms, and when he's stop to pull them out, to keep them from ripping holes in him, they'd hook into the tips of his fingers. By the time he'd get loose he'd be falling behind again and would have to hurry to catch up. His arms and the fronts of his legs were crisscrossed with scratches that stung with the sweat that was pouring out of him from the heat and exertion of their steady uphill climb. He hoped they got to the top soon. They were going to break for lunch there. So they could sit down and scan the area with their binoculars for a while, to see where the game was. He wiped the sweat out of his eyes and was rewarded for his trouble by being bitten on the back of his neck by a fly.

"Owww. You son of a bitch." He muttered, under his breath.

If Africa had a soundtrack, it wasn't the throb of drums or the roar of the lions. Nope, it was the buzz of these God damned flies, he thought to himself. They came for the moisture and salt of his sweat and the smell of his blood. When they bit it felt like someone was driving a nail into you.

He was too old for this kind of stupid shit. What in the fuck was he doing there? He cursed and fumed with every step. He wondered if it would be too much of an embarrassment just to call it quits now. Then, over this running conversation, he became aware of another sound, a sound that was growing louder than the buzz of the flies and of his own breathing. It was the sound of something moving, it was coming from their right and behind him. It almost sounded like something was dragging itself through the brush.

"Fritz...Fritz...Fritz..." each whisper got progressively louder, as his adrenaline level rose and his heart pounded in his ears. It seemed like hours until Fritz turned.

Ray pointed in the direction that the sound was coming from. They stood silently, listening, and then Fritz motioned to Bao, and the three of them crouched behind an anthill that they had just passed on the trail. Whatever it was, it was traveling on the same game trail that they were on. They sat and waited. The dragging gave way to thrashing of the bushes and low guttural coughs. In a few minutes the elongated, almost alien face of a hartebeest bull came into view, Ray remembered it from Pete's, he remembered it exactly because it was so strange.

But something was wrong with the way it was moving, it would jerk and when it did the brush behind it would move. It was moving slowly towards them, until it was only twenty-five to thirty yards away. Ray could see that blood was streaming down its shoulders on both sides. Through the binoculars he could see a loop of metal wire. Either it had gotten tangled in a fence somehow or it had been caught in a wire. Whichever it was, the bull had been strong enough to manage to escape by breaking it, but in doing so had pulled the wire so tight that it had cut the poor animal's neck to the bone. The wire'd broken so that he still drug a long length of it behind him, and it was tangled now with branches and grass, which caught in the thorn bushes, causing it to cut further into his flesh with every step. The flies that had been tormenting Ray all morning covered everywhere there was blood, and every time the animal had to stop, they rose and swarmed into it's eyes and nose causing the animal to snort and shake its head, trying to do anything to get some relief.

This was a shot that Ray understood without needing to be a hunter, it was a shot that had to be made, for the sake of the animal. Ray brought up his rifle, but he was too quick and the bull saw the motion and lurched sideways off of the trail.

"Damn," Fritz cursed almost inaudibly.

"We have to stay on it," Ray whispered. "We can't leave it like this."

Fritz nodded. So they moved out from behind the anthill and kept on its trail. It was easy enough to follow. Even Ray could see it clearly, going deeper and deeper into the bush. But the animal was hurt and it had seen them. So now it was being cautious and moving away from the trails.

"It's going to be nearly impossible to get a clear shot." Fritz whispered. "I'm not going to have time to tell you when to shoot. When we get to that anthill over there, the tall one, we'll climb up and see if we can see him."

From the anthill Ray could see the bull ease into a small clearing, a tiny hole in the brush, only ten yards across. The bull stopped and stood, he coughed and a cloud of pink spray escaped from its nose and mouth.

"Bring your rifle up behind me and rest it on my shoulder." Fritz ordered.

Ray did as he was told. There was no nervousness. There was no joy or excitement in this. He put the crosshairs behind the bulls shoulder a third of the way up his body as he'd been told and slowly, slowly squeezed the trigger. The bull's front legs buckled and it fell without taking another step.

Fritz grabbed his arm and shook it. "Good job. The damned wire had cut into his windpipe. The poachers don't care, they catch some, they lose some. They just set another snare."

Bao moved up behind him and slapped Ray on the shoulder and nodded solemnly.

"Thank you," Ray answered.

"He's a good bull. A gold medal bull, but you won't be able to do a decent shoulder mount. He's too torn up from the wire." Fritz said as they moved up beside the downed animal. "You don't have to pay if you don't want to. You don't have to take this one as a trophy. I'll square it with Walt when you go."

Bao took his stick and touched the open eye of the bull. There was no response.

"It's dead?" Ray asked, feeling the responsibility of what he'd done. There was a sadness to it that he hadn't expected.

Bao nodded.

"His neck's a mess." Fritz pulled at the wire trying to get it loose to slip it off the animal's head, but it was wedged in the bone. He fished into his pack and came up with a pair of folding pliers, and cut the wire as close to the animal's neck as he could. "Do you want to take some pictures? At least you can have that."

Ray shook his head, "No, I'll take this as a trophy. This is one I want. It's the first thing I've ever killed, and he was...brave, I don't know what I'm trying to say..."

"I do." Fritz answered and nodded.

Now, came the hard part, they were about half of forever away from the truck. There were two choices, carry the four hundred and fifty pound animal along the twisting game trails or go and try to find a way back here with the truck. The answer was obvious to them all since they would be the ones carrying the bull.

"We can't leave him in here alone. The jackals and warthogs will strip him clean before we get back. One of us has to stay here, and I need Bao's eyes to watch for the trail markers we're going to leave on the way out. That kind of leaves it up to you. Can you do it? You don't have to. We can try covering it up with my jacket, but it's going to be hard as hell to find it again in here before dark without someone to guide us."

"What do I need to do?" Ray asked, trying to sound like he was okay with it.

"It may take a little while, so sit back and relax, but don't go to sleep. Keep an ear out for the truck, and when you hear it, tie your shirt to your gun barrel, then climb up as high as you can on the anthill, and wave like crazy, so we can find you. If we go past you, shoot."

"Sounds simple enough."

Fritz gave him some sandwiches and a bottle of water before they went.

Ray watched anxiously as his companions moved out of sight, then he sat as still as he could and listened to their progress until the sounds of that dwindled to silence. He kept listening until all that was left was the insects drone and buzz as they gorged on the dead hartebeest's blood. At least it was keeping them away from him.

Sitting there as the afternoon passed he tried to occupy his time by eating and then he tried reading from the travel guide he found in the bottom of his pack. He fooled with his binoculars, but there wasn't much to look at, so he climbed the anthill and looked around. Mostly what he could see from there was the tops of the thorn trees, and the summit of the hill that they'd set out for when they left the truck.

As the sun moved closer and closer to the horizon Ray's mind wandered. He could imagine any number of unpleasant outcomes to this little adventure. He was sitting next to a four hundred and fifty pound chunk of raw meat with a blood trail leading straight to it and less than twenty-five feet of visibility in broad daylight thanks to the dense brush. He could reasonably assume that the visibility would be getting a lot worse after it got dark. There was no one to blame except himself. He'd been the one to pull the trigger.

He heard something nearby, low to the ground, a warthog maybe? He hoped it wasn't a jackal or a hyena. Were there hyenas in Namibia? That was something he should have looked into more carefully, so he could know what he had to worry about. He should have asked Fritz about it before he left. He had seen a documentary on hyenas on Animal Planet. They were disgusting and awful and the idea of them being out there in the dark scared him to death.

He had no choice but to sit there and wait, what else could he do? The chance of him finding his way out of where he was before dark, by himself, was close to zero. He had no idea of where he was, or how to get back to the road. He could try to walk downhill, but he didn't think the road up here ran parallel to the hill. It would be easy to miss it in the dark. His only option was to wait it out. As the light faded Ray was on top of the anthill for quite a while before he heard the truck or saw its lights.

Ray came back to camp more than a little disappointed with himself. He was no great white hunter. That was for sure. Ernest Hemmingway had never written about being scared out of his wits, hiding on top of an anthill, or depressed over killing an injured animal. He wasn't sure he was cut out to be a hunter.

Ray listened to the day's stories from Bill and Skip, and how they had both gotten a blesbuck, shooting at the same time. He made the appropriate comments, but his heart wasn't in it, so he gave up and went to bed.

There was a fatigue that came from prolonged tension. It set in full force as Ray walked across the compound. He felt like he could barely lift his feet. He was asleep as soon as his head hit the pillow and he didn't even roll over until he heard Josh rapping on his door as he made his way outside for his morning smoke.

He and Skip were hunting with Josh as their guide today. They stayed around camp until it was light and then drove slowly along the perimeter fence. The fence around the compound had an area in a low spot where it almost formed a right angle to follow the contour of the land. With the steep hillside it formed a funnel with only a narrow opening as a way out. It looked like a perfect trap. As if it had been designed to be one. As they approached, they could see that the ground in the center of the funnel was covered in blood.

"I thought I heard something in here last night." Josh said, stopping the truck. "Looks like a lion. Smart fellow isn't he? Using a man-made trap to help him hunt. Your hut's right over there, about a hundred and fifty yards." He raised his arm and pointed.

"He's taken the twins." The old Ovambo guide, Christian said, pointing at a huge eland cow.

Josh explained as he picked up bits of the chewed on carcass of one of the calves. "See her? We call her Mrs. X. See how her horns cross? It makes her easy to recognize. She had twins this year. Now she's by herself."

"Two calves, he must have eaten the one here and taken the other one home with him, like a doggy bag." Skip said, digging a toe into the dirt. "See the drag marks?"

"None of you got a lion tag reserved do you?" Josh asked.

Ray and Skip both shook their heads.

"Think about if you want to. Ray you got the time, you're here for ten days. We can upgrade you if you want."

Ray felt his throat tighten, "Let me think about it. How much?"

"Probably about four or five thousand total, daily rate would go up, trophy fee, a few things like that. But this is about the best chance you're going to get to get a lion. We can set up right here."

"I'll have to see how much I've got left." Ray said, unenthusiastically. He'd come to Africa to find out how much he had left, to try and find something inside himself. God knows he didn't have much else. At least he could come out of this having some respect for himself. Then he remembered the official at the airport. "Can I hunt a lion with the Blaser?"

"Oh, hell no." Josh brayed. "I don't know how you managed to kill the hartebeest with that little popgun. Maybe you could borrow a real gun. Got to have something bigger, a three seventy-five or better. We'll talk to Fritz tonight. Have to see if you can even shoot a big gun. Last thing I want is to get chewed on by a wounded cat somebody shot in the gut, because they didn't know what they were doing. Oh, hell no," Josh repeated as he climbed up into the cab of the truck.

The day's hunt was endless. Ray was backup. That meant that he was walking with Chris, and in contrast to Bao, the younger boy never shut up. It was an endless stream of cigarette smoke and complaints. Ray didn't know how anybody ever killed anything with him around, which was probably why Josh spent all morning motioning for them to fall back.

Lunch was not much different, back at the truck, on the fence line, Chris sat beside him in the bed smoking and jabbering away the whole time. When they were finished picking up all their paper and nesting their cups Josh decided that it would be best to leave Ray and Chris on the fence line for the afternoon hunt, one facing each direction along the road until he and Skip got back.

"Just sit up on the deck, use it like a stand." Josh instructed.

Great, Ray thought, an afternoon trapped in the back of the pickup with a hebephrenic smokestack. Hunting had not turned out to be as much fun as he'd expected.

Within the first hour the unthinkable happened, Ray found himself wishing he were alone in the thick brush again. Fear and flies were better than this. Any animal that came along would have to be deaf and have absolutely no sense of smell not to know that they were there.

Chris was explaining how tips should be given for the twentieth time.

"See, if you just give the whole tip to Josh or Fritz they just keep the whole thing or most of it anyway, they could care less about us, or the skinners. Just split it up yourself. See I'm the one guiding you today, so you shouldn't even think about tipping Josh. What has he done? ... You don't know any way that I could get to America do you?"

"For crying out loud, just be quiet, just shut up and don't smoke for a few minutes." Ray blurted, before he could stop himself.

Chris looked hurt, and Ray felt bad. "Look just take a little walk down that way for a few minutes. I'm sorry I snapped at you." He cast around trying to come up with some justification. Other than, I can't stand this anymore. "Look, my wife left me. I'm kind of upset. I just need to think a little. I don't even care if we kill anything today."

Where in the hell had that come from?

"Well, I can understand that quite well. I have several girlfriends, and they never leave me, but it would probably be very upsetting for a man if they did." Chris said climbing down and starting away. "Just don't shoot anything. You are not supposed to shoot at anything without a professional hunter."

Yeah, like you're a professional hunter, Ray thought. He watched as Chris walked a few hundred yards and then laid down on the side of the road propping his feet on a rock before lighting his next cigarette. He could hear him talking to himself. He looked up from Chris and saw the white flash of the horns. It was a kudu, as big as the one that Bill had taken the first day. Ray watched silently as the horns moved through the brush, making a wide circle around the yapping, smoking "professional hunter". He got his first good look at the bull as it came alongside him about a hundred yards out. Still he didn't move. He didn't want Chris to see him raise the gun. So, he followed the bull with his binoculars as it continued to circle.

When it was behind a large bush, he picked up his rifle and slid out onto the road, keeping the truck between himself and the bull. He crawled along the fence line until he was where he thought the bull would come into the road. He rested the fore end of the gun on the lower strand or wire and waited.

Just when he thought that the bull must have changed directions while he was getting into position, it came out of the cover. With a single shot it was over. The bull looked up at the shot and then collapsed where he stood. He could hear the boy's shouts behind him as he stood up. He didn't listen. He moved slowly to the bull, it was magnificent, the biggest one he'd seen in camp. And he'd done it alone.

Josh and Skip showed up shortly, they'd heard the shot and were back to see what had happened.

"Damned fine bull, damned fine." Josh repeated several times while they cleaned it and loaded it into the truck.

As they raised it into the bed a pool of blood in the chest sloshed out and ran down the right leg of Ray's pants.

"It'll come out in the wash. Damned fine bull, worth a little trouble. Shot him right beside the road, early day…and with Chris. When I heard the gun I thought you probably shot him. Shot a fine bull though. I don't know if it was luck or magic." The old man said rinsing the blood off of his own hands before he got into the truck.

They rode in silence. Skip had been skunked and Ray was listening to Chris in the back telling his father about how he had told Ray to lie in the fencerow and wait. That he had seen the bull and knew that if he walked that way it would circle around into the clearing. That he should be getting a good tip for that. Ray had a tip for him all right.

When they got to the skinning shed Fritz was already there, and Mrs. X hung upside down on the skinning rack, Ray recognized the distinctive shape of her horns.

"You shot the cow?" Josh asked Bill critically.

"Naw, they came and got me." Fritz answered before Bill could speak. "The lion again I guess. Ran her into the fence, she split it five feet up. Broke her neck. She was half in and half out. They heard the pop up to the house. The lion was gone by the time they got there with the car. We're going to have to fix the fence."

"No sense letting the meat go to waste." Josh agreed.

"She weighed eighteen hundred pounds dressed out."

"That's a lot of meat. What'll you do with it?" Skip asked.

"We'll go ahead and dry it, and take it in with this weeks load to sell it."

"So you can sell the meat?" Ray asked.

"We keep what we need. The rest goes to the market." Josh explained. Then poked Fritz in the arm with his big index finger. "Look in the back. Look at what this one shot." He nodded at Ray.

"I thought you were backup?" Fritz asked.

"He was, shot the best kudu so far this year with me gone and Chris with him…with Chris I tell you. Less than no help. With the damned loading boy."

They all looked across the yard at Chris, who was in animated conversation with the skinning crew.

"The hero of the day." Fritz said smiling.

"Couldn't have done it without him." Ray said returning the smile.

"Yeah, I bet. You ought to get changed before dinner." Fritz said pointing at Ray's trousers leg.

"I will. I just wanted to take a couple of pictures of Mrs. X and the fence, a lion killing something of that size is incredible...the fact that it used the fence as a tool, that's really something."

Ray stuck his rifle and backpack in his room and grabbed his camera, after a series of photos of his own kudu and the unfortunate Mrs. X he headed down to take the pictures of the fence.

When he got there, the fence gaped open where it was split from the ground to his chin. Ray took pictures of the rip, then tried pulling the wire together to close the hole as well as he could. He looked for a piece of wire long enough to try and approximate the two sides. He'd start at the top and pull the two sides together as he came down, to where it widened out. Like sewing up a laceration. He saw a pretty long piece of the wire, and was bending over to get it when he noticed the eyes. Yellow and intense, they seemed to emanate from the grass itself. It took a second before he could make out the rest of the lion. It was a juvenile male. He had a mane, but it was wispy and thin. It was crouched in the grass and was almost invisible, it never moved, it didn't even blink. He could see the muscles of its shoulders tightening as it gathered itself. Ray moved the camera to get a shot of it.

He knew he was experiencing some bizarre form of disassociation, he knew that the lion was clearly stalking him, but he had become somehow detached, the world moving in extreme slow motion. He saw the lion but couldn't really process it, so he snapped the shot.

As the shutter tripped, Ray noticed a flash out of the corner of his eye and without thinking automatically fell back away from the fence. Just as a second lion, one he'd never even seen, hit the fence, right where he'd been standing a moment before. Lying there on his back he drew his only weapon, the hunting knife he'd used on the kudu. His mind spun, but he had no frame of reference to judge what it was he should try to do. He knew he needed to come up with some plan before one of the lions figured out that they could easily push through the break and get to his side of the fence.

He looked at the knife and then back at the lion. It opened its mouth wide and bit at the chain-link wire of the fence. It had a whole mouth full of weapons a lot more dangerous than his puny little steel claw. The leg of Ray's pants was still soaked with the blood from the kudu.

Ray was prey. They smelled the blood. They thought he was something to eat. Lying down was the worst thing to do. He had to be a man. If he wanted to live he had to stand up and be a man.

"Arrgh," he screamed as he got to his feet. "Get out of here you two. Fritz, Josh I found the lions." he screamed at the top of his lungs and walked straight at the fence, eyes locked with the closest lion. There wasn't fear or anger there, just intensity and concentration.

"Hey, hey get out of here."

"Get on."

Everyone in the camp came down the hill. He could hear their movements and their shouts. Then a gun fired into the air. Ray's eyes never wavered. When the near lion looked back for its partner, it was already gone. Then Ray saw the resolve fade, then the uncertainty. Another gunshot and the lion turned and fled into the grass.

After that, Ray knew that bravery wasn't an issue when it came to lions or even to death itself. There was almost no chance he would have survived an encounter with these two lions out in the thick thorn brush. Even with the rifle in his hands, sitting on the anthill, ready to shoot the lion that he could see stalking him, the second lion would have gotten there and killed him before he ever made the shot, and somehow, that was right. That's what hunting should be. It's what a fair chance means. You're never sure who dinner will be. It was why he'd come here in the first place.

Thirty-Three

Everyone in the compound slept late. Nobody was hunting today. They all got up and put on travel clothes, had a leisurely breakfast and piled into the little Subaru station wagon, that Fritz had pulled up in front of the main house. Instead of knives, water, cord, ammunition, and binoculars, the daypacks were pretty much empty, except for cameras, money, and passports. It was a sightseeing day. They were going to the market in Okahandja for some souvenirs. Then if they had time, they'd swing through Etosha for some sightseeing on the way home. They'd get to see a lot of elephants and some of the bigger stuff there. Hunters usually shot more pictures there than anywhere else.

With only three hunters in camp they were taking the car. It would be only the four of them going. Josh bitched that he was a hunting guide and not a tour guide, but the truth was, as soon as the hunters were gone, Josh would get cleaned up and head home to see his wife. Fritz couldn't blame him. He could use some female company himself.

He'd get a chance to stop in and see Reese when he dropped off Bill and Skip in a few days. It would probably be the last time he'd ever see her again, one way or another. He hoped she wasn't too sad when she found out that he was dead. He liked her, even if he didn't love her. She was a good kid and a lot of fun, but she was the kind of girl that wouldn't waste away too long once he was gone. She'd move on and be just fine. He hoped he survived his death as well as she would.

There were still some things that had to be attended to. Hopefully they'd be able to get them taken care of today.

"Let's get loaded up boys. Old Bill's got a hot date with Bink's cook." Fritz said as he walked across the porch. "Bill, you want to use the facilities before we go. Just in case."

Ray spit a mouthful of coffee out as he choked on it laughing. Sally walking across the yard changed direction to investigate. Fritz leaned down to scratch her behind the ears and she purred her growling purr. Each one of them in turn rubbed her head as they climbed in the car. She looked in each door as she walked around the car, then sure nobody was getting back out to pet her any more she stalked off, smacking at Rex as he ran up looking from side to side. Always a day late...Fritz thought. He and Rex were a lot alike.

"Everybody got their money and papers?" Fritz asked as he started the engine. Everybody did. Now he just had to get the set he needed.

Fritz kept up a running travelogue as he drove. "See those, in the trees? Those are communal weavers nests. They're small birds that live in one big nest for safety. It's kind of like a bird hotel. Sometimes a mamba will live in there with them. The mamba eats a few of the birds, but the rest of them stay safe, because the snake's there...The mambas have a distinct smell. Nothing else comes around when they're there...You never want to stand under one of those nests, in case the snake decides to drop out and go for a crawl...They're one of the longest snakes in Africa. They can get twelve or fourteen feet...A few years ago a friend of mine was driving along in an open Jeep with his wife, it was during the rainy season. Snakes were on the move. He was coming down this hill here, and when he got to the dip at the bottom it was flooded. He hit the gas to run on through the water and there was a mamba swimming along. Came right up over the hood, over the windshield, right between the two front seats, and out the back. Good thing he didn't decide to take a right or a left turn on the way through the car..."

After a while they'd all pretty much had enough of talking, so he quieted down and let them talk. Most of the talk on the way down centered on the old woman who had whopped Bill with the broom, of course. As they pulled up in front of Bink's, Bill made a big point of how she'd probably gotten so scared because she'd never seen anything so long and thought a mamba had gotten into her kitchen.

"More likely she thought it was a mouse." Skip corrected.

"Better watch out, she might have set some traps." Ray warned.

This had been a good bunch. They'd gotten along well. Nobody had gotten too moody or caused any trouble.

"Alright boys. Keep an eye on each other. The market there has a lot of the regional stuff. So the carvings, and those sort of things you can get there. If you want to get some of those orange shoes, like Josh wears, the stalkers, made for you we can get you measured, if you want to, at the old man who makes them's shop later. Then we can check out the tannery and see what kind of skins they have to sell, if you want a couple for rugs or something. Why don't we try to get away from here in about an hour and a half? Just meet me back here." He watched as they walked across the road and then headed inside.

His brother, thin and ill, leaned on the bar drinking a soda.

"He has it in the bag?" Manfred asked, without preamble.

"I think so.'

"But you're not sure?"

"No," Fritz admitted.

"We can't afford another foul up, like at the hotel. We aren't going to get another chance on this. If we try and take it at the ranch there's no chance he's going into the desert with you." Manfred rapped his knuckles on the bar while he thought. He looked at Bink.

"We could just kill him, and drop him in the desert." Bink suggested.

"That doesn't help us set up our story very well, does it?" Fritz asked.

"No it doesn't." Manfred agreed, and frowned. "Is the boy coming straight here with it?"

Bink nodded.

"All we can do then is to turn him around. If his papers aren't in there, we send him right back with the bag and have him drop it at the closest stand to where he snatched it. When he hears a commotion, he can hold it up and ask 'is this it.' Then maybe he gets a little tip for his trouble anyway."

They all looked at each other.

'Then what, a pickpocket?" Bink asked.

"Why, you got one?" Manfred sounded hopeful.

"This is Africa, isn't it? Every other kid hanging around those stands is a pick pocket." Bink confirmed.

"Harder to cover, harder to recover too. Remember we want to get the stuff back in his possession once we get it copied. We need him to think that everything is just fine...until this is over at least. That means we need a minimum of three documents to pull this off. The doctor's original passport which we will need to destroy once he's dead, Fritz's license to leave with the body, and the new passport from the U.S. Embassy with the doctor's data and Fritz's face on it."

"You have someone in the American embassy?" Fritz asked surprised.

"I have someone in every embassy. I have to know things." Manfred shrugged. "You just have to remember to leave your license and pick up his original passport, leave your hunting pack and take his, go through his pockets and be sure that there's nothing to identify him as the American doctor, then head for the pick up."

"Alright..." Bink started, and then stopped, as a thin ten-year-old came through the back door with a backpack. The boy held out his hand as Manfred approached. His face fell when he was relieved of the backpack without being paid.

"Mister Bink say..."

Bink laid a heavy hand on the boy's shoulder. "Shhhh, boy. You'll get paid. Let the man see if he has what he needs."

Manfred went through the backpack, lifting out a carved elephant and a warthog with ivory tusks. "Never get these through customs," he murmured. "Here they are. Alright, we need to get rid of the boy for the next little bit. In case one of them saw him. When the doctor gets here take him to the police. I'll get on the road with these."

He walked straight to the back door as Bink pushed the boy after him.

"I'll let him off down the road a little. I'll give you some extra money to get home. That okay?"

The boy nodded, and followed Manny out the door.

"So, what do we do now?" Bink asked as they resumed their seats at the bar.

"I suppose we have a beer and wait." Fritz answered.

And so they did.

It took longer than Fritz expected for the three hunters to show up. When they did, they all tried to talk at once.

"Whoa now boys, whoa. You didn't have another run in with old Lolie again did you?" Bink asked.

"No," Bill said, "Somebody stole our stuff."

Fritz looked at Bink and raised his eyebrows. "What was stolen?"

"Somebody took my backpack. I only sat it down for a minute, while I was looking at something and when I turned around it was gone." Ray explained.

"Who else is missing something?" Fritz asked, looking at the other two.

"Somebody grabbed my pack, too." Skip offered.

"For crap sake, you can't trust those little bastards farther than you can throw a damned elephant," Bink spat, honestly disgusted. You couldn't even trust them to stick to the deal you made with them. Always trying for a little extra, something more than they were supposed to get.

"So both of your backpacks are gone?" Fritz asked. He was starting to get nervous. What if Manny had the wrong one? He didn't know what Ray even looked like, did he? He might have seen him from across the room at the hotel.

"We found mine, but it was empty, all of my stuff had been taken out of it." Skip explained.

Fritz breathed a secret sigh of relief and turned to Ray. "Did you find yours too?"

"No we never found mine." Ray answered.

Bink rubbed his forehead. "We need to talk to the police. You're not going to get a straight answer out of any of that bunch if you're white. Don't think it's going to be that straightforward with the police either, though. You'll have to grease the wheels there, if you want to get your stuff back."

"What do you mean, 'grease the wheels'?" Ray asked.

"He means bribe 'em." Skip answered.

Bink nodded. "That's kind of how it works. Don't get upset about it. At first they're going to try to rob you. They want to get as much for themselves as they can. They'll have to pay a little to find out anything, but not as much as they're going to ask for. Let Fritz and I handle it when we get there."

The five men walked together down the dusty street to a small house with a single door labeled POLICE. An old and thin black man wearing a khaki uniform shirt sat on a wooden chair behind a battered desk as they entered.

"Officer Tombo." Bink greeted him.

"Hello Mister Bink. I see you have some friends with you today. How may I help you?" The old man asked formally.

"Two of these fellows had some of their things misplaced while they were shopping at the stands on the road." Fritz said.

"Well, if they have been misplaced, perhaps I can be of some assistance in helping you find them." Tombo replied, and looked at the three Americans. "And where are you gentlemen from?"

"Mississippi," Ray answered

"America?" the policeman asked.

"The United States." All three men answered at the same time.

"So you are Americans." The policeman fished around in his desk for some papers. "And there are two of you who have misplaced their belongings?"

"No. I didn't misplace anything. Some son of a bitch took my backpack and then stole my camera, my binoculars, and my money out of it. Then they threw my backpack in a garbage can." Skip said angrily.

"Those are serious accusations. Things that are stolen are much harder to find, you see, because that is a criminal charge. It would take a great deal more to get someone to answer questions about something, if it were such a serious matter." The policeman explained.

"He misplaced them." Bink shot Skip an angry look.

"That will be much simpler. Each of you fill out on the form what you are missing and I will ask around to see if anyone may have found them."

"But I lost my passport." Ray blurted.

"Are you leaving in the next few days?" Officer Tombo asked.

"No sir." Ray answered.

"Give me a few days then. Passports are usually easy to find. The other things are harder. Money is the hardest. Did you lose all of your money that you have with you?"

"I didn't lose any of my money." Ray answered honestly.

"Then you should think of leaving some of it with me. Sometimes money will help things be found. Money motivates people to look."

"How much should I leave?" Ray asked.

"For your things, because they will be simple, only a few hundred dollars and the things should be found. For your friend, the one who had his things stolen it may take five hundred."

"Why don't you take a hundred American dollars and see if you can find something out while we drink a beer?" Fritz suggested.

"I'm not sure I can find out very much for only a hundred." The old policeman said frowning.

"Try and see. If you don't find anything out today, some beer may help you tomorrow."

"A police officer may not drink beer while he is working." Officer Tombo rebuffed him.

"Then perhaps you should take it with you when you come. So you can drink it at home."

Officer Tombo nodded as he thought about it. "I'll walk over to the road, and see if anyone may have seen anything that can help me. I will come by and tell you on my way home."

Skip was disgusted as they left the police station. "That old bastard is just as much of a thief as whoever stold my stuff."

"Yeah, but he's the police." Bill observed.

"Let's hold it down until we get past where he can hear us at least." Fritz warned. He had no use for any trouble with the police right now. "We should go ahead and head back. Bink do you mind handling things on this end?"

"It'll make it easier if you're gone. He knows it's not my stuff. Why would I give him any more money?"

"Do you think he'll really find it?" Ray asked.

"I have confidence that a hundred dollars is going to at least find your passport. What in the hell are they going to do with it?" Bink assured him.

Thirty-Four

Ray worried about his lost passport all night. He'd finally decided that if they didn't find it by the time Bill and Skip left to go home tomorrow afternoon, he was going to ride into Windhoek with them and go to the U.S. embassy. That way he could at least start the process of getting a replacement.

He talked to Fritz about it at breakfast but Fritz wasn't too worried, he was sure the passport would turn up by tomorrow afternoon. If it hadn't, they could go straight to the city after they did their desert hunt for the gemsbok. Ray wasn't sure about waiting. If it would only take a few days to get a replacement that was one thing, if it was going to take two weeks that was something else entirely. Whatever the time frame was, he wanted to get the embassy started on it as soon as possible. He could always get the desert hunt in once they submitted the paperwork.

Today, he was the number two hunter again. So he had plenty of time to think about all the different things that could go wrong while he walked along behind the rest of the party.

At least they didn't get his wallet, so he didn't have to worry about trying to cancel his credit cards and thank God he'd left his cell phone in camp because he didn't have a way to charge it. The last thing he needed was somebody running up one of those twenty thousand dollar cell phone bills you read about on the Internet. So, it was far from as bad as it could have been, and there wasn't anything he could do to alter the outcome, what so ever. Either the police would find his stuff or they wouldn't. He was taking as many pictures as he could with the little back-up camera he'd brought, in case he didn't get his Nikon back.

If he got his passport back, the rest of it was just stuff. He tried to pass the time by taking pictures, and trying to stay out of the way while Skip hunted.

As they came across a rise, Ray was walking to the side of the others, to keep below the horizon, when he saw something about a hundred yards away. He couldn't tell what it was because it was partially obscured behind some bushes. He didn't have his binoculars any more to take a closer look, so he waved for the others to stop and then pointed in its direction. He brought up his rifle and looked through the scope. He couldn't find anything, not even the bush. He looked at the scope and saw that he still had the power ring set at ten X. No wonder he couldn't see anything. He turned the magnification ring down to the lowest setting and scanned the bushes until he found it again. He could tell that it was spotted, but he still couldn't make out what it was, but with the spots it had to be an animal. Maybe it was a fawn or something? He slowly eased the power ring up to increase the magnification, but still couldn't make out a clear outline.

He was concentrating so hard on the scope that he nearly jumped out of his skin when something touched his back. He heard Bao laugh in his ear, and flushed with a wave of embarrassment, but the little bushman only patted him on the back and motioned for him to put down his gun. When Ray lowered the rifle Bao walked right past him and straight to the place that he had been studying so intently. When he turned, Bao was holding what looked like a bloodstained rag up with his out-stretched hand. He took a few more steps and held up the head and one front quarter of what looked like some kind of a cat. He, Fritz, and Skip all moved to have a closer look.

"It's a young cheetah." Fritz said, squinting.

"What happened to it?" Skip asked as they looked down at the scene in the grass.

The cheetah had been torn to pieces, and just left there. It didn't look like something a human would do, and it didn't look to Ray like anything had tried to eat it either.

Bao stretched out his fingers and slowly moved them around his face facing outward.

"You're right, I think it was lions." Fritz agreed.

"I never heard of a lion eating a cheetah." Skip said.

Fritz moved a piece of the carcass with the toe of his shoe. "He didn't eat him, did he?"

"Then why do it. Why go to all the trouble of tearing it to pieces?" Ray asked.

"Because it was a group of lionesses, not a single lion. A male lion would have just broken the cheetah's neck. The lionesses pulled it apart to be sure it was dead." Fritz speculated.

Ray looked up, "I still don't get it. Do lions usually kill cheetahs?"

"If they can catch them. Cheetahs are fast, so a single lion usually can't. But they don't have much endurance. A couple of lions can wear him down. Then they can catch him." Fritz explained.

"But why would they kill him at all?" Skip joined in.

"They hunt for the same food. The lionesses want to be able to feed their babies. To do that, there has to be enough food. So, whenever they can, they eliminate the competition. Africa's too hard. You choose yours. You do whatever you have to take care of your own." Fritz looked hard at Ray, like he was trying to tell him something, but Ray wasn't sure he understood what.

They didn't find anything the rest of the day, and walked forever. Ray was ready for a bath when they got back to the camp. He filled the tub with hot water and bent down to pull off his boot. When he pulled on the boot a curious thing happened, or more accurately didn't happen. His boot wouldn't come off of his foot, he pulled and pulled, but except for a dull pain in the middle of his foot nothing happened.

"I'm a doctor, I know about things, shoes don't just get stuck on people's feet." He said out loud. Then he started to examine the boot to try and figure out what it was that was holding it in place. Feeling along just below the laces he found the tip of a thorn poking up through the leather. Ray twisted his foot over, and there, embedded in the sole of his boot, was the thorns base.

He'd gotten his tetanus booster before he left the U.S. so that wasn't a problem. But he still had to get the boot off of his foot. He tried walking on it. He barely noticed it, but knowing it was there, he could tell. He walked back to his bunk and looked into the side pocket oh his duffel bag and found the set of Leatherman pliers that Pete had suggested. A sharp jerk, and the problem was solved. He held up the bloody thorn and looked at it. So sharp that it had pierced both boot and foot when he'd jumped off of the truck, and he'd never even felt it. He climbed into the tub and washed his foot as well as he could. He poured on some Betadyne and then allowed it to soak in the tub until the water got cold. When he got out of the tub he went ahead and started some antibiotics. The last thing he wanted was an infected foot.

The next morning, his foot was sore and swollen. He had a lot of pain when he walked on it. He talked to Fritz and Josh about it at breakfast. They decided that it would be best if he and Josh rode out to a water hole, with a camera. He could sit in a blind and get some close up pictures of whatever came by to get a drink. By lunch he'd seen more species of animals and birds than he would have ever imagined, but in the high desert water was a universal need. Once his camera was full of pictures, they headed home for lunch and an afternoon nap.

As they got out of the truck Ray grabbed his rifle. He'd left it in the gun rack of the truck all morning. It had been soaked by the dew then covered with the fine powder of red dust that covered everything in this place. He knew he needed to wipe it down with a little gun oil to keep it from rusting, so he unloaded it and carried it back to the garage.

As he approached the door Josh was standing there shaking his head disapprovingly.

"You didn't leave the door open this morning, did you?" He asked.

"Nope, I came out before you did, remember."

"Damned cook." Josh muttered to himself.

Ray walked into the small bedroom, closed the door behind him, and tossed the rifle onto the spare bed.

That's when all hell broke loose.

Three adult warthogs darted out from under the bed. Ray screamed like a girl and jumped onto the other bed, and five or six warthogs ran out from under that bed to join the other three, which were now running laps around and around the room.

Ray jumped over to the bed with the rifle, startling the already upset pigs even more, and started fumbling in his pocket for shells. Luckily, common sense overcame him before he found any. He was in a small room with a cement floor, and tin walls. If he fired a gun in here somebody, and probably not a pig, was going to get hurt. He jumped back to the first bed keeping the rifle with him to use as a club and tried to reach the door, too far. He tried to push it open with the barrel of the rifle. The pigs, un-use to people jumping and swinging guns around them, started to vocalize, in huffing squeals, snap at each other, and make little rushes at the bed Ray was standing on top of.

This was not good. Ray did the only thing he could think of. He started hollering at the top of his lungs for Josh. When the old man opened the door to see what all of the hollering was about, he was almost bowled over, as three of the warthogs made their escape. The rest ran back under the beds.

"What in the bloody hell are you doing in there?" He shouted startled.

"I'm jumping from bed to bed. What in the hell does it look like I'm doing in here?"

"But, why are the pigs in there, and why did you throw your clothes at them?" the old man asked, truly puzzled.

"That would be a good question, and no I didn't throw my clothes at them. I guess they were trying to get the gum and candy I had in my suitcase." Ray replied.

"They must have rooted under the break in the fence back there. We haven't really got it fixed right to keep 'em out."

"I don't care how they got here. What am I supposed to do about them?" Ray shouted.

Well you need to get 'em out of there." Josh suggested.

"You're the professional hunter, how do you suggest I do that?"

"Well, for starters I wouldn't get off of the bed."

"I don't think that's something you're going to have to worry about." Ray said looking down to see glimpses of snouts and tails under the bed across the room.

"Second thing, put down the gun." Josh ordered.

"Like hell I will." Ray countered.

"Look, I'll throw you a broom. You drop the rifle, and you'll ruin the scope entirely and that will be the end of your hunt, you don't have iron sights on that thing." He explained patiently.

Ray thought about it and then laid the rifle gently on the bed. "Toss me the broom."

The next thirty minutes was spent jumping from bed to bed, poking the porkers out from under one bed only to have them run under the other.

"Okay, run in here and jump on this other bed." Ray suggested, "Then you can keep them from getting under the bed you're on when I get them out from under this bed."

"I have a better idea." Josh replied rubbing his chin.

Through the doorway Ray could see Josh throwing a pail of corn down in the courtyard, then he walked back to the room and poured a trickle of the corn as he walked. When he got to the door he poured the last of the corn onto the floor and then he went back out into the courtyard. One by one, the remaining porkers scooted out from under the bed and set about eating the corn. Following the trail until they were out the door. When the last one was gone Ray hopped to the other bed and looked back just to be sure there weren't any stragglers before he darted to the door and slammed it shut.

As he did, he saw a car he didn't recognize parked in the yard.

Thirty-Five

Manfred wasn't sure what it was that he was watching. As they got out of the car they'd heard the shouting coming from the garage.

Bink craned his neck to try and see what it was that was going on. "Wonder what they're doing over there?"

"No telling. Josh is doing something. Maybe they found a snake or something." Manfred answered.

"You want me to go over and check it out?" The big man asked, eager to get into something.

"No, we want a minimal profile. I don't want to draw any attention to the fact that I'm here. I need to sort things out, talk to Fritz, and go. You can handle giving them their things back."

Bink carried the doctor's backpack and the other fellow's camera. The shouting continued as they crossed the porch and into the dining room.

Manfred let his eyes accommodate to the darkness of the room after hours in the sun. "Put them on the dining room table, for now. It doesn't look like Fritz is back yet."

Bink set the things he was carrying down. He held up the camera, and switched it on to see if it still worked. To be sure, he looked at a few of the digital pictures of men hunting. "The guy Skip is going to leave happy about getting his camera back anyway...why didn't we bother with the binoculars? Then he really would have been happy."

"There were a couple of reasons. First it keeps up the idea that this was all about the theft, and second, it doesn't matter. He wants the camera. He's done hunting. He doesn't need the binoculars. He can buy some new ones when he gets home." Manfred explained.

Through the window a new commotion was developing. Old Josh and a bunch of the blacks from the skinning shed were chasing a bunch of warthogs around in the courtyard. It wasn't clear why. It looked like they had baited them in with some corn or something.

Without any warning Sally rushed out from under the porch. Maybe she was just trying to help, but her whirling and snarling at the hogs and slashing at everything around her wasn't really conducive to getting the hogs to cooperate.

Bink was laughing at what was going on outside of the window. Manfred joined him to watch for a minute himself. If he'd been stronger Manfred may have considered trying to help. As it was, he was glad that he was inside, watching it all through the window.

The man that he recognized from the documents in his pocket as Ray Moffett was looking out of the door of one of the rooms along the side of the garage, but he wasn't making any effort to help either. He should have been out hunting, but, of course, if Josh were still in camp, one of the hunters would have to be there with him.

A heavyset skinner grabbed a broom that the doctor held out to him and made a rush into the mayhem. Sally swatted his feet out from under him and he went headfirst into the warthogs. Manfred saw the doctor look in their direction and stepped away from the window.

"That's enough of that." Manfred said firmly, grabbing Bink's arm. "Go and see if you can get Fritz on the radio, so we can get out of here."

"You don't want me to see if I can help them?" Bink asked, anxious to get in on the fun.

"No, just get Fritz please." The last thing Manfred wanted was to spend any time with the hunters, the less people that knew that he'd been there the better. He sent Bink into the kitchen and sat down at the table to sort through the different sets of documents.

There was the doctor's original passport, there was the new duplicate with an image of Fritz inserted, and there was Fritz's license that they'd used to get the image for the passport. The latter two items he put into an inside pocket to give to Fritz in private. The doctor's passport he placed on the table.

The map he'd brought with him had the set checkpoints marked, so all that was left to worry about was an accidental run in with a patrol, and he should be able to be sure that there was an open window from that standpoint as well. He'd send the patrols north and have Fritz come in on a little side road from the east to bypass the checkpoint. He'd put the detail on the main road in the morning and switch them to the side road in the late afternoon. By then Fritz should be past them and into the restricted zone.

Absorbed in his planning, Manfred was surprised when the door opened and Ray walked in.

Ray saw the backpack on the table and smiled. "Is that mine?"

Manfred nodded.

"Are you the police?" Ray asked him.

"Something like that." Manfred answered uncomfortably.

"Oh, you're Fritz's brother aren't you?" Ray asked suddenly.

"I'm sorry..." Manfred was dumfounded.

"Sorry, occupational hazard. Fritz told me that his brother had lung cancer and was getting radiation treatments. I saw the markings for the portal on your neck." Ray explained.

Involuntarily Manfred's hand moved to cover the blue mark, then realized it was unimportant. If one of them were going to know who he was, it might as well be the one that wasn't going to be able to tell anybody about it later.

"Yeah, I am. He asked me to see if I could recover your items for you." Manfred answered.

"I don't know how to thank you..." Ray said opening the backpack and beginning to look through it.

"Is this what you're looking for?" Manfred asked holding out the passport.

Ray opened the passport and shook it, "Yes! That makes it a good day, even if I did have to jump around trying to get away from those damned warthogs."

Bink returning from the kitchen slapped Ray on the back. "That's the funniest thing I ever saw."

"It wasn't quite as funny from the inside." Ray said.

"Kind of like a crocodile. Funny to look at, but..." Manfred said.

Ray looked at him quizzically.

"...not quite as funny from the inside." Manfred completed the joke.

"I get it. That's a good one too, but not near as funny as these guys." Bink said, motioning towards the window.

"Did you get up with Fritz?" Manfred asked.

"Says he's twenty to thirty minutes out." Bink answered.

"I guess I'll go ahead and head back. Well, doctor, I'm glad I was able to help you. Will you give Skip his camera back please?"

"No problem." Ray responded automatically.

"Then, I guess I'll go ahead and go. I have a long trip. I'm sure you know the radiation and chemotherapy are difficult." Manfred explained. "Bink I'm going to go ahead and go straight back to the city. You don't mind riding back to Okahandja with my brother do you?"

"I don't guess so, but I can drive you that far if you need me to."

Manfred shook his head. "Thanks, but I think I can make it okay. Tell Fritz that I'll be at the hotel tonight, if he'd like to have a cup of tea after he gets his hunters settled for their flight out tomorrow." He said carefully.

"Yeah, a cup of tea is exactly what he'll want..." Bink started, but the look that Manfred gave him stopped him cold. "Sure thing Manny, I'll tell him when he gets here."

"Doctor it was nice to meet you. I hope you enjoy the rest of your hunt. I hear you're going for the real trophy, the desert Oryx?" Manfred asked.

"I guess we will, now that you've found my stuff."

"Well, that's what I was hoping for." He shook hands with Ray and turned to the bar owner. "Bink, thanks for driving me up, hope to see you again soon."

With that he turned and made a determined exit. As he turned the car around, they were finally herding the last of the warthogs out of the front gate. He waved to Josh as he passed and slowed down to keep the old man from having to breathe more dust than he already was.

Manfred had been asleep for some time when the knock on his door woke him. The trip had taken more of a toll on him than he'd imagined when he planned it. He put on his robe and slippers and turned the knob without speaking.

"Hey Manny...you look pretty rough." Fritz said as the door opened.

"It's almost over. One way or the other." Manfred said sleepily.

"I hear you wanted a cup of tea?"

"You want one? I can call downstairs?" Manfred asked, momentarily confused.

"No, don't bother on my account. Bink just told me that, about ten times on the way down. I supposed it had some meaning since you took off without him."

"Oh yeah," Manfred said remembering the instructions he'd given. "That was just to make sure you stopped by here before you went home. I didn't want to go over any of this with a bunch of distractions. It was like the circus maximus up there."

"I heard about that."

"The doctor knew who I was. He recognized me, from the marks." Manfred pointed at his neck. "Did he say anything to the others?"

Fritz thought for a moment trying to remember. "Just that you'd been there, and that you looked like you'd had a hard time with the cancer."

"He said that I'd been there to the other two hunters." Manfred asked.

"Yeah. Skip asked me to thank you for finding his camera."

"Damn, I would have preferred everyone just thought it was Bink that found things. We don't need anything to look suspicious."

"What looks suspicious? You came up and helped your brother?" Fritz asked.

"That I came up there sick, that I spent time with you, that you turn up dead, and a bunch of diamonds are missing. How is that not suspicious?" Manfred said, angry at himself.

"That's kind of a stretch, isn't it?"

"I'd see through it." Manfred said emphatically. "If I found something like this I'd at least keep looking until I was sure it was nothing. I'd go to the people who could forge the papers. I'd ask around, offer some money, see what turned up. We have to be really careful."

"I know." Fritz said wearily, it had been a long day already and he wanted to get home to Reese. "We don't want me to really end up dead, or you to end up in prison."

"No, either of those are things that might happen anyway. We could both end up dead. What we don't want is for Gretchen to struggle through the rest of her life or for Fritzy to end up with a life like you and I had growing up. That is what we have to remember. That is why we have to stay focused. That's the only reason we're doing this." Manfred explained.

"Okay, I've got it. What do I have to do?" Fritz asked.

Manfred picked up a locked case and set it on the bed beside him. He knew why his brother was in a hurry.

"I know you're going to want to spend some time with the girl, the one you're with now, but don't say too much. You don't want her telling people about the premonitions you had about dying or anything, so keep your good-byes to a minimum."

Fritz nodded.

"Will she be alright?" Manfred asked.

"She'll be fine. Invite her to the funeral so she can show out a little as the bereaved. She'll move on just fine."

It was Manfred's turn to nod as he concentrated on opening the lock. "I have all of the stuff here in this case. It's been locked so nobody could fool with it. Here's the receiver and the GPS. Go to the coordinates on the map and turn on the receiver, it's already set, it has four directional arrows. Follow the arrow. On the map, I've got where to go and when to do it. I've got the patrols all arranged to let you get through. Take Bao with you. I'll have two other bushmen that are local to the area meet you here, just before you go into the zone." He pointed to a red star with a set of GPS coordinates. "Get rid of the doctor in here." He swirled his finger over an open area on the map.

"These are his altered documents, with your picture on them." Manfred said handing the passport to his brother. "Memorize everything so you can rattle it off without thinking. Practice an American accent. Pay attention to how you speak, remember everything that he's told you about his personal life. Give the all the doctor's original documents to Bao, passport, license, anything he has that can identify who he is, Bao knows to hide them and to bring them only to me. Don't forget, don't keep them with you, they're your greatest liability. Use the doctors credit cards, to give an electronic profile of his movements, remember you are now him."

Manfred returned to the map. "Here's your route out. Here's where the boat will be. The marine maps are all on the boat. You've got a weeks worth of provisions and a GPS on there too, set for Saint Helena. Anything else we need to think of? Anything that you can think of that I've forgotten? Any problems?"

"I don't want to kill him." Fritz said flatly.

"I understand that. I met him this afternoon. He seems like a really nice fellow, but we don't know how long all this is going to take, and we can't have him showing up at the American embassy or going through customs as himself, if you're supposed to be him." Manfred explained in as logical a fashion as he could. They had to get past the emotional aspect of this. They had to stick to the plan.

"There's got be another way." Fritz insisted.

"Then tell me what it is? I've been through this plan every way I can think of. We don't have room for mistakes. If you can think of a way to do it fine. I can't." Manfred looked at his brother expectantly.

"Well, I can't just kill him." Fritz said almost pleadingly.

"Fritz, you've done this sort of thing before. You just have to look at it as your duty. Just like it was your duty to kill the enemy when you were in the defense force. This is your duty to your family."

"But it was different…it was different."

"How then?" Manfred asked. He could see the plan crumbling to pieces in front of him.

"I didn't know them. I did…I didn't like them. They weren't my friend." Fritz stumbled over the words.

"So your friends come before your family now?" Manfred asked harshly. "If you can't do it yourself, then take Bink. I've had him watch over you since you went into the defense force. Take him…he'll do what has to be done."

Fritz knew that he would. Ray would have no chance with Bink in the mix. He'd do it himself before he allowed that to happen. At least if he were going to do it he'd be sure that there were no other options.

Manfred got to his feet and put his arm around his brother's shoulder. "Do you think I wouldn't take this from you if I could, that I wouldn't do it myself. Look at me. I wouldn't last two hours in the Namib. It almost killed me to drive up to camp today. God damn it, I don't want to risk your life. I don't want to make you kill your friend. I don't want any of this. I just want to take care of my own. That's what we have to do. Do you understand?"

Fritz nodded and lowered his eyes, not wanting to look at his brother.

"It's not like you have to shoot him. Give him your pack, with your stuff in it. Give him some water, and leave him alone in the desert. Leave it up to God. That's what I have to do right now. I don't know how things will come out. What could be fairer than that?"

Thirty-Six

"Sixty-five Centigrade. That's like a hundred and sixty-five in Fahrenheit." Fritz explained as they coursed along the ridge of a dune following the tracks of a group of five gemsbok. They'd caught sight of them for the first time about a half-hour ago, as they crossed a dune far in front of them. The animals were about two kilometers in front of them now. They'd never catch them before dark.

"How's that even possible?" Ray asked.

Fritz looked out across the desert. All he could see in front of them was the line of footprints arching out along the line of dunes.

"It must have something to do with time. It's the oldest desert on earth it's been like this for two million years. The plants out here are the same plants that were here when there were dinosaurs running around in the desert. Almost everything that thrives out here is reptile. We're not going to catch up to them tonight." Fritz sat down and opened a bottle of water.

He'd had a plan when they left the truck. But he hadn't done anything, yet. He motioned to the bushmen. It was no use to stay with the gemsbok. It was late afternoon. The wind would die down when it got dark. They'd be better off waiting until morning, when they could read the bushman newspaper, the record of undisturbed tracks that would be left on the sand overnight.

What in the hell was he thinking? He didn't give a damn about finding the stupid gemsbok. He'd already wasted a half a day. He was supposed to be rid of Ray by tomorrow morning.

They had to move tomorrow to stay ahead of the patrols. They had to hide the truck and get into position before dark to give them time to make the recovery and get out before it got light. And now, sometime in the middle of all that he had to find a way to do something about Ray.

He handed the water bottle to Ray first, and let him drink what he wanted. He drank next and then each of the bushman took their turn until the water was gone. When the bottle was empty he put it back into his pack.

He looked at the bushmen Bao, like Bink before him was his guardian. There were no worries there. H'ung and Gan he'd never seen before. What was he supposed to do with them while he was killing Ray? This whole thing was crazy. He didn't really have any idea of how to do something like this.

Maybe he should just shoot him. That's what Bink would do. Take the gun and pop him in the back of the head when he wasn't looking. That would be the easiest thing. No need to talk, no need to explain to him why it was that he was going to abandon him in the desert. The problem with that was that the authorities would need a corpse to declare him dead. They had to find a corpse, that's part of why the bushmen were here, so they could bring the authorities once everything was picked clean, a bullet hole would ruin that.

His original plan was just to bump him down the lee side of one of the dunes. Find a nice tall one. The slipsand and the thirty-five degree angle would do the rest. It would take him an hour to get back up. He'd leave him some water and go. The only problem was that unless there was wind, there was no way to hide in the Namib. Anyone could just follow your footprints to wherever you ended up going.

Even if he beat him back to the truck and drove off, there was still a chance that Ray would make it to the road, which made it possible that he'd get picked up by a patrol. Then everything they'd planned would fall apart. He should have let Bink do it.

The only other thing he could think of was to just keep Ray with him. How long could he do that if they weren't hunting? What was he going to tell him? Oh no, we're not hunting today, today we're stealing diamonds. Then what was he going to do? Take him with him to the boat? Throw him overboard on the way to Saint Helena? Tie him up on board and send him off into the middle of the Atlantic when he abandoned ship? Manfred was right. It was going to come down to a choice. And as far as he could see, there weren't any of them he could think of that were going to turn out well for both of them.

He wondered if the bushmen had any poison. They were famous for that. Made it up by crushing up beetles and fermenting the juices. That's why they were such successful hunters out here. All they had to do was nick an animal, and then follow its tracks until the tracks stopped. That's where the animal would be. He could slip some of it into his food. The problem with the white poison in humans was that it took a couple of days to kill you, and he didn't have a couple of days.

He'd put it off for now, and come up with something tomorrow.

"Let's head back to the truck. If we start now we should make it by dark." He said.

They spent the night under a sky that can't be understood by anyone that hasn't slept in the desert. "That's the Southern Cross." Ray said raising his hand. There was still more dark than stars, but the profusion of them that stretched across the pitch black sky made it hard to swear to.

Dinner was a simple pot of sausage, beans, and rice with a loaf of hard bread. Fritz savored it, knowing that it would be the last regular meal he'd have until he made it to the boat. After tonight it would be the bushman's hunting rations. Which meant mostly hoodia. Hoodia's a plant that looks like a cactus, because it has spines, but it isn't. It stores moisture in the stems and it keeps you from getting hungry. If you mix in some moths, a few grasshoppers, and a handful of grubs it's enough to keep you alive, for a while.

"You want to sleep on the ground with these guys or you want to sleep in the back of the truck?" Fritz asked as he tossed Ray a bedroll.

"I guess the ground will be softer." Ray said as he shook it open.

"It probably is, but I'm sleeping in the truck, too much stuff on the ground."

Ray hesitated. "What kind of stuff?"

"Scorpions, spiders, sidewinders…stuff like that."

"Then why don't they worry about them?" Ray asked pointing at the bushmen.

"They hope critters show up. Then they have breakfast." Fritz answered as he climbed into the bed of the pick-up.

"Pick a side then, I guess I'm sleeping up there too."

Fritz lay on his back looking up at the stars, trying as hard as he could not to think bout what it was he was going to have to do tomorrow. He didn't have much luck.

The bushmen were already gone by the time Fritz opened his eyes. He'd told them where to go and what he wanted them to do when he woke them at two. The weather had changed. The wind had picked up and was building. He'd told them to head out at first light. It looked like they hadn't waited. Fritz placed his license and some other papers with his name on them into his pack along with some water. He didn't bother to pack a lunch. He put Ray's doctored identification into the glove compartment. He had to be back to the truck by one, at the latest, to get into position to be where he was supposed to be tonight.

He knew what he had to do. He woke Ray as soon as he could make out shapes in the darkness. They were moving through the dunes following the center set of tracks thirty minutes later. By seven-thirty the wind had picked up to the point that the tracks were gone on the windward side of the dunes, and they were filling in quickly on the ridges. They were following broken tracks now. It wasn't long before Fritz began to see the trail marks that Bao was leaving on the lee side. He followed them for another hour before he stopped on the ridge of the highest dune that they had crossed and broke out the water and handed it to Ray.

Ray drank it quickly. It had been a hard walk up the ridge. "I haven't seen any tracks for the last hour."

"There aren't any." Fritz said flatly. The time had come.

"Then how do we know where we are?" Ray asked.

"There are marks on the bottoms, on the lee side of the dunes. Look there you can see the last one." Fritz pointed.

When Ray got up and moved to the crest to look over at the bottom of the steep grade, Fritz moved. He snatched up Ray's rifle and pushed the cocking mechanism forward.

Ray turned immediately at the sound of the click.

"Don't move Ray."

Ray looked down quickly. "What's going on Fritz? Is there a snake or something?"

Fritz held the rifle steady, aimed straight at the center of Ray's chest. "I want you to step off of the crest of the dune."

Ray's eyes widened. "You've got to be kidding, it's three hundred feet to the base."

"You'll make it Ray. You'll hit the slipsand and slide the rest of the way down. Then you can climb back up here, Ill leave you my pack with the water." Fritz pointed to his pack.

"What if you don't..." Ray started.

"I'll send it down first then." Ray kicked the pack over the crest of the dune. It fell briefly and then hit and rolled down the steep surface almost to the bottom. "It's down there waiting for you. Get it. Follow the markers back to the truck. Bao will find you there."

"Why can't we go back to the truck together?" Ray asked.

"Because, I'm not going back. I'm going on. There's something I have to do." Fritz answered.

Ray swept his arm across the barren horizon. "What could be out there that you have to do?"

"I have to die Ray. For the sake of my family I have to die. I have to die in the desert where I can't be found."

"Fritz, no matter what it is, suicide isn't the answer. There's no way I can find my way back. You're killing us both."

"This isn't about us Ray. You remember the cheetah? The one that the lions had killed?"

Ray nodded.

"It's just like that. You have to do what's best for your own. The lions didn't have any feelings about it, they just did what they had to, to protect their own."

"Who are you trying to protect? You can't help your brother like this. How does you dying help him? He's going to need you soon."

"It's not about Manny, he'll be alright. He knows what he's facing. This is about his son. About what's right for him. About making sure things are okay for him."

"Fritz, this isn't going to help his son. His son needs his uncle."

"The boy has his father. Step over the crest Ray...NOW Ray...Don't make me shoot you."

The time had come. He had given Ray every chance that he could. Fritz's right thumb moved forward to be sure that the safety was off before he squeezed the trigger. When he did, the gun decocked. He felt it slip below his thumb and the mechanism dropped with a loud click. Ray leaped forward and grabbed the barrel of the gun. Fritz jerked the trigger once, then twice and nothing happened. Fritz pushed wildly on the cocking piece as Ray pulled the rifle. And then the sand under his feet was moving, and then they were falling. Locked together by the gun. His back hit the sand first and then Ray fell on top of him. Somehow, in the middle of it all, the rifle went off, and with a brilliant flash Fritz's world disappeared.

Thirty-Seven

Ray felt the concussion of the blast hit the right side of his face and felt the blood splatter across it and into his eyes. He rolled back hard snatching at the rifle. It came away loose in his hands and he slid away from Fritz's limp body. They both continued to slide down the dune face, but now they were falling in different directions. Ray could only keep track of the rifle as he rolled, out of control, for what seemed like a hundred miles.

When he finally stopped he was so dizzy all he could do was try and feel his face with his hands to see if he was injured. Finally the dizziness subsided and he was able to catch his breath enough to get to his knees. He drug the rifle by its barrel as he made his way to where Fritz was lying face down, in an awkward position, his neck bent and his head covered by his arm. Blood soaked the sand around him. Ray could see that Fritz was still breathing. Then felt a pulse in his carotid. He moved his hand to the back of Fritz's neck to palpate for fractures. When he didn't feel any he gently straightened the neck, and rolled him over onto his back.

Fritz had been hit in the left side of the head by the gunshot. The entry wound was just in front of his left ear. The left side of his face was already badly swollen. Blood was still gushing from the wound. Ray took off his shirt and pressed on the wound. As he pulled the cloth back two sprays of blood jetted from each side of the wound, arterial bleeders. He'd try compression. If that didn't work he'd have to tie them. He pressed the shirt back into the wound and secured it by tying the sleeves around Fritz's face, across the eyes. So he could still breath without difficulty.

Ray looked up the slope for the pack. But the pack was still forty feet above them. He started the climb to retrieve it, but the soft sand gave away and he slid back down to where he'd started. He tried running and got a little higher, so he tried running harder. It didn't help. He tried twice more with the same results before he decided that running harder wasn't the answer. He dropped to his knees and tried crawling, with much better results. He inched closer and stretched out his hand. He immediately slid backward. He stopped himself and crawled slowly, slowly upward, but this time, as he neared the backpack he laid flat on his stomach and belly-crawled the last five yards up the sand until he got it into his arms.

As soon as he closed his arms around it, he turned and slid back down the slope on his butt to get to the bottom as quickly as possible. He jerked open the pack's flap and found a water bottle. He carefully removed the shirt that he had used as a makeshift dressing. He pulled it away from the tissue gently, to avoid dislodging any clots. He used the water sparingly to gently wash out the wound. The bleeders held off. Maybe they'd retracted back into the tissue and the swelling had compressed them.

He couldn't see much and he didn't want to force water into the opening because he didn't want to wash debris into Fritz's brain. There was only one thing to do. He washed his hands as well as he could and stuck his index finger into the wound. He could feel bone fragments almost immediately, and the wound was deeper than that. He had to assume that the bullet went into the brain. Without a skull series, or a CT there was no way to assess the depth of the wound any further without the risk of contamination. He had no choice. He had to get Fritz out of there.

Carefully, Ray tore strips of Fritz's outer shirt, to use as a bandage. He found a small cloth in the pack and soaked it with a clean bottle of water. He gently packed this into the wound to try and protect it. Then he used the strips of shirt to secure it in place.

Ray struggled as he tried to pick up the limp body, but the dead weight made it impossible to move through the sand. He tried pulling Fritz's arms over his shoulders, and getting him on his back. That worked better, but he still couldn't make any progress up the dune. After falling and dropping Fritz twice as he tried to skirt the base, Ray realized that he was probably doing more harm than good and that he'd never get either of them back to the truck if he kept on like this. The only thing left to do, was to try and go for help. His medical kit was in his duffel bag at camp, but if he could get to the truck, he could send the bushmen back along his tracks to try and bring Fritz out while he took the truck and went for help.

He placed Fritz with his head uphill. That was the only thing he could think of to reduce the swelling. Use gravity to pull the fluid toward his feet and away from his brain. He made sure that he was in what little shade he could find and left a bottle of water beside him, in case he woke up.

It took him forty-five minutes to get back to the crest of the dune. He jammed the barrel of his rifle down into the sand and tied the bloody sleeve of what was left of his shirt to the stock. It was the only way he could mark which dune.

They had followed their shadows all morning, so they'd been traveling west. The road had run north and south. The wind across the top of the dune had already erased their tracks. All he could do was to head due east, maybe a little north, that way he would know to head south when he hit the road. His shadow was short so it was near noon. It had to still be morning, so he would walk away. He started fast, sure that he was on the right track, but within an hour he had to slow down. The sun was straight up. His eyes were killing him from the glare and the blowing sand. He wasn't sure where his shadow was any more.

This was a heat beyond heat. It was an absolute dryness that sucked the moisture out of you. His mouth was so dry that moving his tongue felt like he was splitting leather. His tongue was glued to the back of his throat and the roof of his mouth. The pain was unbelievable.

He drank the last of the water in the pack. He shouldn't have left the other bottle with Fritz. Then he let the pack slip from his fingers and fall to the sand. He kept walking. He couldn't think of anything else to do.

It was afternoon now, he was chasing his shadow, when his shadow fell across footprints, a man wearing shoes' footprints. It couldn't be Fritz, and it wasn't the bushmen. Whoever it was they had to have come from somewhere. He looked at his shadow. The footprints were kind of going in the right direction, so he followed them, until it was dark, and then he laid down. He took a coin out of his pocket and tried to suck on it. Just to get some moisture into his mouth. The metallic taste was overwhelming and he couldn't get it to go away. He tried to spit the coin out but it was stuck to the roof of his mouth. He had to pry it out with his fingers.

He laid in the dark until he felt a fluttering on his face. He hit it hard and then looked down at the little stunned lizard lying there on the sand. He snapped its neck and twisted off its head. He sucked all of the moisture he could out of its body and then skinned it and chewed up the rest. He felt a little better. He could almost feel a bit of moisture in the air. Maybe it was just getting a break form the heat. In the morning he would find the truck.

The sunlight woke him, and again Ray followed the tracks, it didn't take long until he knew where he was. As he came up a high dune he saw it. He wasn't sure at first, so he pushed himself on until he was. Then he fell back on the sand laughing. There on the next dune was a rifle with a shirtsleeve tied to it sticking in the sand.

He was weak, he was tired, he was almost dead, and he was right back where he'd started.

At least there would be water, and he could check to see if there was any reason to hurry any more. There was no way Fritz could still be alive in this place. He made his way up the dune and looked over the lee face…to see nothing. He had to be here. He pulled the rifle out of the sand to be sure it was his. It looked like his. Ray walked along the crest looking as he went and still no sign of Fritz. Even if he rolled, or slipped where could he have gone? He still should have been able to see him. He worked his way back down dragging the rifle behind him, or using it like a cane when he stumbled. He searched along the base of the dune and found nothing. There were lions in the Namib, and jackals. Suddenly Ray felt panicked. He had to get out of there. He struggled against the sand until he fell, and then he crawled until he couldn't move, finally he rolled over and just lay there cradling the rifle in his arms like a treasure.

He stared up at the sun and felt himself start to relax. He could feel his eyelids drag and stick on his eyeballs when he blinked, so he stopped blinking. And the yellow sun became white. He was looking across a great white plain, and everywhere he looked there was only the light. He was alone. The light began to dim to yellow and then red and then black. He breathed out with a breath that was so pure and so restful that he couldn't help himself. He just slipped away.

Thirty-Eight

Lisa stamped her foot on the floor of her car as she drove. Where in the hell was he? He couldn't call? He couldn't answer? Maybe he was just paying her back for the way she'd treated him during the divorce, but she'd left so many messages, really sincere messages, asking him to call her.

She pulled up in front of what used to be their house. His car wasn't there. The newspapers hadn't piled up and there wasn't a bunch of mail sticking out of the mailbox, so he must have been there at some point. He must have gotten back from Africa safely.

She tried her key in the kitchen door. To her amazement, it still worked. The house didn't look any different than it had the last time that she'd been there. When they'd taken the furniture. Ray hadn't replaced any of it. Everything looked clean, like the maid had just left, but Amanda wasn't due until tomorrow. Unless he'd fired her. The newspapers were stacked neatly on the counter and the mail covered the kitchen table, so someone was bringing it in for him.

She looked at the blinking light on the answering machine and felt a momentary twinge of guilt as she pushed the "play messages" button.

"Messages full. You have one hundred and twenty nine unheard messages. Last message…"

Most of them were from the hospital asking him to call them back, several were from Ray's partners, a few were hers. Two were from Anne. Nobody knew where Ray was. Apparently, he'd never come home. She dialed the number for his cell phone for the thousandth time in the last two weeks.

"I'm sorry, but the number that you have called is not currently in service…" She hung up the phone and threw it into her purse. No, she didn't want to leave a message. She wanted Ray to answer the damned phone.

Ray may be a lot of things but irresponsible wasn't one of them. She didn't think he'd ever missed a shift without checking in, arranging coverage, something. She came to the unavoidable conclusion that Ray was…in fact… missing. He might avoid her. He might be upset about the divorce. But he wouldn't just, not show up at the hospital. Something must have happened. She had to find out what.

She searched the house. She was relieved when she didn't find anything. Every door she opened, every piece of furniture she looked behind she had an unreasonable fear that she'd see him lying there. She knew it was ridiculous, but she couldn't help it. Amanda might not move a dead body to vacuum under it, but she would surely have noticed one and at least have said something to somebody about it. Plus, there would have been a smell or something.

She sat down at Ray's desk. His laptop was gone. He'd taken it with him, so that wouldn't help. There was nothing there, no papers, no scribbles, nothing.

Millie drove her to the hospital in her new Mercedes. They came into the emergency department through the staff entrance. From the hallway Millie pointed to a young woman sitting in the nursing station, writing on a chart. Lisa took it from there. She entered without speaking and walked to the side of the woman sitting at the desk writing. Anne was as young and pretty as Lisa had feared. It tore her heart to look at her.

"You're Anne, aren't you? I'm Lisa Moffett."

The woman's face fell, and she stood up quickly. It was then that Lisa noticed her stomach.

"Is it his?" She blurted. She couldn't help it.

"I'm sorry?" Anne said, confused.

"Your baby. Is it Ray's?"

"No, it's my husband's," she answered, without anger.

"Do you know where Ray is?" They both asked at the same time.

"No." They answered in unison.

"I need to try to find my husband." Lisa said after a moment's silence. "I don't know where he is and I don't know anything about what he was doing. A lot of that's my fault. Some of it's yours. But worrying about whose fault it is doesn't help me. I need to find out what it is you know that I don't. Things like: When he left? When he was supposed to be back? Has anyone heard from him? Anything that you can think of, so I can have some idea of what I'm talking about when I go to the police. I guess I should go to the police. Where else would I go?"

Anne thought for a moment before she answered. "Namibia, maybe."

Thirty-Nine

It had been a difficult time, but Manfred was finally finished with the radiation and the chemotherapy. Today he would be finished with the Kimberly investigation.

Manfred smiled as he walked out of his office for the last time. It had been his life for too long. Everything was changing, but that was something he'd have to accept.

Medical retirement wouldn't be such a bad thing. He'd filed for it two weeks ago. He'd get to spend whatever time he had left on this earth with Gretchen, and no man deserved anything better than that.

Now all he had left to do was complete his testimony, and that wouldn't take long. He walked to the conference room and sat down beside Mister Bierstadt, the head of the consortium in Namibia. The three investigators from the World Trade Organization sat across the table.

Bierstadt had already testified before the Kimberly Process and denied the existence of any Zimbabwean diamonds in the official stores. He had testified that here in Namibia they were in the process of moving away from in-ground mines altogether. That ninety percent of what they'd harvested in the last few years were marine diamonds. He didn't understand when he said it, that those were the exact reasons that the investigators would have no trouble finding any artisanal diamonds that had been hidden. The tool marks made it easier, artisanal diamonds were dug with a pick and a shovel not a machine.

Manfred had always been resourceful and had always worked in the interests of the consortium. He still would. He'd decided that it was in the best interests of all concerned if he just took the blame himself.

Sitting at the table across from the investigators, he wasn't nervous, he'd decided that he wouldn't lie about anything, he'd simply tell the truth. Well, ninety-five percent of it anyway.

"Look, the company gave me a job. They asked me to come up with a way of stopping the flow of black market diamonds into the world market. The only thing I could think of was to buy them. So I bought them." He looked at Bierstadt who nodded imperceptibly.

"That was why the Kimberly Process was started." A small man on the far end of the table said. "To stop the flow of conflict diamonds into the market. To stop any unauthorized flow into the market."

"It didn't appear to be working. You turned a blind eye to Zimbabwe time and again. You were supposed to deal with them in November and you didn't." Manfred answered.

"This was going on long before November," the man continued.

"We have brought our concerns about the Zimbabwean diamonds to you many times over the years. " Bierstadt said firmly.

The small man stood and pointed his finger at Bierstadt. "No one authorized you to act on your own behalf."

"I didn't know we had." Bierstadt answered.

Manfred spoke again. "It was easy to hide. It was a blip on the budget. We paid pennies on the dollar."

"And how did you bring them into the country undetected?" The man across the table from Manfred asked, he was a South African.

"They were brought in through Zambia and Angola, along the same channels that my brother had used to move guns, horn, ivory, and money during the war times and after."

"Your brother is Fritz Dietrich?" The third investigator, a black woman, interrupted him.

"Yes." Manfred answered.

"I thought so. That had to be difficult for him. Your brother was wanted for murder in every country outside of Namibia. How did he do it?" she asked.

"You must be the representative from the aggrieved party." Manfred answered coldly. "I'm not sure that you're allowed to ask questions."

"Yes, I am from Zimbabwe, if that's what you are asking, and yes as a member of this team I am allowed to ask questions. Your brother murdered six policemen in my country. He was a murderer. He was wanted for murder in Zimbabwe, Zambia, and Angola. These are facts. There is no question to them. And you expect us to believe that he traveled freely in each of these countries?" She pressed angrily.

"I didn't say that he did. I said that I used the same channels." Manfred returned her look defiantly.

"And where is your brother now? Let us hear what he has to say on this matter. Better yet, let him come to Harare and answer the questions." she spat.

"That would be a bit of a difficulty." Manfred was leaning forward over the table now.

"I don't think we need to pursue this," Bierstadt said calmly. "Mister Dietrich's brother is dead. He buried him last week. He died in the desert, in our country, in a hunting accident. Shot in the head by a client."

"I'm terribly sorry for your loss." The South African took over the questioning. The woman from Zimbabwe tried to speak again, but he raised a hand and silenced her. "If you would just explain to us how it was done."

Manfred forced himself to calm down. "It was simpler for me, I already had my brother's contacts, and all I was asking them to do was trade rocks for money. No guns, no one trying to shoot them, and all of it under the protection of the most powerful force in southern Africa, the consortium's security apparatus."

"So, no one ordered you to do this thing?"

"They asked me to stop the uncontrolled flow of diamonds into the black market. They didn't tell me how to stop it. No one gave me directions. No one told me to purchase or to move the stones. That was completely my decision. I didn't feel like I needed any further authority to implement that decision. I'm sorry, to Mister Bierstadt, to the company, and to the Process if I overstepped the boundaries of what's acceptable. I was just trying to address a problem that I could find no other answer to. If someone has to be at fault, then I guess the answer is that it is me and I take full responsibility for my actions. " He looked and saw the flicker of a smile cross Bierstadt's face.

"And where are these diamonds now Mr. Dietrich?" the representative from South Africa asked.

And then he dropped the bomb. He told them the truth. "They are in the ocean. It was my job to keep them from entering the market, not my job to keep them. They went into the water, along the Skeleton Coast, there's no way to recover them from there, so the market remains safe at the present time."

What he didn't tell them were minor things. Things like, that the best and most saleable diamonds weren't lost, or that he'd received a coded message from a Dr. R. Moffett in Antwerp this morning confirming their sale to a private investor, or that the proceeds from the sale had been wired to Russell Bank & Trust in Scotland. He had sent the certification documents to Antwerp in advance. Manfred knew the investor and he was a man in no hurry, the diamonds would trickle into the market, there would be no flood.

It was over. The President, the country, and the consortium had what they had to have, deniability. They were off the hook. They'd lost the diamonds, but they wouldn't face any sanctions.

The Kimberly Process only controlled the sale of diamonds, they could certainly blame him, they could forbid him to have anything to do with the sale of diamonds ever again, but they had no authority to punish him further, and he could accept that, he was already retired.

The Zimbabweans were beside themselves, but they had no way to detail what had been lost.

"They weren't there to see any more so they couldn't be counted." That was the key. All he'd had to do was to be able to look past himself. It was his ego that had made him think he could hide what they'd done, when, in truth, the only answer was not to try.

Yes, there had been hard times. The cancer had tried to kill him, so had the doctors. He hadn't been able to swallow in weeks. He'd been so weak that he collapsed when they told him his brother was dead.

Having to bury an empty coffin was hard on Gretchen and Fritzy, but he was relatively happy with it. They declared Fritz dead based on the doctor's testimony. The doctor had wandered out of the desert after more than three weeks lost. No one would have believed he could have survived that long, certainly not Manfred. He'd been living with some bushmen who had walked him to safety.

It had been on all of the television channels, the whole world was talking about it. You couldn't turn on the news for the last week without seeing him there, sunburned and thin with his wife beside him. Who knew where she'd come from? The doctor was supposed to be divorced. It was a good story. He could see why people liked it. Why they wanted to watch it.

The doctor would tell how he and Fritz had been hunting in the desert. How they'd fallen over the crest of a dune together and the rifle had gone off. That he'd gone for help.

Who knew what had really happened? The doctor didn't know where they'd even started. Where they found the truck was a hundred and twenty kilometers north of where he said they'd been. The bushmen had said that they'd found the doctor asleep under a dune, which dune they did not know, a dune ten days away. It was hard to get them to be more specific, it could have been almost anywhere in the whole desert. When the patrols found them, the doctor and the two bushmen had just walked up out of the desert, waved and said, "Hi," like they were running into somebody on the street corner or something. The patrols had looked for Fritz, but they never found his body. The bushmen said they hadn't seen it.

Yes, the treatments had been hard, but they'd finally done the MRI of his head and it surprised him that nothing was there. Gretchen had said that it didn't surprise her at all. He wasn't sure what she'd meant by that, but she and Fritzy had laughed when she said it. The CT scans were good too. So, that meant he had time, and time was really all that any of them could ever hope for. A bit of time to thrive, for a while, before the hard times came again.

About the Author:

(the truth this time)

Russell Scott Anderson, M.D. is a Radiation Oncologist who serves as the Medical Director of Anderson Cancer Center in Meridian, Mississippi. He is a former Navy diver who worked in operations in the Middle East, Central America, and in support of the Navy's EOD community, SEALS, the US Army's Green Berets, the Secret Service, and the New York Police Department at various times during his time in the service.

The father of seven has written the family oriented literary columns Una Voce and The Uncommon Thread in the JOURNAL of the Mississippi State Medical Association. He has also served the JOURNAL as the Chairman of the Editorial Advisory Board. A collection of his columns was published as, *The Uncommon Thread* in 2012. He has also written as screenwriter R. S. Anderson on several feature films, he is the author of the novels *Timedonors Wanted* and *The Hard Times* under the pseudonym Russell Scott, and is the Editor of the literary journal China Grove.

SOME WORDS:

There are too many people to thank to ever do an adequate job of it. This book has been finished for five years and because it is a glimpse into both interior and external worlds I have inhabited at different times, it is personal in a different way from other things I have written, and so I have been hesitant to put it forth. I have to thank my dear, dear friend Ellen Gilchrist for her insight in moving forward.

I thank Shawnassey Brooks for her guidance and help in finding the stones in the mud. I need to also thank Marly Rusoff for her words which have helped my feet to find this path.

To Luke Lampton, M.D. my partner in China Grove Press and editor for the last ten years, I say, this is as much your fault as it is anyone's, you're the one that made me think I could write. To Kevin Ivey and Jackson Anderson, my former writing partners, I'm sure I've borrowed something, thanks, I appreciate your taking the time to read and critique this, time after time after time. To my Dad, thanks for your advice and input. In retrospect, I suppose the original version of the book, in which everyone died, may have been a little depressing.

To my children, I know that when I'm writing I'm not there. I know none of you would ever take advantage of my inability to focus on two worlds at once to do things you weren't supposed to, even if I told you, you could, because I wasn't paying enough attention when you asked me if you could do it. So... don't do it any more, and don't tell your mom.

To my wife, The Amazing Charlo, thanks for everything, I can't even say what or how much, but you make everything I do possible.

And my deepest thanks to any of you who are reading this, I hope you liked the book.

Scott

CPSIA information can be obtained at www.ICGtesting.com
Printed in the USA
LVOW10*1950230815

451073LV00002B/3/P